Praise for *Simone LaFray and the Red Wolves of London*

What do London, chocolate, espionage, a chandelier, a watch, a Maestro, *la Volpe Rossa,* a wolf pack, and a key have in common? You will have to read this magnificent book to find out!

Move over, Nancy Drew—Simone LaFray is coming! I had been eagerly anticipating the release of this sequel, *Simone LaFray and the Red Wolves of London,* and author S.P. O'Farrell has exceeded all expectations with this literary masterpiece! Dive into this delightful journey encapsulated by vibrant prose, a witty narrative, and an atmospheric radiance. Throughout the story, this phrase totally resonated with me: *"Don't be afraid of change, Simone. Change happens—but the strong are ready."*

If you love reading middle-grade mystery novels that feature a strong young heroine unraveling clues and secrets, these books are for you and your entire family! A highly recommended, charming read. I dare you to put this book down!

—Lali A. Love, *The De-Coding of Jo*
(the *Ascending Angel Academy* series)

This sequel does not disappoint! Simone LaFray is a sweet, sharp spy on her newest assignment in London—accompanied by her best friend, who knows nothing of her secret mission. With smart dialogue, a scrumptious plot, and plenty of sugary treats, this is a mystery that will leave you wanting at least one more nibble by the end. *Bon appetit!*

—Danielle Dayney, *When Love Sticks Around*

Simone LaFray is the secret agent every middle-grade-mystery lover should know! In this spectacular sequel, the stakes are higher as Simone is sent to a prestigious London school on a top secret mission to find the coveted OmniKey and uncover information on the whereabouts of a missing student. Family and friendships are a real focus in this coming-of-age story wherein Simone blunders her way through some situations and shines in others; and we not only witness the extraordinary array of Simone's secret-agent sleuthing capabilities, but also see a relatable side to the young teen as she flounders when forced out of her comfort zone and into the spotlight. O'Farrell's writing style is sophisticated, witty, and charming; and like every great mystery series, this story wraps up with just enough loose ends that the reader will be waiting in anticipation for Simone's next great performance. An endearing and fantastic upper middle grade mystery!

—E.S. Christison, *The Blameless*

What a grand slam of a sequel! With threads of *Madeleine, Nancy Drew, Sherlock Holmes,* and *James Bond,* this series has massive crossover appeal for audiences of all ages. It deserves an army of an audience, and I have no doubt *Simone LaFray* will be Disney's next big thing!

In *Simone LaFray and the Red Wolves of London,* Simone travels from Paris to London and enrolls in a British boarding school. Cyberattacks plague London, unknown artists graffiti the city with copies of famous paintings, and the Red Fox weaves a tangled web. As a junior spy, Simone must use her brilliant and beautiful mind, along with her astute attention to detail, to solve her mission. She is particular and passionate, specific and precise—yet above all, caring and protective. Family comes first, and the members of Simone's family elevate each other as Simone searches for clues while her father opens a new bakery in London. While the first book incorporated music, the second book references works of art, and I love the cultural layers these elements add to the work.

Throughout the book, Simone grows as a spy and as a person,

gaining confidence and embracing herself. My absolute favorite part of this series is the treatment of Simone's neurodivergence. Her differences make her stronger, and intelligence is her superpower. It is so refreshing to have such stellar and authentic representation. As the parent of an autistic child, I am beyond thrilled that I can point at Simone and say to my daughter, "That can be you. You can do that." Simone is truly a superhero and role model, and many will find a friend in her.

Hugely entertaining and cinematic, Book Two expands the scale and raises the stakes with plenty of intrigue, mystery, suspense, action, and adventure—plus wicked cool spy gadgets. We also meet wonderful new characters and reunite with returning legends—all hail the V!

All in all, this series is extraordinary. Simone LaFray is a contemporary classic, and O'Farrell has the rare and remarkable talent of relating to all ages across all boundaries. This author is one to watch.

(DISCLAIMER: May crave chocolate after reading.)

—Halo Scot, the *Rift Cycle* series

Readers who love bestselling books like *Nevermoor, Charlie and the Chocolate Factory*, and the award-winning novel *Chasing Vermeer* by Blue Balliett will devour the *Simone LaFray Mysteries*.

As readers learned in *Simone LaFray and the Chocolatiers' Ball,* Simone is a junior spy for the Ministry of Foreign Affairs. In this exciting second installment of the mystery series, duty calls when Claire, a fellow junior spy, goes missing from the posh Claymoore School in London. Simone readily accepts the assignment to find Claire and uncover the hiding spot of the dangerously inexplicable OmniKey, but her newfound popularity since her triumph at the Chocolatiers' Ball provides some challenges.

With so much at play for a young girl—including a new school, making new friends, navigating school rivalries, and a possible first crush—going undercover becomes complicated, and Simone finds herself questioning loyalties and keeping secrets from those she values. Whom can she trust? And who is in this vigilante group known as the Red Wolves of London that only comes out at night? Could *la*

Volpe Rossa (the Red Fox), the most well-known thief in the world, be involved in Claire's disappearance? Is he after the OmniKey, too? There's also the opening of a new LaFray's Patisserie in London to oversee!

Once again intricately interweaving mystery, art, music, and confectionery, S.P. O'Farrell's masterful storytelling builds to a spectacularly satisfying grand finale that unpacks the mystery neatly (although crucial characters find themselves in quite a tantalizing mess). Simone's character is well developed, and tween readers will be lured in by the relatable friendship struggles and inspired by the way she steps up and out of her comfort zone.

Filled with stunning sentences that set every scene, *Simone LaFray and the Red Wolves of London* has been created with care, and readers will be left ravenous for the next *Simone LaFray* mystery.

—*The Children's Book Review*

A fast-paced junior sleuth novel perfect for mystery lovers of any age!

Nancy Drew meets the *Great British Baking Show* in this delicious and adventurous spy story set across an iconic European backdrop. *Simone LaFray and the Red Wolves of London* is a fast-paced junior sleuth novel perfect for mystery lovers of any age.

A spot in the limelight has never been on Simone LaFray's bucket list, but after her success at the Chocolatiers' Ball, she takes her newfound notoriety in stride. With a mind like an advanced computer processor and a similarly mechanical set of social skills, she is able to hyperfocus on her spy work, minimize the traumas of petty school rivalries, balance delicate relationships, and even get her homework done on time. No easy task for a teenager who works as a covert junior spy for the Ministry of Foreign Affairs. Ever eager to be of service, Simone jumps at the chance to help recover a kidnapped fellow agent and at the same time locate a mysterious technological weapon called the OmniKey. With dangers lurking in the shadows, a disturbing change in her mother's health back at her Paris home, the opening of a new family patisserie in London, and emerging half-truths threatening to compromise her mission, it's difficult to imagine how Simone will find the time to complete her assignment—especially when allegiances are called into question and friendships become strained.

With a nimbly paced plot and plenty of clever deceptions, O'Farrell's second in the captivating *Simone LaFray Mysteries* series pairs refined opulence with mischief, making for just the right combination of controlled chaos and vintage charm. The supporting cast is as engaging as Simone herself, especially the bubbly best friend, known as the V. The relationship between these two girls adds depth and tenderness to the story, especially when the V opens up about her feelings of abandonment surrounding her adoption, and then again as their friendship is tested to the limits of their trust.

Quirky and agile, *Simone LaFray and the Red Wolves of London* is a delectable story that will leave you hungering for more.

—Jennifer Jackson, *Indies Today*

S.P. O'Farrell

SIMONE LAFRAY

and the

RED WOLVES OF LONDON

Brandylane
Publishers, Inc.
Publishing books since 1985

ISBN: 978-1-953021-36-6

LCCN: 2022902036

Cover illustrated by Kelly O'Neill
Cover and interior designed by Michael Hardison
Project managed by Erin Harpst

Cover fonts: Adorn Expanded Sans, Cambria, Chennai Slab, and Parisish
Interior fonts: Adobe Caslon Pro and Qokijo

Printed in the United States of America

Published by
Brandylane Publishers
5 S. 1st Street
Richmond, Virginia 23219
brandylanepublishers.com

Brandylane
Publishers, Inc.
Publishing books since 1985

For Emily

How sweet it is.

Overture

"**B** onjour," or should I say, "Hello."

On the heels of my family's triumph at the Chocolatiers' Ball, the only thing I wanted to do was fade back into the shadows—but it was not to be. My actions that evening had several unintended consequences—two of particular note.

First, I became somewhat of an international musical sensation. Word of my performance circulated fast, and I soon found myself bombarded with opportunities to sing throughout Europe and Russia, as well as offers of tutoring from a multitude of the continent's most gifted vocal instructors. Flattered though I was, my family and I agreed I needed to become more comfortable with my newfound gift before sharing it with the world. However, when I was presented with a unique mission that would require my newly discovered talent, we agreed to make a single exception—which was how I now found myself backstage at the Vienna Opera House, awaiting my cue.

The second consequence was the one I found most grueling. Despite years spent cultivating anonymity from the back rows of the Elizabeth of Trinity School for Girls, observing everything and avoiding eye contact, I was now . . . popular. Not in the sense that everyone liked me, but in the sense that everyone *knew* me. News of Father winning the Chocolatiers' Ball and me stealing the show had gone viral, and on the first day of school, I was met by a line of starstruck kids asking for my mobile number. At first, I found it unnerving. Now, two months into the school year, I was just getting used to the attention—sort of.

My training as a spy continued—though I had not been back in the field since the Ball, instead performing surveillance and data analysis from a secure room at the Ministry of Foreign Affairs. I loved being a spy, but I had a special fondness for this aspect of the job: it was quiet, predictable, and entirely *sans* spotlights, and poring over details, finding anomalies, and seeing the unseen was where I excelled. My mentor, Eloise, was pleased with my work, and assigning me more challenging cases.

Father was on his own trajectory—and loving every minute of his newfound celebrity. I had never seen him so excited. A week after the Chocolatiers' Ball, he had received a Ministers Citation for Extraordinary Contributions to the Arts and Cultural Advancement of France—and two weeks after that, finalized an agreement with the Fontaine Corporation to open a series of LaFray's patisseries throughout Europe.

Once diametrically opposed, Father and Sugars Fontaine had been kindred spirits since the Ball. The famed sweets magnate often came by the store to whisk Father away to fancy parties and high-profile meetings. Initially, Father had despised the idea of creating a chain of franchises, but Sugars had convinced him every store would be not only unique, but distinctly LaFray.

My parents spent night after night debating the merits of this venture. They even asked for my opinion—which was well-thought-out and succinct, but alas, carried little weight. The agreement was made too swiftly for my tastes, but in the end, Mother could not deny Father this opportunity—while Mia, of course, wondered what took them so long to say *yes*. Despite my aversion, a powerful light was now focused on our shop at 7 Rue Clodion.

After the decision was made, the work progressed at breakneck speed. The first franchise had passed the design stage and was scheduled to open in London on December sixteenth, just in time for the holidays. Already it was the talk of England, and indeed, the whole confectionery world: nearly twenty-eight hundred square meters of a sweet tooth's nirvana, standing front and center on Sloane Street. Madame Fontaine was sparing no expense, with crews working around the clock and Father hopping over the Channel twice a month to oversee construction. However, though the building was magnificent, with a soaring central atrium and balconies that would have dwarfed our store in Paris, I had to admit I rather preferred the original.

There was one benefit to Father's frequent absences: Mother had been home much longer than usual, looking after us in his place. I was delighted to see her more often—though now that I had the opportunity, I also found myself worrying over her in a way I hadn't expected. She seemed scattered and oddly forgetful, without her usual energy and focus. Years of service were catching up to the world's finest spy, and though she insisted all was well, I wasn't convinced. Something was wrong—and I couldn't help but wonder whether it had to do with the failure of our efforts to capture the Red Fox.

The blow still smarted for me as well. The slippery subject of our last mission had gone underground since he'd slunk off into the shadows with *Blue No. 2* tucked under his arm, and to this day, the Ministry was unsure how he'd managed it. One moment, the painting was there, less than six meters from the LaFray display at the Chocolatiers' Ball; and in the next instant, it was gone—vanished into the sweet, chocolate-rich night. Security camera footage from the evening had proven unhelpful, but the Ministry's agents surmised he had fled through an abandoned basement corridor they later discovered behind a pile of smashed plaster and a heavy door with a broken latch. Eloise seemed certain he would resurface soon, though the Ministry as a whole gave little regard to the stolen painting. After all, analyzing foreign intelligence and simultaneously executing multiple covert missions was far more pressing than retrieving stolen art.

Still, the Fox's words—*You have no idea how big your role will be*—still rang through my head, and had kept me up many nights. What role was waiting for me? And how did he know so much? I couldn't get it out of my head.

The weighty complexities of my life would have proven excruciating without my best friend by my side. The V and I were inseparable as always, and spent most of our Saturdays exploring Paris. Twice we got our nails done, and in a moment of spontaneity—or perhaps weakness—we purchased boxes of coloring and dyed our hair bright red. She went first. "*Red for fall!*" she had exclaimed. The experiment was an unparalleled disaster, and our furious mothers had immediately marched us to Nina Le Salon to salvage our looks and our locks. Only last week had we started to be able to laugh about it—but that was how things always ended up with the V. She was the one person who made me feel safe and on edge at the same time, the one that made school tolerable and weekends exciting. Nothing could come between us. At least, that was what I'd thought. . . .

But wait. The lights are dimming. That's my cue.

Deep breath. The show is about to begin.

The Maestro

The hot white spotlight crept slowly up my gown—another Marcel creation, designed and hand-delivered by my family's friend in *haute couture* especially for my debut. The accompanying singers who flanked me gave encouraging smiles as the eager crowd supplied a respectful opening applause. In an instant, the orchestra pit came alive, and the massive room was captivated.

Breathe, Simone. You have four minutes and twenty-three seconds before you come in.

Time to get to work.

I would like to tell you I was onstage in this magnificent hall out of pleasure—but that would only be partially true. Actually, the entire evening was a ruse—a trap to catch a thief. Months of planning between the Ministry, MI6, and even the CIA had led me here—stage left, standing over a dot of white tape as the spotlight crested my glasses.

The thief in question was none other than Felix Ludwig, son of the notorious cyberterrorist Klaus Ludwig. East German by birth, the senior Ludwig was widely regarded as the world's foremost hacker. Once a budding journalist, he had an oeuvre of promising early work; but his quest for the truth had quickly led him into ethically murky waters, and soon money and power eclipsed any thoughts of a Pulitzer. Sport overcame justice, and he developed a propensity for creating experimental technical devices to help carry out his capers. His investigative drive, combined with his exceptional computer skills, eventually made him one of the most dangerous men in the world. He knew to mine for the real gold, the most valuable currency in the world—secrets.

And Ludwig was always ready to shine a light or extinguish the flame—for the right price. But compromising credit cards, draining bank accounts, and stealing identities became *passé* over time, and soon he had caused four power grid collapses, two stock market crashes, and eleven satellite losses, in a seemingly endless trail of terror. He worked under hundreds of anonymous tags online, and his most prevalent moniker was "The Maestro," for the ease with which he orchestrated fear. Rumor had it he'd even developed an OmniKey—a device that could access any computer or network. While the existence of this key was probably more rumor than reality, the mere thought of such a device made many in my field more than a little nervous. The information we gathered was more precious than money—as we'd all been reminded after a momentary breach at the Ministry last year, though Eloise assured everyone no files had been compromised.

As for Ludwig's son Felix—or *Das Flustern*, "The Whisper," as he was known—he was refined and worldly, and perhaps even more diabolical than his father. A genius, he had obtained multiple degrees, including a doctorate in computer engineering, before he was twenty-three. Creating—and then profiting from—international conflicts was his favorite business model.

But while fear and miscommunication were his specialties, there was one thing Felix could not resist: opera. Rumor had it he was first introduced to it in the crib, and as a result, learned both German and Italian by age five. In addition, despite his corruption, he was rumored to be one of the world's most prolific patrons of the arts. The various international spy networks agreed it was inconceivable he would miss the only public performance of the opera world's newest star—me.

He was sure to be somewhere in the audience. The trick now was finding him.

There were 1,432 seats in the Vienna Opera House, and every one was filled—a sold-out show. I had been studying the profiles of all the ticket holders for the last two weeks, and was confident I would recognize any swaps or substitutions, though the low lighting might make them difficult to distinguish. Of course, the Ministry had others working the case: most of the venue's staff had been replaced by agents, and the surveillance equipment they'd placed in the entry hall would have detected an ant walking across the carpet. But I knew these efforts wouldn't matter—not to someone as savvy as the Whisper. No, it would not be that easy; he would anticipate these, and would almost certainly come in disguise. But I was up for the challenge. He would get through somehow—and I was going to find him.

The seconds peeled away. *Four-twenty, four-twenty-one; deep breath, and remember to project. I'm on.*

I stepped up to the microphone and began to sing—and to surveil.

I had been given the lead role in a choral ensemble performance of *Aida*. (A theatrical performance was out of the question, as it would be far easier for me to study the crowd from a stationary position.) The stage was expertly decorated in an ancient Egyptian theme, with several large, aged columns and oversized models of Ra and Osiris. The ladies were styled like Cleopatra, and the men sported linen robes and heavy eyeliner. As for me, I had been in hair and makeup for two hours, and the experience had left me searching for the door. My stylist had given me heavy extensions that looped around my head to cover an earpiece nestled in my left ear, which would allow Eloise to communicate with me during the performance. The hairstyle served its purpose perfectly—but even so, I couldn't wait to brush it all out.

"Simone, have you spotted anything?" Eloise whispered through my earpiece. The connection was starting to develop a faint amount of static, but I could hear her well enough.

I stepped back from the microphone as my part ended. "No, nothing yet," I whispered into my drop earrings. A tiny, ingenious microphone had been planted in each of them. I'd been practicing with them for weeks. "I'll keep trying."

Breathe, Simone.

By the time we were midway through the first act, I had vetted half the theater, and still managed to hit all my notes. The music was intoxicating, and the audience was sitting at attention. Despite myself and my assignment, I was enjoying the evening.

I glanced up at box 3A, seats 1, 2, and 3, where Mother and Father were soaking in the experience while Mia turned to take a selfie against the sea of glittering dresses and upswept hairdos in the seats below. Father noticed the flash and swooped in to snatch her mobile away, sparking a brief protest and a crossing of the arms.

Mother didn't react. She was also monitoring the guests, and whispering into her own earpiece. We had organized the seats into a grid system, which she was scanning along with me. I was thrilled to be working the field with her—especially since she'd been staying home so much lately.

Now, however, Mother was back in her element. With the two of us in the field, there was no way the Whisper would slip away.

The music hit the height of its crescendo with a triumphant D major chord, ending the first act, and the curtain dropped to roaring applause. My choirmates turned and congratulated me, but I'd never been one for the "rah-rah" stuff. I was here to do a job, and Eloise would be checking in at any second.

"Simone, we are so proud of you," Mother said through the earpiece as I caught my breath. Though my mind was already occupied with the balcony seating chart, a warm smile crept over my face. This was praise I could appreciate.

"*Merci,*" I whispered as I tugged at my waistband. It had ridden up four centimeters during my high note, and stubbornly refused to return to its rightful place.

"Yes, yes, we are all enormously proud; but have you seen anything suspicious?" Eloise interjected. "There was one rather tall gentleman in balcony seat 36H who did not match his seat assignment. However, a petite lady who was to be seated directly behind him negotiated a trade before the curtain call. Both checked out."

"Yes, I saw that too," said Mother. "That was nice of him. Nothing the Whisper would do," she added. "I'm afraid I'm at a bit of a disadvantage from my viewpoint—and I don't want to miss your performance, Simone. We're so proud of you," she added again.

The stage manager waved to me. "Ah, I have to take my place. The curtain is about to go up."

"Drink some water, dear, and take a breath. You're doing great," Mother added.

The curtain rose once more, and I returned my attention to my grids. *Three over, one back. Three over, one back.* The words echoed through my head as I scanned and cataloged each row, moving from left to right and back to front. I'd gotten though the second balcony, and so far, all the seat assignments were accounted for. *Where is he?*

"Smile, Simone," Eloise whispered. "You're too tense."

I took another breath and obeyed, allowing my attention to drift slightly as I began my favorite aria of the show. I'd first sung this song when I was six, but I'd never thought I would belt it out with ease and conviction in such an enormous hall. My waistband started to ride up again as my ribcage contracted and expanded with increasing force. This was my moment.

As I hit the C#6, the crowd erupted, jumping to their feet in a standing ovation. Every hair on my body stood up, and I gazed out over the adoring crowd, feeling empowered. I was receiving this attention on *my* terms, and in that moment, the spotlight routed the shadows.

Then the curtain dropped again, and the intermission was upon us.

As my troupe scurried to the makeup station for touch-ups, several performers patted me on the back. I did my best not to recoil. When an attendant arrived to re-pin my hair, I acquiesced reluctantly, hoping it would be over soon.

I was enduring my fifth minute of prodding and poking when Mother whispered through my earrings. "Simone, that was marvelous—absolutely incredible. You must be—"

Eloise cut her off. "Still nothing in the balconies, though we did question a page who was replaced at the last minute. Are you to the floor seats yet?"

I breathed a sigh of relief as the attendant finished with my hair and left to see to others. "No, not yet. But everyone checks out so far."

"We're doing a full sweep of the lobby now, but Felix is smart. He knows how to hide in plain sight," Eloise said. "Stick to the plan for now. Maybe he'll make a mistake." With that, she signed off.

I peered out from behind the curtain toward box 3A. "Mother, why are you still in your seat? I thought you had a post during the intermission."

"One of our agents took it for me. I'm still a little tired from the travel," she replied.

Tired from the travel? On assignment, Mother would spring into action after flying as many as twenty hours, and our plane ride last night hadn't been nearly that long—only one hour, fifty-seven minutes, and twenty-six seconds, to be exact. My brows furrowed in concern—but a sudden hum interrupted my thoughts.

I glanced down and pulled up the long sleeve of my robe to see a notification on the face of my Ministry-issued spywatch.

"How's it going? The art project is going great!!!!!!! — V."

Per usual, the V and I were partners in art class, and our term project on a Byzantine painting was due Monday. Our teacher, Madame Parks, was a new arrival at Trinity and had high expectations; but in the face of my many Ministry-related obligations, my enthusiasm for the project was waning. Byzantine art lacked a certain *je ne sais quoi* that the V was trying to make up for with rhinestones and glitter—though thus far, the effort seemed hopeless. I predicted the final product would secure us a firm 92 percent, which was fine with me. Though I would of course have preferred my normal 100 percent, I was busy enough that the V would have to carry some of the load on this one.

It was sweet of her to check in, but I needed to focus. Quickly, I typed out a message—"Good. Talk to you later— S."—and hit Send.

But as the curtain went up again and the warmth of the lights bathed me, I couldn't stop thinking about our assignment. *Maybe the V will come through and follow my directions for once.* It was a long shot, as the V tended to do the exact opposite. "I go where the inspiration takes me!" she often exclaimed. I preferred to rely on careful planning rather than inspiration—but it was out of my hands now.

As the music swelled again, my eyes raced through the floor seats. *Three over, one back. Three over, one back.* On and on it went, until I had cleared the room. All grids were accounted for, but not a Whisper among them.

Nevertheless, he was here. I knew it—but where could he be?

As the tenor began his solo, I whispered, "I've cleared my grids, but no sign of him. Perhaps I should start over?"

"We've pulled a young gentleman in for questioning," Eloise replied. "He could not produce his ticket when returning from the lobby, so we escorted him to a private room."

"It's not him," I murmured. That would be too easy.

Sure enough, as the tenor concluded, a whisper came through my earpiece. "He checks out. Work the balcony again—the Whisper has to be here somewhere."

Three over, one back. Three over, one back, and on and on, until I had cleared the room again and the curtain dropped. Only one act to go.

"Mother, have you seen anything?" I asked.

"No, dear, nothing—but the concert is fantastic. We are enjoying it immensely," she replied. Her voice had all the warmth of fresh bread coming out of the oven. "You should be proud of yourself, Simone," she reminded me again.

A faint smile cracked my face—but I had a job to do. I tried to return to my grids, but they blurred before my mind's eye, into that darn art assignment. In my opinion, the Byzantines needed a lecture on impressionism—though without the influence of their "style," the Renaissance might not have been necessary. I pictured our painting again—an angel bringing tidings to a young Mary. Why couldn't I let this go?

The final act commenced, and it was back to *three over, one back; three over, one back.* A constant dialogue was now running in my earpiece, making it harder for me to sing in time with the music. Though I was hiding it well, I was becoming fatigued, and frustration was setting in. *Where is he?*

I was almost through the floor seats again when a terrible thought occurred to me: we might not find him. Color rushed into my cheeks, and a few beads of sweat formed on my brow.

Even worse, my hair was starting to fall into my face. I'd already swept it away once, but the effort seemed hopeless.

"Your hair, dear. Pull it back," Eloise instructed. *I know, I know!*

I pulled my hair back over my ears. Our strategy wasn't working. I needed to try something else—but that painting kept dominating my subconscious. There it was: big, lifeless, and *blah*. What was my mind trying to tell me? *I never get off-task!*

I closed my eyes, took a breath, and let my mind wander. For the next forty-eight seconds, while the mezzo-soprano had the lead, I pored over every detail of the painting: the brushstrokes, the color palette, the texture, the . . .

Wait. That's it! It's not the details, it's the full frame. Concentrate on the full picture, not the details!

My eyes opened just in time for my final aria. I had three minutes and thirty-seven seconds to find him.

This time, as my voice filled the theater, all my senses felt heightened. I could smell the perfumes, the colognes, the faint burnt odor wafting from the heating system. I could distinguish every note from each instrument as it emanated from the pit, and hear the soft rustles from the audience as their clothes shifted with each movement. The room was in balance now.

Less than two minutes left.

I glanced up at Mother, who was looking back with adoring eyes. She could see me—the real me, confident and engaged.

The conductor's wand caught my eye, flashing up from the pit below. He was a fraction of a second behind on his cadence, but this was a challenging piece. As my part came to its crescendo, I surveyed the musicians, all playing in perfect time. I was living the joy of the music and lifting my voice to the rafters, even as I gazed down into the orchestra accompanying me. The violin, the bassoon, the oboes—

Wait. Why is there a second oboe? This performance doesn't call for one. I stared at the extra man among the woodwinds. Though he held his instrument properly, he wasn't playing. He was only listening.

I see you, Whisper.

I hit the final note—a C#6. The music concluded in a thunderous roar, and the house once again erupted. But as I locked hands with the cast for an impromptu closing bow, my mind had room for only one thought.

"The second oboe—he's the second oboe!" I gasped into my earpiece.

"Are you sure, dear? We thought he had given us the slip," Eloise replied.

My hair escaped its pins again, falling into my eyes as my choirmates' hands pulled me into another bow—but I still managed to catch a glimpse of the man's face. "I'm sure! It's him—the second oboe!"

In the next instant, nine agents dressed as hall pages converged on the pit. I raised my head just in time to see them closing in on the Whisper, whose face suddenly filled with alarm. Still clutching his oboe, he spun on his heel and made a futile attempt to hop out into the audience—but the orchestra pit was too tightly packed. The agents quickly surrounded him, and I saw a set of handcuffs flash.

As the Whisper was escorted out through the cheering crowd, he glanced back at me coldly. His jaw clenched, and his nostrils flared. Despite the triumph surging through me, a chill went down my spine.

Then the agents pulled him into the hall, and he was gone.

Seeking reassurance, I looked up at Mother, only to find her clapping and cheering. Her smile warmed me instantly, and I couldn't help but return it. *We did it!* it seemed to say—and we had.

A swell of pride filled me as I gazed out over the adoring

crowd. Our mission was over, and it was time to take a bow.

"*Merci! Merci!*"

My return to school the following Monday was far less exciting, if not downright mundane. The thrill of our success was still wearing off, and I couldn't wait for my next assignment.

The V and I were the last students to present our term project for art class. It took us several minutes to carefully remove the trifold canvas from a bag and place it on the easel at the front of the classroom. I took my place behind the easel, shielded by the array of sequins and assorted feathers that adorned our Byzantinesque masterpiece, though at least seven sequins and four feathers had already hit the floor. The V stood in front, presenting, and I reached around the sides of the canvas to point out details as she discussed them.

While I was sure our project would only garner us 92 percent of the full marks we could have earned, the V was doing great, and selling it like a pro. Although she tended not to follow directions, I was glad to have her help in this—despite my success in Vienna, I still didn't consider presentations my forte.

"...So in conclusion, when we study these boring paintings, we don't see *blah!* We see potential—lots of fabulous potential!"

With that, the rest of the students burst into applause. The V lingered at the front of the room to soak up the accolades, bowing and waving to the students in the back row. As for me, I immediately made a beeline for my seat.

"Great job, Simone! You and the V are so talented. Wow!" cheered the girl to my left as she clapped mightily.

Ugh. "It's only worth ninety-two percent," I murmured to myself.

Madame Parks rose from her chair and took a closer look at

the piece. "Well, it's apparent you've been busy, and your presentation was inspired." Her unruly blonde mane flopped into her face as she bent over her clipboard and wrote down her assessment. The rubric was clear, but she was taking longer than I'd expected. *Hm.*

Still at the front of the room, the V craned her neck, trying to sneak a peek at the score sheet. Finally, Madame Parks straightened and looked up to make her final remarks.

Here we go: ninety-two percent.

"Attention, students! After thoughtful consideration, this project, entitled 'Byzantine Be-Dazzled,' is awarded a score of ... ninety-three percent!" Madame Parks proclaimed.

The room clapped again, and the V took a bow, exaggeratedly signaling to me to stand and join her in basking in our success. But that wasn't going to happen.

Ninety-three percent? The rubric for this assignment was clear: five points deducted for less than four cited sources, and three points deducted for not using a direct quote from each. Our project, with its three sources and absent quote, should have been easy to assess. *Perhaps she rounded up? Maybe the V changed something at the last minute?* I had to analyze the score sheet!

The V savored the collective praise as she returned to her seat. "Ninety-three percent, Simone! Isn't that great?"

"Great, V. Maybe we'll frame it," I answered. *Ninety-three percent?*

Now firmly irritated, I raised my hand.

"Madame Parks?" I asked politely. "May I ask you a personal question?"

"Well, of course, dear. Please come forward."

I made my way to the front, skirting groups of girls who had broken into chatty packs. No one paid me any attention. Behind me, I heard the V exclaim, "NINETY-THREE PERCENT!"

I slid my index finger over the face of my watch. Under the

right circumstances, this piece of advanced Ministry technology could launch and navigate a rocket, but right now, I only needed to take a simple photo.

"Yes, dear, what is it?" Madame Parks asked. As she met my gaze, I let my hand drift inconspicuously toward her clipboard and snapped a picture. *That should do it.*

"May I use the restroom?"

"Simone, class ends in less than a minute. Can't you wait for—"

"Oh, yes, of course. I'll be fine," I replied. I had what I needed, and turned to take my seat.

The V was still staring at me. "N-I-N-E-T-Y-T-H-R-E-E-P-E-R-C-E-N-T!" she mouthed one last time.

I gave her a smile and turned back to the front of the room— only to find Claudia Finke, the girl assigned to the desk in front of mine, staring at me through her oversized glasses. *Geez!*

She smiled widely and leaned toward me. "Simone, my mum packed me an extra pudding. Would you like to share it at lunch?" she offered through a mouth full of braces.

I liked pudding, as it reminded me of our patisserie. "Ah, sure. I'll find you at lunch," I replied. My response was met with an even toothier smile and a slight giggle. This "popular" thing was getting weirder and weirder.

Feeling slightly unbalanced, I turned and started placing my school supplies into my backpack. I was half finished tucking my pencils into their case when—suddenly—the room went dark.

Gasps filled the air. "The power's off!" Claudia shouted, as if excited to share news of what was already evident.

After a few moments, the battery-powered emergency lights came to life. A wan fluorescent glow bathed the classroom as several of the girls huddled and began to whisper.

I saw the V reach for her mobile—no doubt to share the word of this exciting development with her adoptive parents back home.

As she looked down at the screen, however, her eyes bugged. "Hey, my mobile's dead, too!"

A hum rose from the classroom as everyone checked their mobiles, followed by exclamations of dismay. Not a single mobile was working.

Odd. I could understand the power grid failing—but the mobiles? And at the same time?

I thrust my hand beneath my desk and rolled up my worn sleeve to check my spywatch. Its face blinked on, displaying a satellite connection as strong as ever. *Good.*

"Everyone, please—I'm sure it's just a temporary outage. If we all just—" Madame Parks began. Before she could finish, however, the main lights flashed on, and within the next few seconds, all the students' mobiles blinked back to life.

With order restored, Madame Parks began describing the next unit with outstretched arms—only to be interrupted by the bell. Eager to leave, everyone stood, and the classroom emptied in seconds as students dispersed in every direction, rushing to their next classes.

I finished putting my books in my backpack and hurried after the V as she ran out. Our mathematics class was one hundred seventy-two steps away on the second floor of Lyden Hall, through the rose garden and across the lawn, and I squinted as we emerged into the sunshine.

Nestled in the heart of the Montmartre District, the Elizabeth of Trinity School for Girls had stood for over 160 years. With its heavy stone walls and iron front gates, it was a place of fairy tales, where dragons might fly overhead or a princess might gaze longingly out a window of one of the administrative building's five turrets. Old, weathered stone structures with terra-cotta tile roofs and large wooden doors dotted the parklike campus, smooth stone walkways weaving between them like the lattice of a carefully baked pie. And just inside the main gate was the Headmistress's residence—a two-story cottage of impeccable appointment, worthy of a queen or aristocrat.

But my love for Trinity wasn't just for the buildings, the gardens, or the walkways—it was for the scents, the sounds, the shadows. The way the air hung heavy just inside the dining hall's atrium. The echo of footsteps as students walked the ancient oak floors of the dining hall, and the way the midday sunlight refracted through the chapel's stained glass windows. Even my recent struggles with newfound popularity were not enough to quash my love for this school.

"Do you think I should have played up the sequins more?" the V asked as we took our twenty-second step.

"No. You did your—ugh!" As we turned a corner, I walked right into someone—the wrong someone.

Two years older than the V and I, Grace J. Paulson stood at the pinnacle of Trinity's social food chain. She was both a junior prefect and the captain of the field hockey team—distinctions that had been passed to her last year, when former queen bee Celia Merkel had moved to Leon mid-term. We'd all been ecstatic over her departure, but none so much as Grace, who had been Celia's rival since their second year.

And Grace had wasted no time establishing her reign in the wake of Celia's exit. On day one, she'd brutally embarrassed Kimmie King at lunch by pointing out a blemish on her forehead and faint stains beneath the armpits of her sweater. Kimmie had made the tactical error of sitting at table 5, historically designated only for the most popular of girls—but with Celia gone, I guessed she had aspired to move up in Trinity's social hierarchy as well. Grace would have none of it, however. It had been downhill since.

"Watch where you're going!" Grace barked, straightening her

sweater and skirt. Then she recognized me, and a nasty grin spread over her face. "Face in a book again, songbird?" Two of her cronies giggled from behind her.

"Ah, no. Just trying to get to class," I replied.

The V stepped between us, one hand firmly on her hip. "Isn't there a lame rabbit in the rose garden you could pounce on?"

The V must have been the only student at Trinity to remain completely unaffected by the social structure. No matter where she went, she always seemed to fit right in—perhaps because she always lived in the moment; or perhaps because her adoptive father, Monsieur Cantone, was one of the Trinity Seven—a fancy name for the chairmen of the school's financial foundation. Personally, I believed the root of her social ease lay in the fact that she simply did not care. Many times, she'd told me, "I don't do petty." I admired her for that—especially as I tried to get used to my sudden fame.

"Still watching over this loser, Cantone? I heard she lost her voice in Vienna. Poor, boring Simone. I didn't even know she was a student before this year—I thought she was a maid or something," Grace said.

"Whatever. Now run along and mow down some third-years," the V replied.

After a three-second stare-off, Grace turned to her two minions, made some remark under her breath, and walked away, followed by her troupe.

The V turned to me with an apologetic smile. "You know, you *should* watch where you're going, Simone. She's getting bigger by the week, and one of these times, she's going to snap."

I shrugged. It was nice of the V to worry, but Grace didn't intimidate me. She was just a mean girl with no imagination.

We made it to our class and slipped through the door just as Madame Gentzel was pulling it shut. I pulled out a notebook as she addressed the class, and allowed myself to relax into the comforting order of mathematics—simple, straightforward, and practical. I might be popular now, but at least the lessons hadn't really changed.

The same could not be said of other periods of the school day, however. At lunch, I found our table had expanded by several fifth-years, who all looked up as I approached. My heart sank as they pulled out their phones for a photo op.

"Bonjour, everybody," I muttered, setting down my tray.

"I'm done sweeping up, Father, and I just finished dusting the rolltop desk. Did we get any mail today?"

The store at 7 Rue Clodion had been busier than ever, and it had taken me three hours to clean up. The whole time, Father had thumbed through a thick set of architectural drawings for the new store in London. I had never seen him so rapt—at least, not over anything other than chocolate.

Now he looked up, seeming almost startled. "Mail? Ah—I don't know. Did we get any mail today, Garren?" he asked, turning toward a man who was meticulously placing utensils back into the worn drawers of an old cabinet.

Father had hired Garren Barre twenty-three days after our triumph at the Chocolatiers' Ball. The day after Father had signed his deal with Sugars Fontaine, he'd reluctantly agreed he needed someone to help him at the patisserie, as he would be spending a lot of time in London. Once word of the position got out, Garren, who had been born in Paris, had discreetly reached out to Father to offer his candidacy.

Of course, this did not sit well with Madame Bo Cho, under whom Garren had worked as a sous-chef since graduating from Le Cordon Bleu eight years ago. From her perspective, Garren's controversial betrayal added insult to the injury of coming in second to Father at the Chocolatiers' Ball. When Father sought Madame Fontaine's counsel on the matter, however, she replied, "Louie, all is fair in love and chocolate."

Still, Father had given everyone at the patisserie a say in the hiring process—and we'd all agreed Garren was an ideal candidate. Madame Tris, who tended to stare at Garren and commented often on his keen level of fitness, voted an emphatic *yes*. Monsieur John was less inspired, though he also could not deny Garren's talent.

As for me, I liked Garren because he never asked me any personal questions—nothing about school, nothing about singing, nothing about anything. He was all business. Most importantly, Father trusted him. After his triumph at the Ball, Father had decided to preserve the LaFray cookbooks in storage, as we no longer needed to reference them. He and Garren had pored over them just before they were put away, and our new hire proved a quick study.

Garren turned to me. "The mail? Ah, yes—I organized it and placed it in your desk, just the way you like it."

"Thank you, Monsieur Garren," I replied, going over to my desk and rolling up the front. Father and I had briefly discussed moving my old rolltop desk out to make more room, but we simply could not bring ourselves to do so. It had sat in this spot for as long as the shop itself had stood—nearly eighty years.

As I fished out the mail, the door to the back staircase flew open, and Mia's friend Riley came running into the store, with Mia herself in hot pursuit. Gigi, our French bulldog, padded after them, wagging her tail wildly.

"Thag, you're it!" screamed Mia, diving over a table and tagging Riley on the shoulder.

"'Thag'?" replied a now still Riley. Both had just lost a front tooth, and were milking it for all the attention they could. *Theater kids.*

"Girls, we're just finishing our final cleaning. Can you play outside?" Father said.

"Ah, I don' wanna play thag anymore," Mia replied with a huff. Riley chuckled and started to hunt around the kitchen for a wayward cookie.

The front door opened, and the welcome bell clanged.

"Bonjour—I'm home!" Mother said as she closed the door behind her and dropped her bag on the counter. She'd been at the doctor's for her six-month physical, a staple for members of the Ministry.

Father glanced up from his blueprints, which spread in a cascade across the table. "Everything okay, dear?" he asked, standing to greet her.

"Never better. Ready to take on the world," she replied as Father kissed both her cheeks. The blueprints slid off the table, startling an unsuspecting Gigi, who had just settled down for a nap.

"I have to show you these revised drawings, Julia," Father said as he walked back to his table. "Sugars is sparing no expense. It's going to be marvelous!"

Mother yawned. "Yes, Louie, marvelous—but I'd like to lay down for a minute or two first. I walked most of the way home, and it's warm today. I just need a moment to recuperate."

Father's eyes darted up. "Of course, my dear. Do you need anything?"

Mother shook her head and turned toward Mia and Riley, who had begun whispering between themselves. "What are you two planning?" she asked. The two girls blushed and started to squirm. "Now, if I had to guess, I would—"

Suddenly, a flash of fiery color erupted at her wrist.

"What?" Mother whispered. She snapped upright and stared

at her watch for several seconds. Then her gaze darted to me, and her eyes widened. "Simone—look."

She pointed, and my eyes whipped down to my own watch. It was flashing red, too.

It had never flashed red before.

Harper Faust

Not more than half an hour later, Mother and I were marching through the principal administrative room of the Ministry's Paris headquarters. Always bursting with agents moving to and from their workstations, this space usually buzzed with the chaotic hum of a kicked beehive—but now it felt more like a boat lost at sea. Each agent was glued to their screens, saying nothing. The tension was palpable. Something was wrong—very wrong.

As we reached Eloise's office, Mother turned to me and pulled several unruly strands of hair from behind my glasses. Then she forced a tight smile, and we went in.

"She's *gone!*" Eloise bellowed from her desk as the door closed behind us. "Gone!"

In all the years I'd known Eloise, I had never seen her display any sense of anxiety or concern. Now, as I studied her face, I barely recognized the person sitting in front of me. Her skin was the sallow color of sour milk, and her hair, which was always pulled back in a perfect bun, was loose and unkempt. Not even her clothes looked right: her blazer was wrinkled and hanging off-center on her shoulders. Panic this extreme could only mean one thing.

"What's going on, Eloise?" Mother asked. "*Who's* gone?"

Eloise looked up at us. Her eyes were wet and red.

"*Claire!*" she said, her voice cracking.

Claire Pilfrey was in her final year at the Claymoore School in London—a posh independent school for the children of privileged landlords, titans of industry, and even royalty. She had been boarding there for three years. I hadn't seen her since I was eight, though Mother had visited her a few weeks ago while inspecting our new store on Sloane Street. After all, she was Claire's godmother, handpicked by Claire's own mother—Eloise.

"Claire—missing?" Mother asked, frowning. "Are her mobile and locator working?"

Locator? Mobiles could be tracked, I knew; but this was the first time I had heard of a *locator.*

Eloise's eyes tracked away, as if she was finding it difficult to focus. "No. . . no. There was concern when she didn't report to breakfast. Her dormitory prefect found her watch with the locator intact on her bed." Her voice came out strained. "We're reviewing all the tapes; we have Scotland Yard and MI6 onsite, and still nothing. Not one clue. She's gone!"

My mind began to race. I remembered Claire as quiet and reserved, but with an inner strength that caused her to exude confidence. Her keen intellect afforded her a certain independence that Eloise fostered.

"Does she have a boyfriend?" The words were out of my mouth before I had the chance to think twice.

Both women stared at me.

"Absolutely not!" Eloise replied. "I know everyone in her life—all her professors, her friends, everybody. There is no boyfriend, Simone!"

Mother pulled her hair back into a knot and rolled up her sleeves. "Well, Eloise, have you started the protocol?"

Eloise's wandering eyes refocused. "The protocol—why, yes, yes. All of the standard response measures are in motion. But it's been too long! It was time to call you in."

"Protocol?" I whispered.

Mother turned to me. "Yes, dear, protocol—in case any junior agents go missing. If they can't be found through their watch, the protocol is engaged. It's been tested before, but Claire is the first to actually have gone missing."

Junior agents? What? Was Claire in the Ministry, too?

As if reading my thoughts, Mother leaned toward me. "I know what you're thinking, Simone. Yes, there are five junior agents in the Ministry. All are of varying abilities and ages, and all are monitored. Even you."

Wait—five?

At that moment, I felt myself grow older, as if a portion of my adolescence had evaporated. Knowing I wasn't unique as a junior spy invoked feelings of anxiety and shared responsibility. *I hope I can stack up.*

"So, Claire—"

"—shares many of your talents, and was making great advancements in her fieldwork," Mother said. "She may have attracted unwanted attention. If that's the case, however, it isn't good. It means whoever is responsible for her disappearance knew enough about Ministry protocol to have removed her watch before taking her."

I stared at Eloise, then looked down at my watch. Suddenly, the familiar technology felt like a handcuff. I'd known the Ministry could use it to contact me at any time, and was not naïve enough to think I couldn't be tracked—but somehow, the word "monitored" shed an uncomfortable light on my position. Although I felt older, I was abruptly, acutely aware of how childish I must appear to the other agents.

A voice broke through the intercom, snapping the rising tension taut. "Madame, we have some information."

Eloise's eyes flew open, and a glimmer of hope returned to her face. "Yes, of course. Come in!"

Mother reached for my hand and gave it a reassuring squeeze as a suited analyst entered, carrying a single piece of paper that he handed to Eloise. "We believe this information to be one hundred percent credible, madame," he said with a curt nod, carefully avoiding eye contact. Obviously, this was not the news the Ministry had been hoping for.

As Eloise hastily scanned the paper, her eyebrows coming together in confusion and anger. Suddenly, she slammed her hand on the desk and looked up at Mother.

"*He* took her! That monster! We should have—"

"*Who* took her, Eloise?" Mother asked gently.

Trembling visibly, Eloise sat upright in her chair. Her voice cracked as she spoke.

"Klaus Ludwig was captured on video this morning boarding a private jet at Heathrow, accompanied by two men and what appears to be a girl. The video is not definitive, and of course the manifest is forged—but the timeline matches. He has her!"

A cold wave of nausea passed over me. Eloise had brought in Ludwig's son, and in return, he had come for her daughter.

Retribution was not a foreign concept to me—indeed, I knew it to be a powerful motivator, though one that often yielded unpredictable and reckless actions. Klaus was a criminal, and I suspected he had accepted a certain amount of risk in his career. But he was known for being calm and calculating. Now, it was clear something in him must have snapped. *What kind of monster would kidnap a fourteen-year-old?* I was uncomfortable even contemplating it—and after watching my mentor wince with worry and uncertainty, I felt my disbelief turning to hatred for him.

"He's been jamming mobile services and power grids throughout Europe for the past few days, but this, this is . . ." Eloise trailed off again as her chest started to heave.

I remembered the outage at Trinity. *The blackout in our art class—that was him!*

"Well, at least we have a motive," Mother said, her voice quiet and cold. She seemed as horrified as I felt, and turned to Eloise. "Eloise, I'm so sorry. If I'd known—"

Eloise shook her head.

"That isn't all. There's something else," she said quietly.

Something else?

"Now that we know it was him, I—I have it on good authority that he might have wanted something else. Something Claire had."

The hairs on the back of my neck rose. I'd never liked surprises.

"What?" asked Mother.

"The OmniKey. We believe it was in Claire's possession," Eloise replied.

What? That's impossible. The key that opens everything? It felt as if Eloise had suddenly announced the existence of aliens, or sea monsters. *It can't be.*

"I thought that was just a myth," Mother said.

"No. It is very real, and he certainly wants it back. We—"

The intercom came to life again, interrupting her. "Madame, we have Headmaster Bailes on a secure line."

"Oh—oh, yes," Eloise replied, regaining her composure. I had never seen her emotions pivot like this before—but I knew trauma could have strange effects. "Julia, I'll brief you this evening. I have to take this."

I looked at Mother. I was bursting with questions, suggestions, possibilities. But I knew it would do no good. We would both have to wait.

Mother and I returned to the apartment in silence. The whole time, my mind swirled with unasked inquiries and unseen phantoms. I barely knew Claire, but I couldn't help but put myself in her shoes—imagining her fear at being taken away, the loss of control. I needed answers. Where was she now? How had she been taken? The Claymoore School was one of the most secure facilities in England. Royalty passed through its halls daily. Someone there had to have seen or heard something. I was sure of it.

My mind kept circling back to the analytics of the situation. I yearned to see the school tapes, establish the timeline, and snoop around the campus. There had to be a clue somewhere—some film or data to analyze—and that was what I did best.

Only a handful of pleasantries were shared at dinner, and both Mia and I went to bed early. My room felt unfamiliar under the weight of Claire's disappearance—silent and serious. Even a fortifying glance over the city lights could not calm me, as the pit in my stomach yawned wider.

"Simone? May I come in?" Mother asked, cracking open the door.

"Of course. Did you hear any news about Claire?" My glasses slid down my nose.

"No, but we need to talk," Mother said. She started to unfold my blanket from the foot of my bed. As I climbed under the covers, she sat beside me and pushed my hair back over my ears. A tear started to form in her right eye, and she quickly brushed it away. She grabbed my glasses and held them up to the light. After wiping them clean, she gently placed them back on my face and stroked my hair.

"Simone, I want you to know you girls mean everything to me. You may not understand, but the pain that Eloise is enduring is a parent's worst nightmare. As a mother, your child's safety is like air. You can't quantify its value, and trying to make any comparison is useless."

I took in her words. Hearing her voice crack, seeing the tears and the sincerity in my mother's unusually tired eyes, something bubbled up in me.

"Let me go," I blurted.

"What?"

"Send me to Claymoore. I can find out what happened to Claire—maybe learn whether she really found the Key, or where she hid it. I could learn where the Maestro took her. I can find her."

"Simone . . ." Mother looked pained. Again, I saw the fatigue that worried me so. "I know you want to help, and certainly we can—"

"I know I can do this. I can search the school and talk to the kids there. I can be on the inside, and there have to be clues. That's what I'm best at—finding clues!"

"Simone—all the way to London, by yourself? I'm not sure—" she began—but my resolve was only growing.

"I'm the right age to enroll there, and Father will be there, finishing the new store. I know I can do this. I know I can find her."

Mother leaned back slowly. She squinted, and I saw more tears beginning to form in her eyes before she quickly turned to look out the window.

"I would do the same in your place," she admitted. "You really are growing up so fast . . ." She turned back and hugged me tight. Somehow, in the strength of that silent hug, I knew we would soon be apart—and that she would no doubt worry about me just as much as Eloise was worried about Claire.

What was I getting myself into?

"You're moving to London!" the V screamed.

"*Shhh!*" several of our classmates hissed.

The day at Trinity had dragged by at a glacial pace. By fifth period, I was more than eager to take our scheduled math test—unlike most of the students, who groaned at seeing our tests waiting facedown on our desks as we entered the classroom.

"Just for a few months," I whispered back.

I would be leaving for London in six days. Mother had briefed me over breakfast and transferred me digital files on all the students, teachers, and staff at Claymoore. There were only 285 of them, so memorizing them would not take long.

The Ministry had quickly agreed to my proposal. I was the proper age to enroll at Claymoore, and I could even continue my schooling as I worked. However, they had two stipulations.

First, I would be given a new watch. After what had happened to Claire, the Ministry had determined an additional layer of security was necessary for its junior agents. Claire had been missing for hours before her disappearance was noted—far too long. My new watch came with a built-in device that would monitor my heartbeat. If I ever removed it without inputting the override first, it would alert the Ministry within seconds. Begrudgingly, I had to admit it was clever—and it would make Mother feel better, at least.

The second stipulation was, if anything, even more significant, and I was still warming to it. For the first time in my career, I would be working with a partner. Higher-ups at the Ministry had agreed that I "lacked certain social skills"—so another junior agent would be on assignment with me.

Junior Agent #4, Harper Faust, had been recruited by the Ministry for her extraordinary social prowess and intellect at age nine. Portions of her file were classified, but those I could access were impressive. Boasting a maturity well beyond her years, she was both a skilled painter and public speaker at the progressive New Age School in Metz. In only two years, she had worked the field eleven times, to enormous success. In many ways, we were exact opposites—but Mother said this would only strengthen our partnership.

Our mission was clear: find the Key, and while we were at it, insinuate ourselves into the Claymoore School and gather as much information about Claire as possible. Who were her friends? Which teachers were close to her? What were her day-to-day habits?—everything. Harper would take the lead in making the acquaintances of our fellow students and establishing relationships, and I would observe and analyze the inner workings of the school. Only Headmaster Bailes would be aware of our operation.

Mother was apprehensive about letting me go, especially as she would stay home with Mia, who was currently embroiled in a casting dispute at the *Loy L'École de Danse.* Father, however, was thrilled. Harper and I would be boarding at Claymoore, but he would be staying only one kilometer away at 6 Aubrey Walk—Sugars' Kensington townhome—while the finishing touches were placed on the new store in preparation for its grand opening in December. If all went well, Father and I would be back in Paris by the end of term with a successful store opening behind us, and Claire Pilfrey would be home for the holidays.

"*Psst!* Simone!" the V whispered again. I glanced in her direction as she began swinging her legs under her desk. "I wish I were going to London. Paris is tired. I need some excitement in my life."

"Eyes forward during your test, Mademoiselle Cantone," chirped Madame Gentzel.

The V rolled her eyes, and begrudgingly turned back to her paper to continue pondering the dynamics of linear equations.

I finished the test's eighteen questions in under three minutes, then briefly rechecked my work, considering whether I ought to answer the extra credit question. My paper was perfect, so I decided to forego the extra question and turned the test over, and my mind to the mission ahead.

After school, I was to take a private car and meet Harper downtown to attend our preliminary briefing. Eloise had amassed hours of material to go through, from the schematics and history of the school's buildings to Headmaster Bailes' shorthaired cat Sophie, who apparently had a penchant for bacon and soft pillows.

I couldn't wait to get started. Between last night's talk with Mother and my own involvement in the case that had brought in the Whisper and inspired Klaus Ludwig's retaliation, the thought of Claire's disappearance was making me ill.

"Ugh, math gets harder every year," the V groused as she passed her test to the front of the classroom. "So, why are you guys moving to London?"

"We're not moving to London," I replied, trundling papers forward. "It's just for the rest of the year. I have an opportunity to study there, and I can also help Father prepare the new store while I'm there."

As I spoke, I became aware of someone else listening with great delight.

"London? Why in the world would anyone want you there?" Grace laughed. "Well, you won't be missed."

The V turned to face her. "She's going to study and help her father there, dummy—and anyway, it's none of your business. Has it occurred to you that you're almost two years older than anyone else in this class?"

"Watch it, Cantone! I might stink at math, but I could mop the floor with both of you in two seconds," Grace replied, staring her down.

I squeezed my eyes shut. *Don't provoke her, V. Just let it go.*

"Girls? Is there a problem back there?" asked Madame Gentzel.

I opened my eyes in time to see Grace force a smile. "No, Madame, no problems here. We were just discussing the test," she said sweetly. Then she lowered her voice to a whisper. "I wish *both* of you would go."

"Whatever." The V rolled her eyes and turned back to me. "London! I was there last spring with my parents. Father goes there a lot on business." She gasped. "I won't see you for *months!* Will you be home for Christmas?"

"I'll try—but don't worry. We can Facetime whenever you want. Mother and Mia are staying here, and—"

"Ugh, I'll be bored to tears here all by myself! And who will be my partner in art class?"

This conversation was starting to get uncomfortable. Even my socks were itching. "It's only a few months—and besides, I can shop for your Christmas gift while I'm at Claymoore. Something unexpected . . . maybe royal?" I replied with a smile.

The V was convinced a mix-up at birth had denied her a royal birthright. She had several fantasies in this regard, and had been plotting her return to prominence for years—though I thought she was doing just fine where she was.

At my words, she perked up instantly. "Did you say *Claymoore?* As in the Claymoore School?" she gasped, her interest returning. "That's where all the royals send their kids!"

"Ah—yes. I guess." Oops. Maybe it hadn't been such a good idea to direct the V onto this line of thought. I was becoming desperate to change the subject. "So, how do you think you did on the—"

"What a place! It seems perfect for me!" the V said, her voice getting louder with every word. Everyone in the class was now focused on us, and their whispers were forming a dull hum.

I slid down in my seat. The school day couldn't end soon enough.

For all its beauty and grandeur, Paris felt flat that afternoon. Even the Eiffel Tower in the distance could not induce a smile, the weight of the moment squashing any excitement.

Before continuing downtown, the private car that picked me

up from school stopped at a hotel in the Champs-Élysées district, where Harper had checked in the night before. I sat in the back seat, my mind still racing. The Ministry's headquarters were only three minutes away, and Eloise was waiting. *Come on, come on.*

I heard a lock click, and turned my attention to the space beside me as my new partner opened the car door and slid inside.

"It's a pleasure to meet you. I have heard so much about the famous Simone LaFray," Harper said, reaching out for a handshake. "Ah—a good grip; and your eyes are beautiful. Have you thought about contacts?" Somehow, she had just paid me two compliments without making me skeptical of her intentions. Well done.

Harper's own appearance was flawless. Athletic, with light caramel skin, soft brown eyes, and a button nose, she was beautiful, but approachable in every way. Her body language was surprisingly unguarded for meeting someone for the first time, and her tone was calm and measured, with no sense of pomposity. Being in her presence was like being wrapped in a warm, familiar blanket.

"Ah, no. I've always worn glasses—no contacts for me," I replied, trying to compose believable small talk as my mouth went dry. We would be inside the Ministry in under five minutes, and I was counting every second.

Three minutes later, as the car pulled away, we stood on the sidewalk and stared up at the nondescript building, its importance well masked by a lack of exterior ornamentation. "I get chills every time before I walk in," Harper said. "Let's go to work, agent," she added, approaching the shabby basement door that led into the building.

Eloise greeted us wanly at the desk within before leading us through the rest of the building and into her office. Her hair was uncombed, and her eyes were dark, as though she hadn't slept in days.

Having abruptly dropped our conversation in the car, I felt I needed to say something to Harper. "I noticed we have the same birthday," I whispered.

Harper tilted her head and said with a smile, "Yes, April twenty-fifth."

Across from us, Eloise closed the file in front of her. "That's Claire's birthday," she murmured.

What? Really? Unbidden, my mind calculated the possibility. If it was true, it was impressive—the odds would have to be about a million to one.

"The rooms are ready, madame," said an agent over the intercom.

Intel Room #3 was thirty-nine steps from Eloise's office and twenty-eight steps down the hall from the outer room. I had been there sixty-three times, and it remained unchanged except for the wall monitors, which were replaced every six months. It was a room designed for concentration: no personal items, no music, no clutter—only data. I could lose myself in there for days.

For the next several hours, Harper and I pored over intelligence on anyone and everyone who spent time at the Claymoore School: roommates, teachers, friends, administrators, janitors, gardeners, anyone who might have crossed paths with Claire. Eloise joined us briefly to immerse herself in the files as an apparent distraction, but her mind never seemed to settle, and she was constantly shifting papers and rubbing her eyes. Her panic seemed to have dissolved into despair, and nothing seemed able to pull her out of it.

After a couple of hours, Harper began to fidget and flip back through her pages. I sensed a question forming, and tensed instinctively.

"Do you always script when you're working?" Harper finally asked.

I waited a moment before answering. We were down to the last four dossiers, and I didn't want to overlook anything. I finished the paragraph and looked up.

"Yes. It helps me focus." As far as I was concerned, there was no shame in saying things over and over again. It kept me sharp.

"It's okay. I just wanted to make sure you were paying attention."

I tried not to take offense, but a swell of irritation bubbled up in me. I glanced up from the file and checked my watch. "In the last seventeen minutes, I have read 8,642 words. I could recite the entire roster of Claymoore in reverse alphabetical order. The room has kept an exact temperature of 23 degrees Celsius, and you just blinked for the 289th time. Yeah, I would say I was paying attention."

Harper blinked again. *Two hundred ninety.* "Oh, Simone—I didn't mean to offend. I was just . . ."

"It's fine. I just don't like to be interrupted," I replied.

We stared at each other.

"I wish I could do that," Harper said.

"Do what? Appear awkward and weird?"

"No. I've met a lot of people, Simone, but no one quite like you. It's amazing. You're the fastest processor I've ever seen. It's like it's effortless. I can read people, but I'm guessing you can do that too. Incredible," she added, glancing over my face. "We're going to be friends, Simone. Even after this is over," she said with a reassuring smile. "Now, let's go over these last few files."

For the next twenty-two minutes, we talked about the mission, our families, and school. She had a younger sister too, and her parents were both professors of literature. I felt comfortable enough to attempt a joke, and when it bombed, she laughed anyway. The conversation flowed, and despite my reservations, I felt we were becoming friends.

Eloise popped in for the last time. Her hair had been brushed and her clothes straightened. This was the mentor I knew.

"Girls, please give me your attention. Despite my insistence, Headmaster Bailes has refused to help us find the OmniKey. He said that the school is experiencing enough commotion and rumor with Claire gone missing, and a full search of the grounds is out of the question. We're on our own, ladies."

Harper and I turned to each other with questioning faces.

"Can you tell us a little more about the Key? There's nothing on it in the files," Harper said.

Eloise took a deep breath. For a moment, she said nothing, seeming to weigh her words carefully. Then she said, "It is no secret that the Maestro had been working on a device that would allow him to hack into any other device or network. An interagency cooperative of the world's finest engineers attempted to theorize how this could be achieved. They concluded that a device with a precise composition of rare earth metals, magnets, and a processor could potentially act as a short-term digital portal. It's simply a conduit to tie into a computer or network, so it should be sleek and unassuming. We've surmised it is about the size of a credit card, and maybe one centimeter in depth. Given its components, our best guess is that it weighs about a quarter of a kilogram."

"And why do you think Claire had this key?" Harper asked.

Eloise pursed her lips.

"Very astute. Claire had been on assignment for several months, and . . . well, I'm not proud to say it, but we hadn't been getting along recently. Our communication had been fractured and sparse, and the strain of spy work was weighing on her. Perhaps when you're both older, you'll understand what I'm talking about. Believe me, it is only making the current circumstance even more painful for me.

"However, just before her disappearance, Claire reported coming into the possession of a high-value asset—something too sensitive to name over the typical lines. We arranged for a plain-clothed agent to meet her and make the drop under the guise of a family visit—but she vanished the night before it was to happen."

"So you believe the Maestro kidnapped her to get the Key?" I asked. In spite of myself, a modicum of relief entered my mind. Perhaps the kidnapping hadn't been a mere act of revenge.

"Yes, we believe this was part of his motivation. Claymoore is one of the most secure places in London, if not all of Europe. He probably had less than five minutes to get in, grab her, and get out. If they'd searched the school for it, they would certainly have been caught looking for it around the campus. If the Key was on her, they would've used it by now; and since her disappearance, there have been no system breaches. No, he doesn't have it yet. She hid it somewhere in Claymoore. Somewhere safe."

Harper hesitated, then asked, "Why didn't she just leave Claymoore and give it to you or an agent at the London office when she first found it?"

"The Maestro has attempted to construct several other compromising devices in the past. We've had the good fortune to obtain a few of them. He places a short-wave locator in each of them to track them should they become lost, and would certainly have done the same for the Key. As he's kidnapped Claire, it's all but certain he knew it went to Claymoore, and his thugs would have had the school under constant surveillance. My guess is that while she was at the school, Claire hid the Key somewhere that blocked the signal, intending to hand it over when it was safe."

Harper squinted and rubbed her thumb across her lower lip. "But how did she get it? Claire, I mean."

Eloise stared coldly at her. "Also classified, I'm afraid. Regardless, there is no way he could hope to break into Claymoore now. Security has been doubled, and the staff is on high alert. The Key is somewhere inside the school, and you must find it."

Eloise turned and grasped the doorknob. Without looking back at us, she said, "We'll revisit this tomorrow. Simone, your car is waiting outside. Harper, you'll be staying with me tonight. Your mother will be joining us in a few hours. Her train was delayed." She paused, and the pain crept back into her face. "Simone, we'll contact you if there are any changes."

Harper and I turned to each other. In unison, we whispered the creed of all the Ministry's agents: "*Protéger les Gens.*"

Protect the People.

"Dinner was perfect, Julia," Father said as we all helped clear the table. A wide smile covered his face. "Your salmon is always grilled just right."

"I'll wash if you dry," I said to Mia as she slipped a chunk of fish to Gigi.

"Okay, but make sure you get all the suds off. My skin is overly sensitive to dish soap," Mia replied.

I rolled my eyes and started on the dishes. No gloves for me.

When the kitchen was clean and all the dishes had been put away, Mother strolled out from the living room with a sweater wrapped around her shoulders. "Would you like to join me on the roof?" she asked.

On rare occasions, Mother and I would shimmy out her window onto a catwalk and climb up to the roof. Paris on a fall night was one of the great pleasures in life. The air had a slight chill, but the energy of the city acted almost like a warming lamp. You could sense the year winding down, and feel satisfaction and contentment in knowing you were a part of it.

I followed Mother out the window and onto the roof. After gazing out over the city for a few moments, we shooed away some pigeons and took a seat.

"Eloise said you and Harper make a formidable team. That's good—working with someone who makes you better," Mother said. She seemed to consider something, then sat up straight and grasped my hand in both of hers. "I didn't think you needed a partner on this one, but Eloise insisted. I understand her point—but don't think for a second that you're not good enough to go it alone. I'm not sure if I tell you often enough, but there's nothing you can't handle. You're as strong as they come."

She smiled at me. "Over these last few months, I've been taking stock of my career, our family, everything—and there's not one thing I would change. Not one. But change happens anyway, Simone—sometimes when you least expect it. It happens, but the strong are ready. We're ready for this."

I looked into her eyes and nodded, matching her energy. But I caught a flicker in her gaze, and something in me wondered:

Is she trying to reassure me—or herself?

That night, I lay in my bed, gazing at my watch and hoping for good news. I wasn't scared about the mission in front of me, but Eloise's panic and the weight of the last few days were taking their toll.

Around midnight, I heard footsteps at my door, and hastily buried my arm beneath the covers, pretending to sleep. The door creaked open, and Mother came in. I tried to slow my breathing, though I wasn't sure whether it was convincing to such a decorated spy. But if she saw through my ruse, Mother didn't say anything at all. She only stood beside my bed, looking over me as she had when I was still a toddler.

Finally, after what felt like hours, I heard her turn, and her footsteps faded away down the hall as the door creaked shut. As soon as she was gone, I pulled my hand out from beneath the covers and checked my watch. Two a.m.

Ugh.

––––––––––––

"Come on, Simone—we need another rack of éclairs!" bellowed Monsieur John.

"And more of the chocolate and almond petit fours," added Madame Tris.

The store was busier than usual, and a line had formed nearly an hour before we'd flipped the sign to *Ouvert*. I looked up from the dusting station and adjusted my glasses. "I'm working on it. They'll be up in a minute."

"Simone, the cooling racks can also be turned over," said Garren.

As busy as it was, I welcomed the distraction from my impending mission. The three hours of sleep I'd gotten last night would be just enough to get me through.

"Three more orders of lemon calissons!" boomed Father, placing the phone back on the receiver. Garren nodded from the back.

"Here you go," I said to Madame Tris as I removed the empty tray from the display and replaced it with a rack of shortbread cookies and scones. The store, while chaotic to those observing from the front, was running on all cylinders. I loved this place.

Madame Tris winked and leaned over to me. "We could use more croissants and macarons too, dear."

"They're on the cooling racks now," I replied distantly. I was distracted by a waving hand that had appeared on the other side of the glass front door.

"Simone! It's me," Harper called out from the door. She looked refreshed, in blue jeans and a light pink sweater. As she entered, a gust of brisk autumn wind followed, and her eyes lit up and tracked to the displays. I was surprised to see her—even a little stunned.

My understanding was that agents rarely, if ever, socialized.

"Now, who is this?" Father asked, approaching from across the store. And standing behind me with his one hand on my shoulder. "Simone, don't be rude— introduce me to your friend!"

"Oh—sorry. This is Harper—ah—Harper Faust. You know, from the . . ."

"Ah, so this is the famous Harper! Well, it is a delight to meet you. What do you think of our humble store?"

"It's amazing, Monsieur LaFray. Like something out of a fairy tale. When Eloise gave me the afternoon off, I simply had to come and visit," she replied, taking a deep breath of the sweet aromas.

"It's Saturday, so we are super busy, Harper. I need to get back to work. I don't know if I can—"

"Nonsense," said Father. "How about helping us back here in the kitchen for a few hours so you girls can hang out?"

Hang out?

Harper's eyes grew big as saucers. "Are you serious? Work at the famous LaFray's!? Where's an apron?"

For the next hour and twenty-six minutes, Harper and I dusted pastries, rotated the cooling racks, and iced petit fours. Father even had her answering the phone and taking orders. She was great at everything, and amid the clattering of the pans and trays, we could talk freely.

As the conversation turned to the Ministry, Harper looked around to make sure no one was within earshot.

"I read about your mission in Vienna—as background for our assignment. I wish I had a talent like yours."

My stomach knotted slightly at the memory of the Whisper. "Yeah—thanks. It took a little longer than I would have liked to find the target, but we were sure he was there," I replied.

Harper wiped her forehead, streaking it with confectioner's

sugar in the process, and put down her sugar duster. "My missions aren't nearly that exciting. Most are actually kind of boring. I hope I start to do more undercover work. Maybe next year . . ."

Her posture changed, and she turned to me. "Don't get me wrong—I love being a spy. It's exciting and fun, but sometimes . . . you know."

I didn't. What was she talking about? I pushed some loose hair back under my toque. I wasn't sure what to say, but I knew I needed to say *something*.

"Well, it can be stressful sometimes . . ."

"No, not that. I can handle that. It's just . . . sometimes it feels so obvious who the villains are. I know we have to follow orders, but sometimes I'm not sure. . . . It just feels too easy. Like I'm only reading half the files, but the full picture . . . it's got to be more complicated than that."

Complicated?

"The Maestro is a bad man, there's no doubt about that. I wasn't talking about him. But I've done some independent research on some of the targets on my missions, and . . . I don't know. They don't always seem so bad." She picked up her duster and started on a fresh rack of pastries.

"Uh . . . I guess so," I replied. It was the only thing I could come up with. I was too blindsided by what she'd just said.

We worked on the next racks in silence, and I pondered her words. *What is she talking about? It's our job to stop bad things from happening, and the data is always conclusive. Aren't all the people we bring in criminals?*

As we finished the fourth rack of pastries, Harper's watch vibrated.

"Oh, look at that," she said. "Eloise has a car outside for me." She untied her apron. "I have to go, but this was awesome." Before I could react, she wrapped her arms around me in a hug.

"We're going to do this, Simone. We're going to get Claire back."

I didn't say anything—just nodded until she pulled away and made for the door. As I watched her leave, my mind returned to her comment.

Half the files? Too easy? It just didn't make any sense.

———

After cleaning up the well-worn store, I ascended the steps to my room to find Mother had already started packing my bags. Two suitcases sat open on my floor, and Gigi had moved into one for the night. Though I wouldn't be leaving for London for a few more days, I was going to miss her.

The next day, I awoke just before dawn. While I'd hoped for good news on Claire, there was no such luck. A day of church and brunch raised my spirits, but I couldn't stop thinking about her, nor counting the hours before my departure.

My last day at Trinity moved fast. I spent most of it with my guidance counselor, Madame Leard, an engaging, bubbly sort who saw the best in every situation. Ever the intrepid mentor, she began our conversation by trying to stay in form, saying, "Now, Simone, you will be representing Trinity at one of the finest schools in Europe." But her eyes sparkled, and she blurted out, "Isn't it awesome!?"

We went over my schedule at Claymoore and discussed the similarities to Trinity's curriculum—of which there were many. As I exited her office, my thoughts drifting to lunch, I saw the V standing across the hall, waiting for me.

"Simone, there's something I have to tell you!" she called out.

As we walked to the dining hall, the V made a compelling case for why she needed to go to London with me. Eagerly, she told me how she had discussed the venture at great length with her parents, and they were on board. "Can you imagine the two of us in London? Think of the people we could meet! The shopping, the concerts we could go to. Oh, oh! We could meet the Queen!"

I endured the next thirty minutes of lunch being barraged with fun facts about London and her deep knowledge of anything royal. Mercifully, when the bell rang, we would be heading to different classes in different directions. I counted down the seconds—but when the harsh alarm sounded and we filed into the hallway together, I was surprised at the surge of emotion that filled me.

This is harder than I thought. I turned to her with a lump in my throat and said, "I'll miss you, V, but this is something I have to do alone."

She must have known it was coming, but it seemed to sting anyway. Her smile faltered, and she glanced at her shoes. But after a brief moment, her bright grin returned, and she looked up.

"You're going to text me every day, right? Oh! Maybe I could come and visit. I'll have to get Mom on that."

A swell of students suddenly filled the hallway, pushing the V farther away. She shouted over her shoulder. "Call me!"

———

One of the Ministry's familiar unmarked cars picked me up again from school and dropped me off in front of Monsieur Leon's newsstand, the unassuming hub of the Paris spy world. I had another few hours of briefing in front of me, and we all agreed I would have the day off tomorrow to finalize my packing and spend time at home before leaving the next day. I was rather looking forward to it.

The sun had just dipped behind the clouds, and a cool breeze rolled down the street. A cluster of fall leaves whooshed by, and I pulled my coat tighter to me.

"Bonjour, monsieur. Copy of the *New York Times?*" I asked as two other men buzzed about the stand. It was a code. Certain papers and magazines had different meanings. The *New York Times* referred to your current assignment. I was expecting him to respond, "Yes, three euros," which meant there had been no changes; or even better, "You're in luck! Free today," which meant that the case had been solved.

Instead, he said, "All sold out."

"*Sold out?*" I replied. *That's the last response you want to hear.* I turned and started for the Ministry's unmarked basement door, only nineteen steps away. *Something's wrong. The mission has changed.*

An agent met me in the front lobby and walked me straight to Eloise's office. As the door opened, I saw Eloise was staring at a medical chart. Once again, her shirt and blazer appeared to have been retrieved from a clothes hamper, and her hair was haphazardly swept back into a tattered bun. She read over the chart again, then looked up.

"Plans have changed, Simone."

My heart sank, and I fought the urge to pull at my sleeve.

"You will still be leaving for London in two days, but something unexpected has come up. We got the results of Harper's physical, and she has the flu. Dr. Oh just forwarded the paperwork. She's not symptomatic yet, but she will be contagious soon. Sending her at this point would be irresponsible." She groaned aloud. "How could this happen!?"

Before I could open my mouth, she shook her head. "Well, your mother said you were ready to do this alone, and it looks like you'll have to. You're going to have to focus all your efforts. It will all be up to you."

The magnitude of the news sank in, and my anxiety bloomed. "You want me to do both jobs?" A swell of nausea formed in my stomach. *She's right—Mother said I could do it on my own.* But could I?

"I'm afraid so, dear—unless you know someone who could leave for London in two days."

Wait. Leave for London? In two days?

My eyes darted up.

"I just might."

The Licorice Whip Quatre

"**W**ow! You'd have to sell a lot of candy to get one of these," the V exclaimed as she stepped into Sugars Fontaine's private airplane.

The deep aroma of fresh-cut flowers and dark chocolates filled the richly appointed lounge area. Although the plane—like its three siblings—was only four years old, Sugars recently had it renovated from nose to tail. From the heavy wool carpet to the exotic wood cabinets to the hand-stitched wall coverings, this was an environment of pure indulgence.

After I'd gotten the news about Harper, Mother, Eloise, and I had weighed the merits of the V going with me. Although she could never know my true intentions or that I worked for the Ministry, she could still be a huge asset to the mission. Within two weeks, she would naturally become friends with every student, opening all lines of possible communication and allowing me to concentrate on finding the Key. However, even more importantly, she would keep me calm and focused. And besides, why wouldn't I want my best friend with me?

Eventually, everyone agreed. Mother called the Cantones to work out the details, and the V's parents were more than happy to let her study abroad at such a prestigious school. When I finally asked her to accompany me, I thought she was going to pass out—but forty-three seconds of bouncing off the walls soon led to sixteen minutes of inquisition, from which I managed to escape relatively unscathed. As far as the V knew, the student who was to accompany me had gotten sick, so the V had to start packing—and that was all she needed to know.

As the V and I gazed about the cabin, the captain appeared from the cockpit, his uniform pressed and his shoes polished as if he had just walked off a movie set. "Please excuse me. I wished to inform you Madame Fontaine is running about fifteen minutes behind, but our flight attendants Joe and Mark can get you anything you might need," he said, signaling to the back of the plane.

As the captain returned to the cockpit, the two attendants emerged from the rear of the plane, dressed in crisp white-and-blue uniforms, and greeted us in unison. "Would you like some juice, water, or perhaps something to eat?" Joe asked.

"Water would be fine," I answered.

"I'd like some juice, please. Traveling makes me thirsty," replied the V. "Do we get our own rooms?"

The attendant laughed affably. "The *Licorice Whip Quatre* has five staterooms, although our flight time will be less than two hours. I'll secure any carry-ons in storage. Please make yourselves comfortable. What type of juice, Mademoiselle Cantone?"

"Pineapple would be fine. I'll take mine in that puffy chair over there." She'd had her eye on an oversized leather recliner since coming aboard. Now she dove onto it and gave it a spin, just as footsteps approached from outside.

"As a matter of fact, I'm starving," interjected Father as he appeared in the open doorway. He was holding one of Mia's old canvas ballet bags, which stuck out like a sore thumb in the pristine aircraft. He dropped it on the floor and pushed his hair out of his face.

"We'll take that bag, Monsieur LaFray. I see you are still traveling light," said Mark. "What would you like to eat? We reordered the roast beef and asparagus you enjoyed last time."

As Father contemplated his order, the V turned to me with eyes ablaze. "Can you believe this, Simone? The two of us in London for the rest of the year! I can't wait to get there. You know,

Grace was super jealous when I told her I was going to Claymoore with you. The whole school was talking about us yesterday." She shifted in her seat so that she could gaze out the window. "Hey, where's Sugars?"

"Father said something about picking up some fabric options for the store cushions," I replied. It suddenly occurred to me that the V and Sugars had never been in a room together. *This could be fun.*

The V turned to me. "Oh, yes! Your store! We'll be there for the opening. I heard even the Queen will be there. I'll have to find the perfect ensemble!"

Ordinarily, I would have dismissed the V's mention of the presence of royals as a flight of fancy—but this time, for once, she was almost right. The grand opening had been in the works for over a month now, and with Sugars taking the lead, no expense would be spared, and no detail overlooked. She'd told Father no one did formal like the English, and that her debut would make a royal wedding look like a weenie roast. It was to be so lavish as to be worthy of the monarch's attention—and in fact, the Queen *had* been offered an invitation, along with several other members of the royal family—though none had committed to attend the event thus far.

"Your roast beef, monsieur. Medium rare, just as you like it." Mark presented the plate to Father.

"Perfect, Mark. This will do just fine."

Mark returned to watering a spectacular array of orchids with surgical precision.

I started to pull at my sleeve as I contemplated whether or not my bed at Claymoore would be as good as the one I had at home. The excitement of the moment vanished as a wave of homesickness rose in my chest. I wondered if Mia would remember to take Gigi on walks.

"Are you okay?" the V asked.

"Yeah—just a little nervous. Maybe a little homesick. I'll miss everyone, you know. But I'll be fine," I replied. I hoped Mother would be fine while I was gone, too.

After another hopeful glance out the window in search of the absent Sugars, the V turned to me, posturing as if she had something to share.

"You know, it's not always easy," she said. "Mom and Dad are the greatest, but lately I've been thinking a lot about my . . . you know."

We had only discussed the fact that the V was adopted once, after her seventh birthday party. Mother and I had stayed after to help clean up, and so that I could play with some of her new toys. The V was holding an authentic African Zulu doll and internalizing the idea of leaving on safari in one week when sadness rolled over her face.

"Do you think they think about me? You know, back in Korea?" she asked, stroking the doll's hair.

I remembered everything about that moment—the temperature in the room, the smell of sugary cake in the air, and the background conversation between Madame Cantone and Mother as they discussed how well all the children had got along at the party. But most of all, I remembered this moment because it was the first time I had ever allowed myself to be vulnerable in front of the V. Seeing the longing in her face, I had held her hand, pushed the hair out of her face, and said, "Of course they think about you, V. How could they not?"

Joe returned with our water and juice. "Here you go, ladies. And if you two are interested, we're stocked with Fontaine Fizzes, a new product Madame Fontaine is working on. We have both cherry and orange flavors."

The V and I smiled at each other for a second longer before

politely declining. Now that we'd been served, Joe returned to fluffing pillows and placing magazines.

"It must be hard sometimes, V, but your family is awesome." *Did I just say 'awesome'? Ugh—Madame Leard!* Still, the V clearly needed a pep talk. "Your parents are the best. And look at what we're doing—two girls off to study abroad for a few months. Anyone would want to be living your life—even Grace," I added, much to her pleasure. But I knew I needed to go further.

"Mother talks about being adopted sometimes," I offered. It was true. My mother had arrived at an orphanage just outside Toulouse when she was only three months old, with no records, no parents reported—nothing. The nuns who ran the orphanage had discovered her on the front stoop, wrapped in a red blanket and placed in a willow-stem basket. They told her she'd never cried—not once.

Mother remained at the orphanage until she was eight. One of the nuns, Sister Corda, always told her that a strong-willed child would be hard to place, so she needed to quiet down during prospective visits. Though Mother never took her advice, she was later adopted by an unmarried journalist named Sarah Dorsey. Described as a scrappy adventurer of exceptional talent, Sarah traveled the world writing pieces on corruption, civil tragedies, and redemption. Mother became her companion, and their lives together were full and exciting, if brief—Sarah died on Mother's eighteenth birthday, the only mother that mine had ever known. Mother had joined the Army the next day and never looked back.

"Oh, yeah, I forgot," the V replied. Her smile had returned. "Does she miss her mom?"

"Of course she does. Who wouldn't? You're lucky, V; your mom's always there for you. And I'm sure your birth mom thinks about you constantly," I assured her.

She started to perk up, and swiveled her chair from side to side.

"Yeah, I guess." The swiveling became more rapid, transforming into impatience. "Now, what's taking Sugars so long? We need to roll!" The V I knew was back.

With all this talk of mothers, my thoughts returned to mine. She had accompanied us to the airport, along with Mia; but her skin looked flushed, and her hair was wavier than normal. She had spent most of the morning in the bathroom getting ready, which was also odd. *I hope she's okay.*

Pop! Pop! Pop! The crisp sound cut through the air as Joe proceeded to open three bottles of chilled champagne. At the same time, the intercom crackled.

"Attention. Madame Fontaine has entered the airport grounds and will be arriving in minutes," the pilot said. Joe poured a generous glass of the champagne, and Mark readdressed the flowers.

"It's about time," the V said.

We looked outside just in time to see an enormous black town car come to a stop at the base of the portable staircase that led to the plane, where three men waited. The driver jumped out and scurried to open the passenger door while the three men removed a collection of luggage from the trunk.

The door opened, and the bottom of a white fur coat dropped to the tarmac as a foot swung out.

Adorned in oversized sunglasses and dripping strands of Tahitian pearls, Sugars Fontaine strode confidently up the steps and into the plane—only to be met by the glass of champagne Joe had poured. After taking a sip, she turned to Father, who was just finishing his steak.

"Well, look at this," she said, gesturing to the V and I. "Do these two know how to wield a hammer? Our store isn't going to finish itself!" she laughed.

"Bonjour, Madame Fontaine," the V and I said in unison.

Perhaps this was out of my character, but my opinion of Sugars

Fontaine had changed drastically over the last several months. Yes, she was brash, unapologetic, and confident; but she had been respectful to my family recently and even showed glimmers of kindness, especially toward Father. While she was far from one of the family, it appeared she was on our side, and that was good enough for now.

Sugars glanced over us with increasing interest. "Bonjour to you as well. Louie tells me you will both be at Claymoore for the rest of the term. That's my alma mater, you know. Yes, eight years at Claymoore . . ." Her voice started to trail off as she scanned the cabin, apparently pleased with the renovations.

"How are my orchids, Mark? You're not overwatering them, are you?" she called over her shoulder.

"No, madame," he replied, exchanging her empty champagne flute for a full one.

Joe approached to take our glasses. "Time to buckle up."

Our adventure was about to begin. The V and I watched through the open cockpit door as the pilot made his last checks. He turned back and gave a thumbs-up. "*Licorice Whip Quatre* requesting runway assignment for takeoff."

As we leapt off the runway and turned north, my mind went on autopilot. I tended to get anxious on planes, and though I had made this trip seven times in my life, this was the first time I'd done so in a plane as small as a Gulfstream III. I calculated the flight time in my head based on the weather report, and concluded we would be arriving at Heathrow in one hour and twenty-two minutes. Our route would take us west of Lille to the coastline, and then over the Channel.

As expected, the plane moved just inland. Six minutes and thirty-three seconds later, minutes from crossing the forty-ninth parallel, we leveled off at 12,500 meters.

The V unfastened her seat belt and started to read a fashion magazine she'd plucked from the coffee table. My focus remained outside the window, on the subtle but spectacular view. Northern France was stunning, full of sweeping contours and quaint villages dotting the expanse of farmland. As we sped north, the landscape became a collection of green and brown rolling fields, genial rural villages, and rivers that snaked their way to the coast.

Soon we started a slow descent as we passed Lille to the east. I could just make out the approaching blue of the Channel, and my thoughts returned to Mother. The distance between us was mounting, and I fought the urge to text her. It would be unprofessional, I knew—but I couldn't stop worrying. Unwavering love and longing coursed through me, even as fear, anxiety, and uncertainty tugged at the edges of my mind.

And then it hit me like a lightning bolt—Eloise, her pain. A mother separated from her daughter. This must be what she was feeling—only how much more, knowing that this separation had not been by choice, but forced upon her suddenly by another? My mentor's life was breaking beyond repair, and my mission took on new meaning. This pain that permeated everything—I was going to make it all go away.

I had to.

The Claymoore School

*T*ick-tock, tick-tock, tick-tock. The mid-eighteenth-century Kipling clock in Headmaster Bailes' office kept a steady rhythm as he peered at the V and me through his thin-rimmed glasses. We were seated at a walnut and leather-topped desk, waiting for our welcome and anxious to get started. Atop a nearby antique credenza, his cat Sophie perched, staring down at us and looking unimpressed.

Lyman H. Bailes had been the headmaster of the Claymoore School for twenty-seven years, and had no plans to retire—ever. After an extended pause, he took off his glasses and removed a handkerchief from the inside pocket of his bespoke tweed jacket.

"You see, ladies, here at Claymoore," he began, before turning his attention back to cleaning his glasses. He started again. "Yes, well, you see, here at Claymoore, we pride ourselves on excellence, and it is simply not . . ."

The V started to fidget. I could tell she wanted to get out of there and make her grand entrance, but that was going to have to wait.

For the next eight minutes and twenty-three seconds, I continued to watch the headmaster's lips as he extolled the history of the school and the accomplishments of its alumni. Impressive, yes. Pretentious, yes. Stiff, yes—and thoroughly old English.

If Trinity was a flowing party dress, Claymoore was a tailored wool suit: appropriate, reserved, and timeless. It occupied a generous plot of fine real estate in the heart of London—one large enough to include even well-manicured sporting fields. Stone-

and-brick structures built by the finest craftsman of their time had stood over the plot since the Renaissance, lining the perimeter of the school grounds and forming an impenetrable wall that separated Claymoore from the outside world. The oldest of these buildings was Jacobean in style and rose to five and six floors before meeting its slate roof caps. These monoliths connected seamlessly into Stuart- and Georgian-style buildings that rivaled the originals. Each gazed down on a series of interconnecting boxwood-lined gardens. Stately oaks and birches older than the LaFray's shop in Paris made the campus feel more like a park, though the trees were losing leaves as autumn rolled in. The uniformity was pleasing—but best of all, no one here knew who I was.

"... and that is why it is essential that you harness all your abilities here at Claymoore," Headmaster Bailes concluded before easing back into his chair with a satisfied smile, apparently proud of his performance.

"Yes, sir," the V and I replied in unison.

"Now, I'm sure that you have reviewed all of our policies and procedures," the headmaster continued, surveying our outfits. "The dress code and code of conduct are nonnegotiable—no exceptions. You will find your uniforms and other campus clothing in your dormitory room."

The V turned and gave me a wry smile as I contemplated the potential meaning of "campus clothing." Headmaster Bailes checked his wristwatch. In the next instant, there was a soft knock at the door.

His eyes refocused on us. "Come in," he called.

A well-dressed girl entered, her hair pinned back in a perfect French braid. "Ah, yes, Miss Kerns." He looked at her with a father's adoration and turned back to us. "Ladies, may I introduce Kirstin Kerns. She is your class prefect, and will be showing you to your dormitory after a brief tour." He began to clean his glasses again, adding, "Your future starts here, ladies. I hope you will make the most of it."

I turned my attention to the newcomer, recalling the details of her file in an instant. Kirstin Lowell Kerns was a duchess from Surrey, and the epitome of privilege. Though less exceptional than most of the pupils at the school, she was one of a small group of friends, together with Charlotte MacLeod, the daughter of an English shipping magnate; and Michele Walsh, the daughter of a senior justice on the High Court. All were well connected, smart, and strikingly beautiful. Together, they were by far the most photogenic clique at Claymoore.

Kirstin began by giving me a firm handshake before following up with one for the V. "Welcome to Claymoore. Please, call me Kirstin. Now, shall we be off?"

We gathered our coats and made our way out of the headmaster's office and into an opulent hallway. Our gracious welcome, however, was short-lived. We'd only made it halfway down the hall before Kirstin turned to us, a decidedly less pleasant expression plastered on her face.

"Look, you losers. I heard you're only here until the end of the term, so don't expect any special treatment from me. I am not your friend, and it is certainly not my responsibility to care for any homesick French girls. I don't really care if you're miserable here. All I expect you to do is remember that at Claymoore, we like our traditions—so don't mess things up! Understand?" she added.

She must have taken our astonishment for acquiescence, because she said, "Good. Now let's go. I don't have all day!" And before either of us could respond, she spun on her heel and walked away.

"Well, she's a delight," I whispered to the V.

"Yeah, a real peach," she agreed as we reluctantly moved to follow our abrasive guide.

Over the next few hours, we crisscrossed the campus. For the time of year, it was a beautiful day in London. The air was crisp, and there wasn't a cloud in the sky. The good weather put an added shine on Claymoore, though it didn't need it: the school was as impressive as my research had suggested, even to my critical eye.

As our tour progressed, I quickly identified the dining hall, the auditorium, and each of the various study lounges as potential hiding places for the OmniKey—though I took care to remind myself it could be anywhere. *Hmm. This seemed a lot easier on paper.*

The sun was now sinking below the rooftops, and I had worn a hole in my left sock. Kirstin's lukewarm tour and pretentious tone had grown tiresome.

"And on your left is the Ingram Library. You'll probably be spending a lot of time there catching up on your studies—end of term is only nine weeks away, and we make no exceptions for new transfers," she sneered.

"*Hmph,*" I murmured.

We passed a group of boys standing under a large oak that was gently shedding its red leaves. A short ginger-haired boy stared at us and elbowed his friend in the ribs. I was unused to having so many boys around—the rowdiness, the faraway stares, the lax hygiene.

"They're all looking at us," the V whispered to me. I already knew—in fact, I'd noticed eyes on us for most of our tour. By my count, eighty-three students—thirty boys and fifty-three girls—had checked us out, along with eleven teachers. Six students had taken pictures of us with their mobiles, though I wasn't sure why; and I'd even caught Headmaster Bailes staring at us from his office window high above the grounds.

"Who's that?" the V asked quietly.

Kirstin glanced over. To my surprise, her mood immediately shifted. She scratched at the back of her neck and began to walk faster.

"Oh, that's Jonas Schmidt and the other footballers. Don't get your hopes up—he'd have nothing to do with the likes of you two."

The V and I looked at each other and laughed as we walked by.

"Isn't this place great!?" the V whispered. "Sure, she's the worst, but nothing could bring me down today."

"Yeah, it's all great," I replied. With my assessment of plausible hiding places for the Key already complete, I began calculating the distance between each point of entry to the grounds and the exact angle of each security camera. Although I had memorized the schematics of the school, walking them myself gave me an enhanced sense of scale. This was going to be a challenge—one I would start to ponder from our dormitory.

Our room, a corner flat on the fourth level of the southern wing of Beresford Hall, was on the top floor, and the ceilings were half a meter taller than the ones in the rooms below ours. By boarding school standards, the space was huge, measuring five meters by six meters; and tastefully furnished, with bathrooms located down the hall. At first glance, I was relieved to see it was not only welcoming, but somehow familiar. It reminded me of home, orderly and inviting. The floors were mellowed oak planks, and a soft woven rug sat between our beds. The walls were painted a faint yellow, the moldings a crisp white. A cream ceiling with the slight roll of aged plaster supported an oversized brass chandelier that anchored the room. Golden daylight poured in through the large nine-over-nine poured glass windows, its warmth washing over me.

I liked this room. It would do just fine. Change was not something I accepted easily, but the few knickknacks I'd brought from home would help ease the transition: a framed picture of my family and a smaller photo of the patisserie for my desk, and the blanket Mother had knitted for me when I was five for the foot of my bed. I slung my backpack onto one of the beds and began rummaging around for them.

"This room is awesome!" the V shouted. She threw her own backpack into the corner and collapsed onto a bed.

Kirstin sniffed at her lack of decorum. "Dinner is served at six p.m. sharp. After announcements, Monsignor Manalis gives the blessing, and the room is excused at 6:45," she barked, as if trying to command our attention—but I was done with her. I already knew the daily schedule from the briefings, including the refectory's full menu for the next three weeks.

Tuning Kirstin out, I found my attention drawn to the slightly open door. Peering through, I could just barely see a figure moving in the hall beyond. As I watched, it approached, stopping at the threshold, and I could make out the face of a girl my age. She hovered there for eighteen full seconds, peering through the crack in the door. Our eyes met.

Behind her, a distant voice with a strong Irish accent called, "Come on! Let's go."

The girl smiled at me, then vanished down the hall.

The sunshine and warmth of the prior day soon seemed a distant memory. The next day, a faint drizzle coated the windows of my world history class, and a chill permeated the morning air. This was the London I knew.

The classroom was quieter than those at Trinity, although several of the boys were huddled in conversation. Having boys in the room would take some getting used to. Most of them had an awkwardness that reassured me—unlike the girls, who seemed so sophisticated and composed, wiser than their years. As I sat in my seat six rows back from the blackboard, awaiting our history teacher's arrival, I took note of seven Burberry and four Rowley scarves with perfect knots that were not to be rustled by a raised hand. Cashmere, lamb's wool, and Egyptian cotton were standard issue, though many of the girls preferred wearing fine silk scarves that conveyed their individuality and social status. Even the basic uniform fit me far better than my old one at Trinity, and the fabric was almost regal to the touch.

Surveying the room, I recalled that another royal was in my year. Two seats in front of me was the infinitely chatty Jillian Auldridge, or "Jilli" as everyone called her. A duchess of Southern Wales, she'd grown up just outside Cardiff. The family estate was well cared for, but in no way pretentious: no nannies, no house staff; only family—oh, and one dog. I believed his name was Chauncey. Although she was a country girl at heart, Jilli's parents could not deny her a spot at Claymoore after her placement scores had advanced her a year ahead of her peers. Based on what I'd learned, I liked her already.

I had read the files on all the students at Claymoore—but I needed to know more. Who were Claire's friends? Who were her enemies? What was she like? Anything could help me discover how she had been spirited away, and where she might have hidden the OmniKey.

"Good morning, all," said Mrs. Boschen as she entered the room at last.

"Good morning, Mrs. Boschen," we replied.

"As mentioned last week, you'll be taking your module test on premodern China today. I'm sure you're all anxious to share your knowledge and validate your many hours of study." She paused. "We also have a new student." *Ugh.* "Ladies and gentlemen, now seated in chair 6 is Simone LaFray from Paris. Please give her a warm welcome."

Most of the class turned and gave me a quick look, but I noticed Jilli's gaze remained just a few seconds longer.

"I will be passing out the tests now. You have the full two hours to complete six essays," Mrs. Boschen said.

Incredulous groans and whispers filled the classroom. I leaned back in my chair. *Six essay questions? Doesn't sound so bad to me.*

Our teacher weaved through rows of desks, handing out packets to less than enthused students before stopping in front of me. "Simone, dear, you can skip the test and make it up next week. I'll make some—"

"That's okay. I'll give it a shot."

She squinted at me. "I can give you something else to read over in the meantime, and we have—"

"No, I'll try it now. We studied that era last year."

"Hmm. I like your spirit, Miss LaFray. Here you go. If you get stuck, just let me—"

I didn't want to attract any more attention. "Okay, I'll try." I took the packet and opened it. The first question read:

In three complete paragraphs, describe the ethnicity and culture of the Qing Dynasty, specifically its leadership. Cite in detail how these factors shaped the relationship between the Qing and the people of China.

Well, this won't take long.

"Alright, boys and girls! I'll be stepping across the hall to attend a meeting on our upcoming All Hallows Eve celebration," Mrs. Boschen announced. Claymoore had a strict honor code that gave teachers the confidence to leave the classroom during tests. "Remember—two hours!" And with that, she stepped out, and the clock began to tick.

I finished the test in under forty minutes and took the remainder of the time to analyze my classmates. By my account, the code was in good condition, although two boys in the back were comparing notes. Based on the content of their stifled conversation, their efforts were futile. Most of the girls were glued to their papers, although Jilli finished her test in just over an hour. Not bad.

During the last minute of the exam, the pressure was palpable as erasers worked at a feverish pace. I didn't want to attract attention by finishing early, so I pretended to still be working when Mrs. Boschen returned.

"Pencils down, please," she said. "Well, now, that wasn't so bad, was it?" I certainly didn't think so, but I couldn't speak for the other students. Most looked as if they had just run a marathon: sweaty, exhausted, and wanting to go home. "That's it for today. No homework tonight—I think you've earned it."

As the class let out and I began putting on my backpack, Mrs. Boschen called for me. "Miss LaFray? Were you able to take a crack at a few of the questions? I'm more than happy to create a make-up test for—"

"I think I did fine." I straightened my glasses. "The extra credit question about the Legalist School's impact on the formation of the Chinese imperial system was broad, so I just focused on its use during a governmental decline. I hope you don't mind me taking that liberty."

She looked at me as if she'd just seen a ghost. "Why, yes—I'm sure that will be fine."

On the thirty-first of October, the school celebrated All Hallows Eve—Halloween—with a ghost walk, followed by a dance on the south lawn. Over a week had passed since the V and I had arrived at Claymoore, and this would be our first social event. Of course, the dance was of no interest to me—in my experience, dances were superficial, silly, and did not supply a memorable experience that I could classify as positive. At all. Besides, boys would be there, which made the whole prospect even less appealing.

The ghost walk, on the other hand, would afford me the opportunity to eavesdrop and further immerse myself in my new environment. Thus far, I had successfully kept a low profile while sorting the potential whereabouts of the OmniKey. The work was surprisingly frustrating. Claire had left few footprints, and the only thing I had ascertained about her time at Claymoore was that she'd spent most of it in the library and the art room.

"Aren't they done yet?" the V asked from her position at our dormitory window, where she was watching a small army of workers carting copious decorations onto the lawns. They had arrived in hospitality vans and had been decorating the grounds for two full days, with no end in sight.

The V let the linen curtains fall together. "And why, again, aren't you going to the dance?"

I buried my head back in my book. We had addressed this subject earlier, and it was starting to pluck my nerves. "We have a lot of studying to make up. Besides, you know dances make me edgy."

The V turned back to the window. "Yeah. Then again, I thought singing wasn't your thing either, but we both know how that turned out." *Touché, Cantone.*

"Maybe I'll swing by the dance after I get these chapters done." Truthfully, I had finished hours ago, but I needed some time on my own. I was also due for a check-in with Eloise. "I'm going on the ghost walk, though."

"Big deal," the V murmured. "That's mandatory, Simone. *Everybody* has to go."

"Yeah, but we get to dress up, don't we?"

The V considered, abandoning the window. "Oh! Maybe we could dress up as twins or something."

"Father had some new chef's clothes sent over to us today. We could wear those," I replied distractedly. My attention was elsewhere: for the last thirty-seven seconds, I'd detected faint traces of movement outside our door—the soft creak of a floorboard as a toe tapped, the rustle of a thick coat, a soft cough. I presumed whoever was there would come in eventually—but then a voice came from down the hall.

"Let's go, Jilli."

The floorboard creaked once more, and the sound of rustling faded as the interloper retreated.

"Okay, let's try them on. I need to make an impression," the V said.

The fresh night air was damp on the south lawn, the faint haze illuminated by an arsenal of strategically placed torches. Groups of costumed students paraded across the grounds, led by animated teachers spinning tired yarns to deaf ears. I pulled back my sleeve and checked my watch. In four minutes and three seconds, we were to meet at the towering oak tree on the south lawn to start our tour.

"These costumes are awesome!" said the V. She cocked her pastry chef hat to the side to give it a little more attitude. The coats were large on us, but roomy enough that we could wear a sweater and fleece underneath. I was grateful—the dampness of the air increased its chill, and the temperature had dropped significantly as autumn wore on.

Our cadre of wizards, witches, ghosts—and yes, two pastry chefs—assembled at the foot of the immense oak. The V nudged me in the ribs. "Hey, there's that Jonas kid again. He sure is easy to look at." I paid her no attention.

"I hope we don't run into any wolves tonight," someone said. A rowdy boy seized on the moment and added, "Yeah, we certainly don't want to be covered in paint." Even more students started to laugh, and someone howled.

"What's so funny about that?" the V asked me. "Is it some British thing?"

I couldn't be certain, but my guess was that it was in fact something of a British thing. Over the past seven months, numerous London-based corporations and banks had been targeted by a group that the media had collectively come to call the Red Wolves of London. Under the cloak of night, the Wolves masterfully painted huge murals that exposed corrupt businesses for crimes ranging from tax evasion and money laundering to fraud and malpractice. Since the only identifier the artists left was a brazen red wolf head in the lower righthand corner of their paintings, it hadn't taken long for a local art critic with the *Evening Standard* to dub the anonymous artist "the Red Wolf"— though it would likely have taken a whole group of artists to produce the paintings so fast. Thus, the more colorful moniker *Red Wolves of London* was eventually splashed across the local papers, and the anonymous group soon developed a cultlike following across social media, where there was a growing competition to see who could discover their latest work first. However, despite the group's increasing notoriety, Scotland Yard placed little priority on catching them, as their actions posed no threat to the public. As for the Ministry, they had opened a file on the matter, but seemed to find it more entertaining than threatening.

"I love your costume!" exclaimed a girl dressed as Little Red Riding Hood, complete with a wicker basket. "I'm Jilli Auldridge," she added, extending a hand. "You're Simone, right? One of the new girls from Paris?"

Interacting with the people I studied often left me tongue-tied and a bit unnerved—but not this time. Jilli seemed authentic, and exuded a welcoming demeanor. "Ah, yes. Simone, that's right," I replied as I took her hand. "I like your costume too."

"Thanks! It's actually a prop from one of last year's school plays, but it matches the costume, and I can use the basket to carry snacks."

The V quickly took notice of our conversation. "Nice costume! Did you bring your wolf?"

Jilli turned to her. "And you must be the V. I think we have a couple of classes together," she said as a group of boys dressed as bank robbers shuffled excitedly through us. "Excuse you!" Jilli yelled.

The V readjusted her hat, which had been knocked askew in the commotion. "Could be. Sorry I'm not sure. I'm still trying to meet everyone. Maybe you could help me?" She surveyed the assembled students, her eyes tracking to a tall girl with what looked like two grey socks coming out of her red hair. "Who's that?"

Jilli looked over and gave a short laugh. "That's my wolf. That's Maeve."

My stomach dropped.

Of all the files I'd studied on every student at Claymoore, Maeve Stahl's was by far the thickest and most interesting. An orphan from Belfast, she had been placed into seven foster homes and expelled from nine elementary schools before she was taken in by a retiring nun, Sister Mary Teresa. A graduate of Claymoore herself, Sister Mary knew the school extended scholarships to impoverished children of ordained alumni. She soon adopted Maeve and crafted a letter to the headmaster, and Maeve was offered a full scholarship for the next term.

But while this story would garner sympathy, a closer look into Maeve's more recent history might do the opposite. Her file was full of "incidents" stemming from her smoldering temper and apparent comfort with violence, and she exuded a strength formed by independence, resolve, and street smarts. She had no loyalties I could discern—and no one to answer to, as Sister Mary Teresa had died just two months ago. I could come to no other conclusion: Maeve Stahl was dangerous. As far as I knew, Jilli, her roommate, was the only person who had tried to befriend her.

The V peered skeptically at Maeve. "Is she really supposed to be a wolf?"

But Maeve had noticed us staring, and begun moving toward us. Now within earshot, she shot back, "That's right, I'm a wolf. Can't you see? Ears." She raised her left hand and pointed at the socks, which I now saw had been affixed to a headband that was barely visible through her thick, curly red hair.

Maeve looked us over critically. She towered above us by almost half a foot, and at my side, the V started to squirm.

"You're not going to blow us down or anything, are you?"

From the details in her file, I knew Maeve was not used to kids being smart with her. Jilli must have known it too, because her eyes darted to Maeve. But Maeve only straightened up and said, "Of course I'm not. Dumb question."

"Well, I think you look great," Jilli hastily added.

I felt compelled to interject—not only to ease the tension, but because I knew I had to start interacting. "So, Maeve—your accent—is it Downpatrick or Belfast?" I already knew the answer, but I thought the question might break the ice.

Her eyes turned to me. "What? It's Belfast, but how did you—"

The V cut her off. "Oh, she knows all kinds of stuff like that. She could probably guess what month you were born in, and the hospital where it happened too." Actually, I would not be guessing at all—the answers were April and Musgrave Park—but I'd keep that to myself for now.

"Ladies and gentlemen, we will be starting our tour in exactly one minute!" Mr. Royce, an English teacher and author, announced, exuding a sense of inordinate giddiness as he approached the base of the tree. As he got into character, launching into a series of exaggerated gestures, the crowd around me snickered. I needed to say something funny to blend in. But what?

Oh! I know. "He's quite the bird, isn't he?"

I waited for some laughter, but quickly determined my attempt at a joke hadn't been funny at all when Jilli turned to me and asked, "What?"

Another girl standing next to her piped up. "Yeah, that weird girl, Claire, used to say dumb stuff like that."

Claire? This was the first time I had heard a student say her name since I'd arrived at Claymoore. I had to capitalize on this.

"Ah, yeah, sorry," I replied. I needed to keep this conversation going. "Claire? Is she the girl that threw up in the refectory yesterday?"

The second girl rolled her eyes and replied, "That wasn't Claire. I think that was that Danish girl. You know, the one with short brown hair? She gave it a real heave. No, Claire's the one who ran away or something a few weeks ago. She's gone."

"Ran—" I began—but stopped as I caught a glimpse of Jilli. She was frowning, her brow furrowing as she looked away.

That's it. She knows something about Claire. I was sure of it—and I had to learn more. I took a deep breath. Without Harper here to help me, I was going to have to do something I'd never done with someone my own age since the V: I was going to have to make a friend.

Suddenly, the bright beam of a flashlight streamed over us, and Professor Royce exclaimed, "Shhhhhhh! You might wake the ghost of Claymoore with your chatter!"

"Oh, brother," the V said to me. The ghost walk was clearly not proving as exciting as she had hoped.

The next thirty-four minutes were filled with an odd mix of hyperbole and oxymorons that left me irritated. I did my best to ignore the professor's tale and mull over what that girl had said about Claire. *Ran away?* That had to be a rumor.

As Professor Royce concluded the tour with a dramatic pronouncement about a lost spirit that still roamed the grounds on All Hallows Eve, the V turned to Jilli and Maeve. "Are you guys going to the dance?"

"No, our prefect told us we needed to straighten our room before we could go. She's the worst," Jilli said. She turned to me. "Do you want to come back and hang out for a while? You don't have to help us clean or anything."

A flush of triumph spread through my limbs. This was my in!

"V, I'm going to hang out with these girls for a while. I'll see you back at the room," I said.

The V was already starting to tap her feet. She loved to dance, and was obviously eager to move on to the more interesting part of the night—along with the several new friends she had made during the walk. But she stopped when I spoke. "What? I thought you had to study. You're going to . . ." Her gaze passed from Jilli to me, and I saw the confusion of novelty in her eyes. She had never needed to share me with contemporaries before. After a moment, however, she forced a smile.

"Sure. I'll see you later."

———

To say Jilli and Maeve's room was merely cluttered would be a vast understatement. A corner unit just like mine and the V's, it was covered in books, piles of clothes, boxes overflowing with art supplies, and oversized posters of polar bears haphazardly taped to the wall next to Maeve's bed. As I entered, the odors of old laundry and perfume assaulted my senses from every corner of the space. I got the impression its inhabitants had few visitors—and even fewer standards.

"So, LaFray, what's the deal with you? You seem like one of those—" Maeve began.

"Maeve, where are your manners?" Jilli interjected. She turned to me with a widening smile and picked a notebook and pen out of the clutter, pushing piles of clothes aside with her foot to make a spot to sit. "I like French kids. The accent, the clothes, the—"

Maeve returned the favor. "Yeah, 'French kids.' That's what I was going to say."

Glancing over the clutter, I noticed last year's yearbook peeking out from the bottom of a pile of sweaters and socks—but something about it was odd. In my briefings, I'd received the last ten years' worth of Claymoore's yearbooks, and committed every page to memory. But by my estimate, this book was at least thirty pages longer than the one I'd reviewed.

Before I could bend to pick it up, the door behind me flew open, and Kirstin Kerns barged in. Ironically, she was dressed as a witch—not the kind with moles and a crooked nose, but the beautiful kind, like Glinda from *The Wizard of Oz*. Her costume was brilliant, festooned with sequins and ribbons, like something from a stage show—or one of the V's art projects. As she entered, she placed her hands haughtily on her hips and peered over the room with disdain.

"What are you up to? Not cleaning, I can see."

"Well, we aren't at the dance, are we?" replied Maeve in an equally snarky tone. "Just like you *ordered*. So what's it to you what we're doing in our own room?"

Jilli gave a short laugh and began to doodle in her notebook, in a pointed show of ignoring her prefect.

Kirstin straightened her pointed hat. "I don't care what you losers do. Stay in here all weekend for all I care." She stopped in the doorway, turned, and took one last look around. "Remember, room checks are in three days. Yours is disgusting. Clean it up!"

SLAM! went the door.

Maeve and Jilli glanced at each other and laughed, and I awkwardly tried to join in. Despite the brief distraction, however, my focus remained on the yearbook.

"Jilli, do you mind if I look through this?" I asked, pointing at it.

Jilli looked up. "Sure. Just make sure the supplement stays with it. I don't want it to get lost . . ." Her gaze swept around the mess.

She now had my full attention. "Supplement?"

Jilli got up and plucked the book from the floor. "Yeah, they published a supplement that covered the last three months of the school year. I think it was the first time they did that. Anyway, here you go," she said, handing it to me.

I took the yearbook from Jilli's outstretched hand and immediately began flipping through the pages.

Maeve glanced over. "See anything interesting in there? A bunch of rubbish, if you ask me."

I was already six pages into the supplement, but so far, nothing had jumped out. "Ah, no. I just like books, and wanted to see what you guys do around here."

Maeve seemed skeptical, but turned her attention from me to a small notepad that lay on her pillow and began to sketch as well.

I continued to investigate the supplement. My heartbeat quickened when I found Claire in two of the photographs—both group shots of the art club. The first photo featured Claire and several other students standing around the pottery kiln, and the second was a photo of the entire club seated. The caption beneath read: "Jillian Auldridge, Lewis Downs, Katie Hart, Mimi Maechling, Claire Pilfrey, and Maeve Stahl. (Mr. Redd not pictured.)"

I studied the page.

"Who's Mr. Redd?" I asked.

Maeve dropped her pencil as Jilli's eyes lit up. "Oh, Mr. Redd is the *dreamiest*. A real—"

"Jilli!"

There was an awkward silence, and then Maeve said, "He was just an adjunct art teacher Bailes brought in for the end of the year. He's nobody."

"Yeah, nobody," murmured Jilli.

Maeve stared at her for another second, then went back to sketching as I flipped to the final page. As I scanned it, my heart nearly stopped.

There, in the middle of the adjunct staff update, was a picture of Mr. Redd—with a charming smile framed by unmistakable, blazing red hair, as if he had been waiting just for me.

La Volpe Rossa!

Lights Out

The next few days passed without incident as I continued my investigations and immersed myself in the school—but my focus was slipping. The Fox's words kept filtering through my head. I could barely believe he'd been here.

After a cursory scan of the library, which turned up absolutely nothing, I finally decided to contact Mother to tell her about my discovery. I'd found a quiet place to talk: an alcove behind a block of mechanical equipment on the roof of my dormitory, which I'd accessed through an unlocked maintenance hatch. The satellite feed was strong here, and I was unlikely to be discovered—I'd left the V holding court in the room next to ours. She'd already befriended no less than fifteen kids from our hall.

"You're sure? You're absolutely sure?" Mother asked.

"I'm sure, Mother. I know it's him," I replied, shivering. The sun was ducking under the rooftops, and I was regretting not bringing my coat. A pigeon stared at me with bewildered curiosity as I fidgeted with my overstarched right cuff. *Why do the shirts here have to be so stiff?*

"But you've never seen his face before. How can you be so sure? Did you scan the photo with your watch?"

"I started to, but Maeve grabbed the book and told me to get my own. I tried to find it online, but it wasn't digitized." I started to unbutton my cuff.

"Maeve?" Mother always perked up when I mentioned a contemporary by name. She had been imploring me to expand my circle of friends for as long as I could remember. "Who's Maeve—a new friend?"

With the cuff now turned back, I was able to focus. "Ah—no. Well . . . maybe."

I closed my eyes to recall the photograph of the elusive Mr. Redd. The image remained imprinted on my mind as clearly as the faint smell of pretzels that had been wafting from a bag on Maeve and Jilli's floor. *How do I know it's him?* I asked myself; but every instinct reassured me: the Fox had been here. But why?

Suddenly, a thought came to me, and my racing mind came to a screeching halt.

Was he here for Claire?

As I stared at the screen, trying to conceal my emotions at the revelation, a familiar face squeezed into the frame.

"So, have they asked you to leave yet? I'm guessing you've bored them all to death by now, so you can come home. My holiday recital is only a few weeks away!" Mia chimed in, flashing a smile that revealed a newly missing tooth. She missed me, I could tell.

"Not yet," I answered, managing an apologetic smile. "I'll be here a while—and Father will be here any second to pick me up." Thus far, the V and I had avoided going on any outings as we'd settled into life at Claymoore, but Father had said we were due a home-cooked meal, so we would all be dining at the Fontaine mansion that evening, after a special tour of the still-unfinished store. I couldn't wait to see more of London, and was quite looking forward to some time away from campus to collect my thoughts. "I've got to go."

"Be careful," Mother said, her voice tinged with worry.

"I will," I promised.

I ended the call and went back to my dormitory to find something to wear on our imminent outing. It would need to be warm:

the building had a chill to it that even the failing rays of the sun couldn't heat.

"This will do," I murmured as I held up a freshly laundered sweater. It was warm, but just fancy enough to pass me off as presentable at the dinner.

"Is your dad here yet?" yelled the V from the room next door.

Predictably, the All Hallows Eve dance had been a productive one for the V from a social standpoint. She was amassing an army of friends and admirers, including the two eighth-year students in the adjoining suite: Anya Swayne, a budding actor from Inverness whose mother and grandmother had both attended Claymoore; and Madison Morrow, a gifted writer and the daughter of a decorated British military family. Both had clean files and, unbeknownst to them, were jockeying for the seventh and eighth spots in their class. The three of them were listening to some pedestrian brand of syrupy pop music that threatened to make my ears bleed, but they seemed to like it just fine.

"Did someone say 'Dad'?"

I whipped around just in time to see Father stick his head into my room and offer a warm smile. It had been almost two weeks since we'd last been together—the longest I had ever been away from my parents. He was electric as ever, and in desperate need of a haircut. "Simone! You look well. Why, you must have grown another five centimeters!"

In the next instant, the three girls who had been in the next room over spilled through the door. "Hi, Monsieur LaFray!" the V shouted. She wore dark sunglasses, evidently pretending to headline her own concert and, in her own mind, destined for pop stardom.

"Bonjour, V," he replied. "So, it appears you are somehow getting through your stay here?"

"Oh, I love Claymoore. It's much better than Trinity!"

"Excuse me, but—are you the famous chocolatier? The one opening the shop on Sloane Street?" asked Anya.

"Ah, yes. Well, I don't know about *famous,* but we are opening a store," Father replied, a hint of arrogance in his voice. It didn't suit him, and although I would cut him a break for now, I'd had enough of this conversation.

I slung my sweater over my shoulders and took Father and the V by the hand. "Okay. Let's see this store everyone's talking about."

⸻

I had studied the London underground before, but this was the first time I had ridden in it. It was exactly as I'd expected, with its clean white tile walls, well-defined signage, and the hum of scattered conversations interrupted by pulsing train engines. The V's voice echoed as she described all her new friends to Father, and I was more than happy to let her steer the conversation.

As we emerged from the tube, the three of us were met with a blanket of cold, moist air that clung to us as we hurried down Sloane Street. Even in a light mist, walking through London was captivating. Like a congregation of well-dressed businesspeople, the perfectly balanced, symmetrical buildings rose three or four stories from the street, their dark color palettes radiating longevity and stature. Pavements of smooth Victorian stone and aged concrete aligned plumb with the shallow curbs, and the streets were full of ragged taxis, red double-decker buses, and old cars—though I never heard a horn. Shoppers bundled in winter coats and hats bustled past, generating only a subdued hum of conversation. No matter what the British were talking about, they always did so with a polite dignity that oozed intelligence and credibility.

Despite the chill, the pavement was crammed with people. The new store was less than six weeks from opening, and it was already the buzz of London. The ovens were being placed today, and Father wanted us to be there for it. I had to admit I was curious to see them—and the opportunity presented a momentary distraction from finding Claire and the OmniKey.

"Have you made any sweets yet?" the V asked Father as over the hum of the crowd.

"No, none yet; but I hope to break the kitchen in next week. Our store manager has already hired seven bakers and chocolatiers, and now she's interviewing potential washers and clerks. Sugars wants to start their training soon." Father stopped, and his eyes lit up. "Oh! And I haven't told you the big news: the Queen has accepted our invitation. Isn't that great!?"

"What!? You're kidding!" screamed the V, grabbing Father's arm.

"The Queen?" I murmured in disbelief. I'd thought the Queen's attendance would be a long shot—but Sugars must have been persistent. A royal presence would be a big deal, and was sure to provide a huge publicity boost. "That's wonderful. I'm sure Mother and Mia are excited to see her," I offered.

Father's expression changed to one of slight concern, and he leaned down to me as we walked on. "Actually, Simone, I'm not sure if they're coming. Your mother has a very full plate—and besides, she wants to make sure the apartment is properly decorated for Christmas when we return."

What? Mother—not attending? Why? Whatever the reason, it had to be serious.

On Father's opposite side, the V continued to shriek. "The Queen! Oh, what am I going to wear? I hope I can get a selfie with . . ."

I tuned her out, still reeling. I couldn't believe Mother would miss the opening of the store. Was something else going on? Was she sick? Or was Father covering something up? Though I tried to push these worries aside, I couldn't help but wonder.

The conversation between Father and the V had now veered into the guest list for the grand opening. I could tell Father was starting to tire, but he could not dampen the V's enthusiasm. As for me, I was attempting to distract myself from my worries over Mother by constructing a list of the Red Fox's potential motivations for being at Claymoore when—all at once—the store came into view behind the crowds.

Oh, my . . .

The shop was located at the far end of the street, now only sixty-four steps away. The illuminated marquee out front was taller than our entire store back in Paris. At Sugars' insistence, it was more Moulin Rouge than LaFray's, its theater-like presence a magnet to anyone walking the street. I was used to lines forming outside our store on Rue Clodion—but those were nothing next to the crowd clustering here, trying to look into the enormous front windows. Five service trucks were parked out front, and technicians buzzed about as deliverymen carted several dollies stacked with enormous crates down from an oversized truck and onto the pavement.

"My ovens!" yelled Father with sudden vigor. Eyes locked on the mammoth boxes, he began to jog, pushing through the crowd as we slipped through behind him. "Oh, look at them, girls! Haller 4000s—six of them. Aren't they amazing?"

The V and I looked at each other, anxious to get inside and away from the crowd. "Yeah, Mr. LaFray, they look great! Can we see the store now?" the V asked.

Father grinned and led us through the masses. My gaze darted over the oversized plateglass windows, "LaFray's" freshly painted on each of them in a stylish black font. *Our name isn't on the ones in Paris.* One would think seeing one's name splashed across such a magnificent façade would be exciting—but on the contrary, the experience left me feeling anxious and exposed.

Remember, it's for Father. Remember it's for Father—oh, Simone, stop scripting. I stopped and took a breath before squeezing inside after him.

"Whoa!" the V exclaimed.

We had only taken three steps inside, but the view was already spectacular. I stood still for several seconds to take it all in. With its extravagant high ceilings and ample lighting, the design evoked grandeur. The walls were covered in a bright white coat of paint, and decorated with French flags and a few well-placed fleurs-de-lis. The cabinetry was painted in alternating black and white, with bullnose countertops of swirling white marble. The kitchen was pristine, every pot, tray, utensil, and towel neatly stored or elegantly displayed. Even with tattered paper still covering the new wood floors, the space was stunning—indeed, almost overwhelming.

But by far the most spectacular aspect of the shop lay straight in front of me.

Placed right in the middle of the atrium, the store's centerpiece was one of the largest chocolate fountains in the world—a series of inverted silver bowls that would have perfectly suited a fountain set in a small park, rather than a store. Directly above it, suspended from the ceiling, was an intricate sugarwork-and-hard-candy chandelier, its multitude of colors and textures providing a stark contrast to the rest of the orderly store. It was unquestionably the shop's focal point, a fascinating piece of art suspended seemingly in midair above the inviting showroom.

But for all the store's splendor, the magic of our Paris shop was missing. Absent were the warm scents of rising pastries, the squeaking hinge on Father's favorite oven, and Monsieur John's shouts of "Who's next?" And though this store oozed with French style, no sunlight poured in through its glass façade—the gray London afternoon would not permit it. As I glanced outside, I saw rain just starting to fall, forming a thick sheen of condensation over the store's front windows.

Father turned to me, hands together. "Well, what do you think?"

I carefully formulated a response as I finished calculating the subtle differences between the schematics I had reviewed and the magnificent architecture before me. I had to lie—but just a little.

"It's perfect—just perfect," I replied.

Father let out a relieved breath. The V, who had already dashed farther into the store, yelled back, "Are you kidding? This place is better than perfect. It's *awesome!*"

I cringed. *Awesome* was not a word I used with much fluency. *Perfect* was justifiable, as the store was perfectly successful in its intent: to overwhelm its customers with a fantasy world that would entice them into buying more overpriced sweets than they could carry. However, other than its apparently imminent financial success, I had to conclude that this franchise bore no resemblance to the store I knew back in Paris—none at all.

Father was still rattling on. "Simone—did you see the table?" The pride on his face was unmistakable, and I turned to look.

At the front of the store, Father had placed a small table and two wireframe seats. They looked uncannily like the ones we had in the shop on Rue Clodion—right down to the names "Simone" and "Mia," which someone had haphazardly carved into opposite sides of the tabletop. I'd carved the originals into our table back home when I was six, and Mia had kept wanting to sit in whichever chair I wanted. To designate once and for all who sat where, I'd taken the smallest knife from the kitchen and done the deed. Though it hadn't worked to stop Mia's fussing, it had seemed like a good idea at the time.

I had to admit the replica was convincing—but while I appreciated the sentiment, in some way, it made me miss home even more. The fake authenticity was making me feel fake too—just like the table.

"And the chairs! I had them made and insisted on their placement in front," Father continued. "Sugars hates them. She says they are taking up valuable floor space she wants to use for a display of impulse items for customers."

Impulse items? I didn't remember any of those back home either.

"This place is huuuuge!" the V called out. She had already ascended to the third floor and was hanging over the polished brass railing, her wide eyes drinking in the store below.

"Well, she seems to like it," Father said to me with a growing smile.

I looked for a spot to call my own—something out of sight. I knew of six such spots in our Parisian store where I could go and blend in if needed. But this place was too new and glossy, and everything was on display. Even as the rain drummed harder on the pavement outside, the cold shine of the store remained unchanged.

The front doors opened again as the deliverymen began wheeling the ovens into the store. While they filed in, I wandered behind the main counter and took in the sheer volume of space. I had a question—well, I had seventeen—but this one was the most pressing.

"How are you going to make enough chocolates and pastries to fill this place? It has to be at least thirty-two times larger than our store at home." Depending on whether you counted the grand staircases in the floor plan, the real number fell between thirty-one-point-three and thirty-two-point-seven times larger—but who was counting.

But Father seemed not to hear me. He was walking in front of his new set of ovens like a general inspecting his troops before battle. I studied him intently. At the end of the row, he stopped and drew himself up, and for just a moment, I noticed a glimmer of apprehension in his eyes.

Is he ready for this?

Father refocused on me, as if he had just registered my inquiry. "What?" He gazed over a large metal racking table and said, "Oh, yes—good question. We'll only make about a quarter of the sweets here. Sugars has contracted a co-packer in Barnet who will bring in deliveries three times a week, and the Fontaine Company will supply the rest."

Co-packer? Fontaine Company?

I didn't think I needed to look for a spot anymore. There was no place for me here. The sparkle of the new store was fading, and I yearned for the squeaky oven doors, precariously stacked pans, and aged floors of our store in Paris, where all our treats were made in the same kitchen, with love and attention to tradition—fresh, and distinctly ours. We'd always made everything by hand, the way Grampy did it.

"Sir—where would you like the books?" asked a deliveryman holding a large box.

Father turned to him. "Ah, yes. Please put them on the front counter. The decorators will be in next week."

Books?

Father's face illuminated as he tore into the box. "You have to see these, Simone," he said. "There are at least another ten boxes coming in. Sugars commissioned a publisher to recreate the entire lot. Aren't they amazing?"

Oh, no—

"Our recipe books?" I gasped. "All of them?"

Father paused to gaze over the first volume. "Yes, dear, all of them." Seeing my face, he quickly added, "Not the recipes, dear—just the covers. The pages are blank. You see?" He tipped the book open and flipped through it. White sheets, as white as the store's walls, flashed emptily before me.

More illusions. We don't belong here.

"Simone, you've got to see this!" the V shouted. "Have you been upstairs yet? There's going to be a whole section for toffies and hard candies—and did you see the fountain?"

I braced myself for a barrage of questions—but suddenly, I noticed something that stopped me cold.

"Excuse me," I said. Trying to stay calm, I walked away, toward the front windows.

It can't be. It simply can't be. My heart pounded. Just three meters in front of me was a message, freshly written in the heavy condensation on the store's enormous front window, and just beginning to drip. It read:

IT'S NOT WHAT YOU THINK.

—R

Adrenaline flooded my limbs. I turned my head from side to side, trying to catch a glimpse of him. That window had been untouched just a moment ago. I'd just been glancing over the chairs in front of it. *How did I miss him? How did he know I would be here?*

Just two meters away, a painter was finishing a doorframe. I rushed over, almost tripping over a pile of discarded cardboard, and pointed at the window.

"Excuse me, sir. Did you see a man with red hair write something on this glass?"

"Ah, no, miss. Seen a man or two with red hair earlier, but I think they were with the electricians."

I whirled away and glanced around. Two repairmen were approaching the front door, apparently going back to their trucks for more tools. "Excuse me, sirs. Have you seen a man with bright red hair? He was just here a minute ago."

"Nah, miss. Not seen anyone like that," the shorter of the two replied.

The enormous room was closing in on me. It had to be the Fox. There could be no doubt. I turned back to Father, whom the V was now bombarding with design ideas.

"Father! Have you installed the security cameras yet?"

Father looked over at me. "No, dear, they go in tomorrow. Why?"

Disappointment splashed over me. He was gone. But why had he been here—and *what* wasn't what I thought?

I collected myself. "Ah, no reason. Just wanted to look at some tech stuff."

I lifted my watch and took a picture of the now nearly illegible message, which had dripped to the sill. *He must have been waiting for us.* But what was he talking about?

As I lowered my watch, I saw a black Rolls-Royce pulling up to the curb. It stopped, and a chauffeur opened the passenger doors. Soon enough, a larger-than-life silhouette piled out and began marching in under the canopy of two oversized umbrellas held by careful assistants. As the trio entered, the umbrellas came down to reveal Sugars, resplendent in a black mink coat and holding a freshly lit cigarette.

"Darlings . . . let's go to dinner!"

Like most of the people with whom she surrounded herself, Sugar's chef, Katherine, was a genius in the culinary arts. I could still taste the evening's decadent beef Wellington and the rich cream of the crème brûlée as I gazed out over a bedrizzled London from the fourth-level terrace of the estate on Aubrey Walk. Big Ben, Tower Bridge, and the spires of Westminster Abbey kept regal watch over the Thames. As much as I missed the view from

Rue Clodion, I cherished this one as well.

The Fontaine family had purchased this lofty townhome twenty-two years ago, and spent four years and a fortune modernizing it in their flamboyant style. From its roof covered in Welsh slate to its hand-dug stacked-stone basement, the building dazzled—though London's architecture and design community had categorically panned the project, describing it as "garish, tawdry, and unrefined." One wrote, "The Fontaines have completely disregarded proper English tradition and have smacked the face of neoclassical excellence with a rude, brutish wrecking-ball sensibility that leaves the historic location desecrated." I thought that one was a bit unfair, but it was so very British. As for Sugars, she brushed it off, saying, "When they pay my bills, they can pick my drapes."

The gentle hum of the city was starting to lull me into a trance when I detected a set of doors opening behind me.

"Are you enjoying the view?" a raspy voice asked between drags of a withering cigarette.

"Why, yes, madame. It's wonderful," I replied as I turned, attempting to keep my nose from wrinkling at the scent of smoke.

I must have failed, because she peered at me. "Don't be so judgmental, dear," she said, twisting her exhausted cigarette into a silver ashtray. "I plan to quit these one day, but for now, I'll make my own choices, thank you."

"I'm not jud—" I began, but she interrupted. I got the sense she preferred a one-sided conversation.

"You kids! Everything is absolutes with you. It's good; it's bad. I love it; I hate it. The candy is too sweet; the chocolate's too rich—ugh," she said turning toward the door. "Brendan! Bring me my nightcap," she shouted to her butler.

A faint reply of "Yes, Madame" filtered upward from at least two floors below us.

Sugars turned back and put her boney hands on the balcony's low granite wall.

"You're unsure about all of this, aren't you?"

I started to respond, but she interrupted again. "Let's cut to the chase, shall we? You don't trust me. Perhaps I *may* have been less than cordial on some occasions, and those times I was thrown out of your store were justified. It's alright. I would be skeptical, too. Your father and I are getting into some pretty deep waters together. Change is never easy, girl; but it's people like us that move the others. The ones that get things done."

People like us? I thought to myself, gazing down at the nine lampposts that illuminated the sleepy street below. The fog had almost lifted. I contemplated a suitable response, but before one could surface, she spoke again.

"I noticed you the first time I walked into that *tiny* store of yours. You were behind the cooling racks, trying to look uninterested and busy. What seven-year-old is uninterested and busy?" She laughed. "Each time, from then on, I noticed you. Looked for you. You were always processing, taking it all in. I was the same way at your age—studying people and why they did what they did. You can't be too careful, even as a child. It's the quiet ones you have to watch."

Faint footsteps approached. "Madame, your nightcap. Should I leave it here on the table?" the butler asked as he appeared in the doorway.

Sugars' eyes never left me. "Yes, Brendan, that will be fine."

As the butler retreated, I made another attempt at a response. "Father is very exci—"

"Save it," Sugars interrupted. "Yes, I'm sure your father is excited. He should be. This is going to change everything for him, for you—but you're smart. You already knew that." She leaned down toward me, just enough for her long pearl necklace to scrape the balustrade. "Look. We need to get something straight. It's a dog-eat-dog world out there, and if you have something, someone is trying to figure out how to take it. Those with the most have the most to lose—and I'm no loser."

She paused, narrowing her eyes at me. "Let me be absolutely clear. I know about your certain *skill set*. I know what your mother does, and I know who you are connected to. My sources might not be as good as yours, but I wouldn't make an investment like this without knowing everything about you. We have to be honest with each other, Simone—which is why I'm admitting to you that I know these things. After all, that's what partners do."

My skill set? Wait—could she really know I'm a spy? I couldn't look at her. I stared at my shoes, contemplating five different responses. She was looking right through me, and there was nowhere to hide. No secrets. Just pure honesty. Somehow, I found it comforting.

All the anxiety I had toward her vanished, and confidence washed over me. I looked up and turned to her. "I understand."

"Good," she replied, and gave a forced wink. Then, with astonishing abruptness, she turned from me and made for the table by the door, looking for her nightcap.

"We made a room for you and your friend on the third floor. Fourth door on the left from the elevator. I think you'll find it quite comfortable," she said, her voice trailing off as she entered the house.

I sighed and turned back to the skyline. The fog had vanished, revealing London in its full beauty. A cluster of colored lights on a high-rise in the distance drew my attention, and I was narrowing my eyes to peer at them when my spywatch abruptly vibrated.

With a few swipes, the face came to life. It was Eloise—and she looked serious.

"Simone? Are you somewhere safe?"

The question was surprising—with the locator, she should have known exactly where I was. "Yes, I'm fine. I'm on the terrace at 6 Aubrey Walk."

"Good. I wanted to make sure you weren't in an elevator," she replied.

"What? Why would—"

"We have it on good authority that the Maestro is trying to hack the London power grid. Scotland Yard and Interpol have reported waves of cyberattacks on the system over the last few hours. He's desperate to get his son back, so he's trying to find bargaining chips to negotiate—"

Before she could finish, London vanished as the entire city went black.

"Brendan!" bellowed a voice from the elevator shaft.

Modern Collage

The blackouts hit that evening—London first; then Amsterdam, Berlin, and Paris. At precisely 10:00 p.m. local time, the cities' primary power grids were crippled by a virus that would leave them paralyzed for four hours. At the same time, the Maestro sent an email to the Ministry's director demanding that his son be released, or the lights would be going out all over Europe. He even shared dates and locations, as if daring someone to stop him. It was a powerful message. The Maestro knew he still had control, and he wanted to flex his muscles.

At daybreak, Eloise reported that all the countries in Europe were fortifying their internal systems. Even the Americans were being brought in. The situation was spiraling. Mother and I both agreed this was just the beginning, and more chaos was on the way. I didn't know how Claire might be involved, but we needed to find her—and fast.

On Monday morning, I sat in a classroom in the northwest corner of the arts building, gazing out the tall windows. With its glazed concrete floor, parged walls, and vaulted ceiling, the minimalistic classroom could have been cold or sterile, but a closer look revealed tiny paint splatters everywhere—on the desks, the floors, and even the exposed ceiling joists. Though it was now well organized and swept, the room appeared to have once housed an army of well-fortified aspiring artists, all trying to be the next de Kooning, Hofmann, or Pollock. It was beautiful—and yet, knowing what I now knew, I couldn't help but feel the effect was ruined by the presence of the Red Fox, permeating the room like the smell of petrol.

My thoughtful solitude was broken by two girls coming into the classroom from behind me.

"Did you hear what happened when the lights were out?" one said in a thick Manchester accent.

"Yeah, another painting. Something about a bank," the other replied.

I tensed slightly.

"Another strike by the Red Wolves. Can you believe it? And at the same time as the blackout. Seems strange to me," she concluded.

Coincidence, I thought; but it *was* strange. Sometime between 10:00 p.m. and 2:00 a.m., a skillful partial rendition of Bosch's *Haywain Triptych* had been painted on the southern façade of Findlay's PLC Bank. Although the bank's staff had already begun painting over the mural, pictures were circulating in all the newspapers—and the bank's executives were going to have some explaining to do, as by now everyone knew what that vibrant wolf tag meant. PLC had been under preliminary investigation for mortgage fraud and creating false consumer accounts, but this hadn't been public knowledge—the investigation was only in its twenty-first day, and no formal charges had been filed. Whoever these Red Wolves were, they had inside information, as well as speedy brushes.

I looked down at the four brushes already on my desk. They were set parallel to one another, with five centimeters separating each: the fan, the angle, and then two Filberts.

As I glanced up and to my right, I saw a tall, lanky German boy staring at me. I recognized him immediately, having read his student profile at the Ministry: Jonas Schmidt, a football player from Baden-Baden. I'd noticed him looking at me earlier, though I'd paid him no attention; but his prolonged interest confused me. Was there something in my hair? Our eyes met, and he looked down at his own brushes. *Odd.*

Jilli and Maeve moved through the classroom. Jilli was speaking. "I did the best I—"

Maeve cut her off. "It's fine; just stop talking about it."

Hmm.

At last, our teacher, Ms. Kusma, entered, holding a ragged binder packed with colorful papers, which she dropped on her desk as soon as she reached it. I recalled her file from my research at the Ministry. She had been classically trained, and her early works consisted of bold cubist murals and modern portraiture. Despite initial enthusiasm from the art world, her career had never taken off, though she appeared content as a teacher and was among the most popular with the students.

"Good morning, friends," she said.

"Good morning, Ms. Kusma," we replied.

Jilli leaned toward me. "Will you be my partner today? Maeve is so picky."

Classroom chatter was not my cup of tea, but it would have been rude not to reply. "Well, okay," I whispered, and she grinned.

As Ms. Kusma began going over the day's assignment—a modern collage—I studied her mannerisms. Standing at about 1.7 meters in her flats and colorful cotton blouse, she commanded the room with little effort. Her warm brown skin was radiant and her long black hair was pulled back in a tidy updo, except for a few stray curls hanging over her glasses. The loose strands made her somehow more approachable—less authoritative.

As I watched her, I imagined the Red Fox teaching here in her place. From what I could piece together from last year's course list, he'd been in this classroom at least forty-two times. I imagined what he'd said and how he'd moved about the room. His presence, the art club, Claire and her disappearance . . . it all had to connect somehow.

A sudden question interrupted my thoughts. "Simone, can you tell us about modern collage?" Ms. Kusma asked.

The class quieted, and all thirty-two pairs of eyes turned to me.

I scratched the back of my left hand with my right index finger. I could tell them anything they wanted to know about modern collage. In fact, I could have gone on for over two hours on the subject; but I didn't want to stand out. Thus far, I had flown under the radar in every class—but this was the first time I'd been called out. I had to say something.

"Well, a collage can be just about anything. Bits of paper, photographs, text; but I like the ones that convey an image that is contrary to the materials used in its design," I replied.

"Contrary? Brilliant! Can you give us an example?"

"Now she's got you," whispered Jilli.

I cleared my throat. "Sure. Hale Scot took photographs of pollution and cut them into tiny strips."

A few girls in the back of the room giggled. "'Hale Scot,'" one of them said in a forcedly proper tone.

"Ladies," said Ms. Kusma as she moved toward the front. She smiled at me. "Go on, Simone."

"Then she took the strips and arranged them into gardens, oceans, landscapes." I had to slow down—I didn't want to sound like a robot. "You know, stuff like that."

Jilli leaned over again. "Good answer."

"Yes, I like that too. Hale is an old friend of mine. It's nice to see a student who knows her work." As the class tittered, Ms. Kusma pushed the stray hair away from her glasses. "Now partner up and start picking your supplies. We have art to create!"

The room exploded into activity. Maeve pushed by me to get some paper from the back, and turned to me. "Best of luck with her. She's hopeless." She cocked her head toward Jilli, who frowned theatrically before abandoning the pretense and smiling.

The time passed quickly as we collaborated on a collage depicting one of the oak trees on campus. Jilli cut small strips from magazines and newspapers, and I pasted them to the board. She was painfully slow—I'd had the whole image in my head in four seconds, but it was taking her more than forty-five minutes to make all the cuts. Still, it didn't matter; we had time, and I liked Jilli.

As I placed the last scrap, I felt someone watching us from behind.

"Pretty good, Frenchy," Maeve said in a low voice.

Jilli looked up. "Wow. You never say stuff like that."

"Thanks," I replied.

Ms. Kusma came over to inspect our progress. "Well done, girls. Very nice," she said, leaning over for a closer look. In the next second, she sprang up. "Still, it needs something. What does it need?"

"It needs texture. Maybe a few swipes with a loaded paintbrush," I offered.

"I tend to agree." She walked back toward her desk, then returned with a Filbert brush loaded with crimson 4 oil. It was perfect. She handed it to me, and I gave the old oak a proper splash.

Later, as I walked out of the classroom, still smiling over the praise my recent creation had garnered, I ran into the V.

"Come on, Simone!" she insisted, grabbing my hand. "I have to tell you something. You're not going to believe what I just heard!"

It turned out to be more Claymoore gossip. The V was now well entrenched in the rumor mill, and was excited to tell me about some incident that had occurred at breakfast when an American girl, of all people, accused Madison of texting her boyfriend. A trivial matter—but hearing the V go on and on gave me a familiar anchor to cling to in the bustling hallway. I disliked crowded places and the accompanying risk of being bumped into unexpected-ly—which was why I nearly jumped out of my skin when, out of nowhere, someone tapped my shoulder.

"Excuse me. Your name is Simone, isn't it?" It was the boy from class—Jonas Schmidt. *Good grief. What does he want?*

The V and I stared at him for a few awkward seconds before I forced myself to respond. "Yes, that's right."

"I liked your tree—I mean, your collage. It was much better than our apple—if you could even call it that," he said with a laugh.

The V had gone silent, and her lips were drawing into a smile. What was going on?

"Yeah, okay. Well, thanks, but we need to go," I said, turning away. The V stood frozen, an odd look on her face. "Come on, V," I prompted, and she followed at last, leaving the boy standing in the hallway.

We'd made it only five steps before the V leaned into me and said, "Okay, I'm not going to freak out here or anything, but *do you know what just happened?*"

I had no idea what she was talking about. I couldn't remember ever seeing her so excited. It was as if she were going to explode. "Let's go, V!" I just wanted to get to our English literature class, but it was becoming much more difficult with her pulling on my sleeve and giggling.

"He was *flirting* with you!" she said, turning around to wave at him. "Oh my gosh, he loves you! He wants to be your boyfriend. Do you love him too?"

"What are you talking about?" I said. *Flirting with me?* "Can we talk about this later?" I replied as we passed Maeve and Jilli, who were huddling just inside the building. Deep in conversation with their backs turned, they clearly did not want to be interrupted. I could relate.

I sat through the next two hours of a reasonably well-thought-out presentation on the late works of George Eliot, but my mind kept wandering back to the Fox. *Teaching? Why would he expose himself like that? What was he up to?*

As Dr. Adams finished his lecture, the class let out a collective sigh, and we proceeded to collect our things and zip up our backpacks. I had three hours until my next class, and wanted nothing to do with the V's attempts to return to the subject of Jonas. Still, I couldn't help but wonder—

Flirting with me? Was he?

"Simone! Aren't you paying attention? Can you beli—" the V began.

I cut her off. "I think I left my pen back in the art room. I'm going to go back and look for it."

The V came to a halt. "Really?" she pouted. "Fine—but we have so much to talk about. I can't believe my best friend is in *love!*"

Ugh. My stomach turned as I foresaw the V's plan for the coming evening: discussing the virtues of Jonas Schmidt, and thoroughly investigating all his social media accounts. But I already knew everything about him from his file, and had no interest in dating anyone—and especially not in having a *boyfriend,* of all things.

I really had left a pen in the art room, in the hope of spending some more time there. Immersing myself in the room might reveal a connection to the Fox, or even uncover a clue about Claire. As I ran back across the well-groomed lawn, I noticed Maeve leaning against an oak. She had been watching me and scribbling in a small blue notebook. *Weird.* There were far too many eyes on me today.

I found Ms. Kusma still at her desk, reading. When I poked my head into the room, she glanced at the door over her glasses.

"Simone, is that you?"

"Yes. I think I left a pen here earlier. Can I come in and look for it?"

"Well, of course. We can't have you without your pen, now, can we?"

I smiled. Ms. Kusma seemed sincere and deeply talented—a rare find. A calm poured over me as I approached my desk, but the spirit of the Fox was still thick in the air.

I sat and half-heartedly rummaged through my desk. I knew exactly where the pen was—but I was stalling to take in the room around me.

Ms. Kusma went back to her reading, her hand straying to a small plastic bag full of carrot sticks and green grapes that I assumed served as her lunch. "Do you like it here, dear?" she asked.

The question startled me. I found my pen, and gripped it to steady myself. "Well, yes. I like it here a lot."

"You're the singer from Paris, aren't you?"

The nerves in my stomach began to flutter. "Yes, Ms. Kusma, I can sing."

She closed her notebook and rested her chin on her hands. "I love Paris. I was there last spring on sabbatical, studying and contemplating new works of my own. Such an inspiring place. Living there must be brilliant."

Last spring? That's when he *was here!* This was my chance to get some answers!

"I love it," I blurted. "It's perfect. My family owns a patisserie in the middle of town."

"A patisserie? Yes, I've heard of this—the same one they're finishing over on Sloane Street. That must be a marvelous place to live."

"So, if you were in Paris, who taught your classes?" I was clutching my pen so hard, I was afraid it would break.

A sincere smile appeared. "Ah, the alluring Mr. Redd. The school lucked out when his application came in. A painter from Florence, I believe. I sat in on his interview—very charming—and his catalog was stunning. The headmaster offered him the job on the spot. I don't blame him—and besides, I was off to Paris."

"His catalog? Did he leave it?" I bit my lip, trying to conceal my excitement.

"A catalog? No, I don't think so; but he did leave a pile of canvases in the storage room. Way in the back, next to the shelves with the biscuit jars."

"He left canvases?"

"Yes—quite good ones. Very talented, that one," she added. "A little bit of everything. You know, we cover a lot in one term."

"Could I see them? You said they're in a storage room?" I had to get to them! "Oh—there's my pen."

"Of course, you can, if you don't mind the mess," Ms. Kusma replied. "I still haven't got around to clearing out all those jars ..." She pulled out a drawer in her desk and took out a key. "Here's the key. Third door down the hall on the left."

I bolted down the hall and turned the key in the lock, flicking on the light switch as I entered. As the recessed fluorescent lights flared on, I scanned every square centimeter of the room.

True to Ms. Kusma's word, it was a disaster: half-open boxes; piles of cans; brushes on the floor; and more than a hundred ceramic jars, each slightly lumpy and covered with a flat, cloudy matte glaze. Over it all, the overwhelming smell of mineral spirits hung thickly in the poorly ventilated space.

I gingerly stepped over the mess and navigated around bins of glazed pots and misshapen jars with flattened sides, eyeing the overflowing shelves at the back of the room. A wool blanket covered something against the wall. *That's it.*

With care, I pulled off the blanket to reveal thirteen canvases of assorted sizes and compositions. The first was a masterful impressionist work depicting a blooming meadow in spring. Though the subject was cliché, the brushwork was exquisite and airy. And there, in the lower righthand corner, was the calling card: no letters, just an unmistakable doodle of a fox's head. A red fox.

Excitement rose within me, fueling me as I went through canvas after canvas. Each one was excellent—the strokes, the color palette, the texture, the composition. The Fox's presence seemed to grow around me. I could even smell his cologne, faint but unmistakable. I thought of the message on the window of the patisserie. He must have wanted me to find these—but what was he telling me?

I uncovered the final canvas. Unlike the others, this was no masterful painting. Instead, a plain off-white canvas greeted me, a blue "2" boldly painted in the center.

I picked up the painting to move it under a light, and found it much heavier than I'd expected. I tilted and turned the canvas several times, searching for a hint, and then it occurred to me: there were *two* canvases stretched over the frame. Something was hidden underneath the first!

Heart pounding, I searched for something I could use to pry off the tacks. A set of old pliers lay on a table behind me. *This will do.*

After brushing aside boxes of charcoal and pencils, I laid the painting on a table and got to work. With each tack I carefully removed, a rush of adrenaline shot through me. Hunting for clues was like opening gifts on Christmas, only much more exciting. My palms had begun to sweat, and my ears grew hot.

As I pulled the last tack out, I took a deep breath and turned the canvas over. This was it. The outer canvas fell to the table, while the hidden one, now separated from its frame as well, remained in my hands. I held it up.

A message looked back at me. In light graphite, it read:

GOOD GIRL.

– R

My feet went numb, and my eyes studied every letter. I almost couldn't believe it. How could the Fox have known I would find this? *This painting must have been here since last spring. He couldn't have known all these events would have led me here—or could he have?* My mind sorted through every detail: Claire, the Chocolatiers' Ball, *Blue No. 2*, Eloise, Mother, and on and on. *How did he know?*

I moved to take a picture of the note with my mobile, then reconsidered. I wasn't sure if I wanted to share my discovery. Mother and Eloise were already worried enough.

"Simone, dear? Are you about done?" called Ms. Kusma from the doorway.

I'd been so focused, I hadn't even heard her approach. "Ah— yes. All done!" I stammered. I took another look at the haunting canvas—then folded it and, with my back to the door, placed it in my backpack.

"What a mess," Ms. Kusma groaned as I waded back through the clutter. "Did you find what you were looking for?"

"Yeah, I saw some of the paintings. They were very good."

She closed the door after me and locked it, shaking her head. "Ugh—all those pots. I'll have to start throwing them out. I've never seen a student so obsessed with ceramics. That Claire did have some strange habits."

Wait. Claire? *Think, Simone, think!*

"So one student made all those?"

"Not all—but certainly most of them. Miss Pilfrey made over

a hundred of them, though she never seemed satisfied with any of them."

My mind raced. *The Key!* What if Claire had hidden the Key inside of one of those pots?

As we started down the hall, I turned to glance at the locked door one last time.

That settled it. I had to get back into that room.

———

I spent the rest of the day trying to figure out how I could get into the supply room to examine the jars, while the V went on about how cute Jonas and I looked together. She'd discovered his birthday was in two weeks, and thought I should buy him something to advance our courtship. She'd also scoured Jonas' social media accounts, and even photoshopped a picture of us together. The scaling was awkward and disproportionate, but she was having fun.

For now, I was positioning to play "hard to get." I'd read about this ritual online, and it made perfect sense in this instance.

After a few hours, Kirstin came to announce lights-out; but though the lights were turned off, my mind continued to churn. The events of the day turned over and over in my head, pushing any chance of sleep further and further away. It would be a long night.

At 11:04 p.m., I detected the V rolling over in her bed. I hadn't slept a wink, and braced for another discussion about Jonas and how I should text him.

Sorry, V, I'm not—wait. Something about the V's breathing was off. It had become short and choppy.

"Simone? Are you up?" she whispered, gulping.

I rolled toward her, peering at her across our shared walnut nightstand. The moonlight washed over her face, and I saw something I had never seen before.

"V—are you crying?" I asked.

She sniffed quietly and said, "No. Not really."

All my focus and attention turned to her. "What's wrong?" I watched her for a second. Seeing her so vulnerable for the first time in our long friendship was making me uneasy—but I had to see this through.

The V wiped her left eye and exhaled. "Do you . . . do you feel like you fit in?" she asked.

My answer came into my head immediately: *No. No, I don't. Never, ever.* But looking at the V, I knew that wouldn't help her. I needed to try a different tack.

"Sometimes," I offered slowly. "But why would you ask? You're the popular girl everywhere you go."

She rolled onto her back. "Do you think my birth parents think about me?"

In that moment, I knew what was happening.

"Of course they do, V. And I think about you too, all the time. You're my best friend."

She seemed not to hear. "How could they give me up? Why didn't they love me?" she asked, her eyes welling again.

Memories of Mother and Father collided with thoughts of Eloise and the pain she was now enduring. The bond between a parent and a child was again on display before me, and the power of it took my breath away. *What to say?*

"Well, maybe they loved you so much that they wanted more for you. Maybe being apart was somehow better than being together." I paused. "My mother says that family is everything and that families love each other. Your parents love you more than anything, V—and we love you too." But even as the words slipped out, I looked at her face and realized even this wasn't helping. The V was my best friend, and I loved her, but tonight, that wasn't going to be enough. Nothing would be.

"Yeah, I guess so. Maybe someday I'll get to ask them. Someday," she said, rolling over. But ten seconds later, she rolled back toward me.

"Simone? Will you sing me something? Something nice. It might take my mind off things—help me sleep," she said.

My heart filled. Sitting up and inching to the edge of my bed, I cleared my throat and took a breath.

———

The next morning at breakfast, a thrumming tension permeated the refectory. The newspapers had announced that another blackout was inevitable, and predicted it would occur later that day. The threat was apparently so severe, Mother called, interrupting breakfast, to brief me: the Maestro was planning to hit the power grids at 5:30 p.m., the height of rush hour. She assured me the Ministry was working the case, but I wasn't convinced the crash would be averted. Neither, it seemed, were the students, as everyone rushed to charge their mobiles.

In return, I told Mother about recent developments, including my discovery of Claire's pottery, but omitting the Fox's paintings. She agreed that I needed to get back into the art supply room to inspect the jars, then announced almost as an afterthought that the papers had reported Findlay's PLC was under formal investigation, and the Bank of England was now taking over all its operations and accounts. The Red Wolves had once again exposed a thief.

For the moment, however, my main concern was for the V. I watched her chat with Madison over breakfast, my scrambled eggs and toast going untouched. Although she seemed back to her bubbly self, it pained me to know something was festering underneath.

Mother said to give her time and just listen if she wanted to talk. Still, this worry was new to me; and worse yet, it was distracting me from my mission: Claire and the Key.

"Aren't you going to eat?" the V asked. "We have gym class today."

I picked up a piece of toast and spread some butter over it. "Yeah. I was just thinking about stuff," I replied.

She leaned over with a growing smile and a sparkle in her eye. At first, my spirits lifted—until she said, "Were you thinking about Jonas? Oh, he is so cute!" She paused. "You know, I could go talk to him for you!"

Ugh.

The next few hours moved at a snail's pace as my mind quantified and calculated the obstacles before me. By the end of trigonometry class, my priorities were clear: get a line on Claire, get back into the supply room, and of course—dump Jonas Schmidt.

Holds and Throws

By midday, the weather took an unexpected turn as a cold front plunged south. London was starting to ice over.

The chill breeze clawed at our faces as Jilli and I walked across the courtyard. I counted every one of the thirty-seven steps to the library doors, anticipating the warmth within with more fervor than usual.

"So, do you like it here?" Jilli said into her scarf. The cold, it seemed, would not deter her from speaking. "The V seems to be fitting in."

"Yeah, we like it here a lot. The V especially likes all the kids," I replied.

Jilli nodded, her teeth chattering. "She asked if we could hang out later and maybe study."

"Hang out? That seems cool." It occurred to me that I had never described anything as *cool* before. How much of myself would I have to betray to fit in? "Maybe I could come."

The library foyer was a welcome sight. The old tile floors were cold, but the air was dry and warm. As the heat of the radiators washed over us, we shook off the winter chill and ditched our scarves atop of a large coat rack. I intended to come back later for a further inspection, but for today, I was just studying.

And I couldn't have imagined a more perfect environment for the task. The Claymoore library was a magnificent achievement. Finished in 1860 in the Néo-Grec style, its central atrium soared sixteen meters high and was lined on all sides by oak-and-cast-iron balconies. Worn leather seats and green desk lamps accented its heavy wooden desks and reading tables, and its tall, ornate bookshelves housed over ten thousand titles. It smelled aged and untouched, more like a cathedral than a library, and was a popular spot for events. Two hundred eighteen wedding receptions for Claymoore alumni had been held here, so its immaculateness was vital—though to be honest, I thought it could use a little less shine and a little more dust.

I counted only eighteen students, one teacher, and two librarians in the room. The cold was keeping the kids away—which was fine with me.

Maeve sat reading at a table in a far corner. As Jilli and I approached, she looked up, peering at us from over the top of her book.

"Well, aren't you two adorable," she scoffed, lowering her copy of *Mrs. Dalloway. Nice choice.*

I carefully placed my backpack on the table and pulled out a chair.

Maeve sat back and crossed her arms. "Aren't you becoming the popular one." It wasn't a question. In fact, it sounded more like a challenge.

I thought of my recent trials at Trinity, where my popularity had quickly become burdensome. I was not going to let that happen here.

I forced a laugh, attempting to mimic Jilli. "Yeah, right."

This must have been the right answer, because Maeve didn't press further. Relieved, I exhaled.

Jilli took out a notebook and pencil. "I like French girls. The V said I had royalty written all over me."

Maeve snickered, and the librarian shot us a warning glare from her desk.

Stephanie Bickford had been the chief librarian at Claymoore for eighteen years, and took considerable pride in her vocation. She liked her library quiet and orderly, and was not one to be tested on this point. We had to be careful—last I'd checked, Maeve had by far the highest number of demerits of any student in the school, and just one more would see her confined to her dormitory for the weekend, except for meals.

Maeve and Jilli leaned into the center of the table, and I had to follow suit. The next fourteen minutes' worth of talk revolved around the week's gossip and the clear injustice of Ms. Marswell's grading policy. I tried to appear engaged, but all I wanted to do was ask about Claire. What did they know about her? I had to think of an opening line.

"Ms. Kusma mentioned that girl who went missing was a brilliant artist. Maybe the best in the school," I said. Then I waited with high expectations, holding my breath.

Silence. The moment stretched thin as neither girl said a word, ignoring my question as they flipped through their textbooks. Finally, Jilli spoke up.

"Yeah, Claire was great. She was really into art, and she could paint anything. Not much of a potter, though. Have you seen all her pots?"

My heart thudded against my ribcage. "Yeah, I saw a bunch in the art supply room. Mostly unfinished. What else did she like to do?"

Maeve glanced at Jilli, then turned her attention to me. "You know, Simone, you seem to be pretty good at art. Do you paint much?"

This was unexpected—but I had to keep the conversation going. "Sure, I like art—painting and stuff." I couldn't believe I'd said that. I could have launched into a dissertation on mid-century Postimpressionist theory, and the effort of holding back had me biting the inside of my lip. *Clear your head. Clear your head.*

"You know, Maeve is a great artist too," Jilli said. "Almost as good as Claire."

"Jilli!" Maeve snapped—too loudly. *Eeek!* Went the librarian's chair as she stood. Her heels made sharp reports as she strode across the tile floor, and whispers began circulating among the other kids. A reminder on library policy—or worse—would certainly be forthcoming. I had to do something!

Mrs. Bickford drew up to us, lips pursed, and placed her hands on the desk. "Miss Stahl, I will remind you that—"

I interrupted. "It was me, Mrs. Bickford; it was me. Sorry. It won't happen again."

Both she and Maeve looked at me with surprise. Mrs. Bickford slowly stood.

"I see. Well, please respect those around you that are here to learn. The library is no place for kibitzing." She wiped off a small smudge on the table with her sleeve, then walked away.

Maeve leaned in. "Why did you do that? I can handle myself."

Yes! This was my in. I shrugged, attempting to appear nonchalant. "I know. I just didn't want you to spend all weekend in detention. I thought maybe we could hang out or something."

Maeve exhaled, drumming her fingers on the table. "Not this weekend, Frenchy—but maybe later." She studied me, and then the corner of her mouth came up in a smile. "And thanks for taking the heat for me. You're alright."

Bingo!

———

When I returned to my room after dinner, I removed my boots and set them next to the radiator, piled my gloves and hat on top of them, and sat in bed with Mother's blanket draped over me. As the November chill fell on Claymoore, this room had become my oasis. Everything on my side had a place, and the V indulged me by keeping her side in reasonable order. More and more, I felt like we were away at camp, having left our regular lives for a while and gained a novel independence. Despite my initial reservations about leaving my family in Paris, Claymoore was growing on me.

The word *Connecting* blinked on my computer screen as I propped up my legs. The V was hosting another small social in the common room down the hall, so I would have privacy.

Finally, the screen came to life. "There you are, dear. Tell me everything that's been happening," Mother said. She was standing in our flat's kitchen, and after careful examination, I could see nothing had changed. It was my window into bliss: the whitewashed cabinets, the oak hutch with *grandmère's* plates on display, and the old teapot on the stove. In that moment, I didn't care about Maeve, the Fox, or anything. I just wanted to hear her voice and see her face.

"Any line on the Key?" Mother asked.

"I can't get back into the art supply room for now, so I'm focusing elsewhere today. The library is next on my list," I answered. "I'm going there again tomorrow."

"The library? Well, that sounds right up your alley. Any leads on Claire's disappearance?"

"Nothing there either, but I am meeting a lot of people. I just need a little more time." I paused, then asked, "How are you feeling?"

She looked down, and I could tell she was calculating her response. "I'm fine, dear. Just a bit under the weather. No worries."

We had never lied to each other before, but now I sensed that the truth might be bending. My stomach turned uneasily. It was time to address the matter at hand.

I reached into my backpack and pulled out the canvas. "I found this behind a canvas painted by the Fox."

Mother froze. Her eyes narrowed as she looked at the message through the screen. "What? Have you told Eloise?"

"Not yet. I wanted to be able to give her more information. You know, with Claire . . ." I trailed off. "Do you want me to?"

"No, that won't be necessary. Just keep the canvas somewhere safe. I'll brief Eloise."

"Okay. I'll hide it in my stuff."

The moment passed, and then levity jumped through the screen as Mother flashed a sly smile.

"So, who is this Jonas Schmidt I'm hearing all about? Is he as dreamy as advertised?"

I almost blacked out.

The view of the library atrium from the top-level balconies was nothing short of magnificent. I could lose myself in here for hours, but I needed to get to work.

In my estimation, the library was not a likely spot for the OmniKey, but I couldn't help wanting to explore it. Merely stuffing the Key between some volumes would be risky, and I couldn't imagine Claire cutting a hideaway into a book. I had activated my spywatch to detect any low-frequency signals, but so far, I'd found nothing. If the Key was here, it was likely encased in a medium that could block signals, as Eloise had initially suggested—something more permanent, perhaps metal.

"I see you're enjoying our early anthropology section," Mrs. Bickford whispered as she made her hourly rounds.

I looked up. "Ah—yes. It's very nice. Well organized, and the selections are excellent." I felt some desire to appease her after falsely taking the blame for Maeve's earlier interruption. Being in the good graces of a librarian was always a valuable thing.

I sensed that my effort was at least partially successful, as Mrs. Bickford smiled and moved on.

I walked around, trying to see the library from Claire's perspective. What would she have found attractive? I knew she liked the arts, but that section offered little in terms of hiding places. There were no short-wave signals there, either. Wherever the Key was, it was well hidden. *After all, Claire was always smart.*

Thirty minutes later, I found myself on the first floor, rummaging through my last stop—the periodicals section—without even a hint of a clue. No, it couldn't be here. The library was simply too orderly and quiet, with no obvious hiding spots. I wouldn't have hidden it here, either. There were too many variables: books were regularly checked out, shelves were cleaned, tables and chairs were moved. It wouldn't make sense.

Mrs. Bickford approached with an armful of new magazines. "You know, you're welcome to check out any books," she whispered to me. Somehow, from her tone of voice, I guessed few students took advantage of the opportunity. It was just too easy to find things online. Personally, I loved the feel of a book in my hands, and hated to disappoint her—but for now, I had more pressing matters in mind.

"None for me today, thank y—"

The doors flew open, much to Mrs. Bickford's alarm.

"Simone! Come on! We're going to be late for gym class!" shouted the V.

Unlike the rest of the classes at Claymoore, gym class was the only period that saw the girls and boys separated and assigned to different teachers. Decked out in sweatpants and a t-shirt like the rest of the girls in my year, I stood watching our coach pace in front of the bleachers—one of the only spaces in the gym not currently covered by thick rubber mats.

"Okay, ladies, just holds and throws today. None of the rough stuff," Coach Dar announced to the group. He stopped pacing as he ordered, "Now, partner up!"

All around the room, girls gravitated toward each other. The V and Jilli teamed up at once, leaving me alone.

I was no stranger to standing alone in gym class. I'd never tried to project athletic competence, as I found games and other physical activities less than rewarding. Still, I could hold my own in martial arts: thanks to my work at the Ministry, I had been studying judo, krav maga, and karate for years, and had earned my second-degree black belt in judo last spring.

"I guess it's me and you then," said Kirstin smugly, sidling up to me.

Ugh. Why did it have to be her?

From her file, I knew Kirstin was an accomplished athlete. She particularly excelled at swimming and tennis, but was a formidable opponent regardless of the arena, and competitive to the end. Second place was not an option for her.

Several of the other students noticed us pairing up, and a faint buzz started. If I didn't want to draw any more attention to myself, I would have to play this down and take some lumps.

"Okay, ladies, you may engage!" Coach Dar shouted. He blew his whistle, and the match was on.

"You might want to take those glasses off," Kirstin said to me.

"I'll be fine," I demurred. In the next second, Kirstin clenched her hands, and her smile dropped.

WHACK!

She kicked my outer left calf, then moved to a basic *tachi waza* technique, pulling me forward and throwing me on the floor. My glasses went flying, and the girls who had seen me tossed started to laugh.

Kirstin gave a sarcastic bow and returned to her starting position.

I looked over at Jilli and the V, who were rolling around obliviously on their mat, giving minimal effort. My calf had begun to throb, and I winced.

Coach Dar blew his whistle. "Not bad! Now, let's do it again."

I found my glasses and put them on, more than a little embarrassed. *Shake it off, Simone.*

We took our positions again. "On my whistle!" shouted Coach Dar. But just as he raised his hand—*WHACK!*

Another kick, to the right shin this time. As the whistle sounded, Kirstin pushed forward, taking advantage as I stopped to rub my leg. She was much bigger than me, so she easily grabbed my shirt and arm and hip-tossed me to the mat with a pronounced *UMPH!*

My glasses flew off again—but I was unfazed. My *ukemi*—my falling technique—had been excellent, I noted with some pride. Kirstin's techniques, on the other hand, were unpolished and predictable—although they were causing quite the stir among the rest of the class.

"You're not going to take that, are you, Frenchy?" shouted Maeve from two mats away, where she had Madison in a headlock.

Kirstin turned to Maeve, re-tying her ponytail, though not one strand had fallen out of place. "Mind your own mat, ginger. She's a big girl."

Maeve frowned. She released Madison and started to walk toward us—only for Coach Dar to swoop in and head her off. "Back to your mat, Stahl."

The pain in my leg pounded. At least a half-dozen other girls were now pointing and laughing at my misfortune. The phrase "turn the other cheek" rolled briefly through my head. I had to be the bigger person.

"Sad little Frenchy—not much more than an ugly cow," Kirstin jeered.

Red. That was the only way to describe how I felt. When Maeve called me Frenchy, it was somehow endearing—but hearing it from Kirstin was insulting. *Ugly cow?* Nobody talked to me like that! *Ugh—that's it!* She was trying to put me in my place, and that was *not* going to happen. *Sorry, Confucius, but this girl needs a lesson.*

The coach blew his whistle. "Take a break, girls. I'm stepping out to collect some volleyballs. No more contact."

All eyes watched him crest the door—and then, as one, they all turned to me and Kirstin.

"Okay, Frenchy. Let's see what you got," Maeve said, folding her arms.

Kirstin made two fists. "No brakes now, Frenchy. Get 'em up." By now, the entire class had made a circle around us and was waiting to see me take a beatdown.

I took a deep breath to clear my head and assumed a perfect starting position—head calm, weight balanced, and hands ready to fly. *Itami ga kuru.*

She leaped at me again, trying the same leg kick; but I grabbed her shirt and rolled her over and onto the mat. If she'd stayed down, I would have let this go—but she popped up, to several snickers from the crowd. A few strands of her hair had come free of her ponytail, and she quickly looked around to see if anyone had noticed.

And it seemed everyone had.

As we circled the mat, her expression turned to rage, and she leapt at me again—a bad move. I deflected her hand, and as her weight easily carried her forward, I gripped her arm and assumed the position for a hip toss. As her body started to fall, I jumped up and tucked my shoulder deep into her chest.

We hit the mat with a thunderous *WHAM!*—and all the air left her lungs.

A gasp came from the crowd as I bounced off Kirstin and skipped up into a respectful *rei*.

Silence fell. From my position on the mat, I turned to see Maeve gazing appreciatively at me.

"What was that?" Jilli whispered to the V.

"My girl is *crazy* like that! Yeah!" the V cheered, slamming a flurry of karate chops into the air. "Anybody else want some?"

Hushed conversations broke out as Kirstin caught her breath and ran toward the locker room. Everyone was staring at me—and for once, I didn't care.

That evening, I sat in bed reading as the V tended to a generous bag of ice on my leg. I didn't need it, but it was sweet of her to go to the trouble.

The rumor that I was some type of assassin had spread quickly throughout the school, and by dinnertime, most of the student body was giving me the cold shoulder—not that I minded. The V was as enthused as ever, and even now, she kicked at the air. "Man, you really showed her what was up!"

I cracked a smile and turned a page of my book. I had almost finished my re-read of *Mrs. Dalloway*. "Yeah, I guess so."

The V stopped spinning and turned to me with all the attention of a devoted mother. "Does it hurt? Do you need crutches or something?"

"No, I'm fine." I grinned, knowing Kirstin would probably not be coming to our room tonight to announce lights-out.

Later, I lay awake in bed, running over the day's events. The V was fast asleep, snoring gently. The lights had already been out for over an hour, and now that my leg had stopped hurting, my focus turned to Claire and the Key. Having eliminated the library as a potential hiding place, I knew I needed to get back to the art closet.

I tossed and turned, scanning the room, which the light of the full moon had filled with a bluish cast. Outside, a few distant boat horns sounded from the Thames. London was calm and clear, ready for a good night's sleep.

In the next moment, however, footsteps stopped at our door. The knob turned, and the door made a faint *c-r-e-a-k* as a figure stepped into the room.

I sat up in my bed, heart racing, and squinted into the darkness.

It was Maeve. Before I could react, she walked toward me and put a finger to her lips.

"Wanna do something cool?"

The Red Wolves of London

A burst of adrenaline rolled through my veins as I watched Maeve step into the moonlight. She wore dark pants, a hooded sweatshirt, and black gloves. Her hair was pulled back, and her eyes were ablaze. *Am I dreaming?*

"Sure," I replied guardedly as the V turned over in bed. My eyes flicked in her direction. *Don't wake up; don't wake up.*

Maeve closed the door, squatted, and brought her face twenty centimeters from mine. Charcoal was smeared under her eyes, giving them a wild look. "There's no going back from this, Frenchy. You're either in, or you're out."

Any remaining levity evaporated from the room. My toes tingled, and my hands went clammy. It occurred to me that this was the first time in my life a contemporary had asked me to join in anything. Sure, the V and I had created a number of "secret societies" growing up, but those had been capped at a membership of two—three if you counted Gigi. This was different.

Maeve looked into my eyes and gave me a devilish smile. "Well?"

My first instinct was to say no, but an inner voice urged, *Say yes, Simone. Say yes!*

"I'm in," I whispered.

I sensed a fuse had been lit, but I didn't know whether to put it out or stick around for the explosion. The feeling was ominous—exciting.

Maeve put her hand over my mouth. "Good. No questions, then. Keep your mouth shut until I say so—not a word."

Removing her hand from my mouth, Maeve stood and glanced back at the door.

"Put on some dark clothes—the tighter the better. You don't want anything to slow you down."

Slow me down?

I rolled silently out of bed and began taking stock of my outfit. As I did, my fingers brushed my wrist.

My spywatch! It needed to stay here. This was an adventure the Ministry did not need to know about—couldn't know about. But the watch also tracked my heartbeat, so I needed to find . . .

That's it!

I removed the watch. The diodes within blinked blue, and I hastily typed in the override code to let the Ministry know I was safe, as I did every time I took it off. Then I crossed the room and carefully attached it to the V's wrist.

Don't wake up—don't wake up.

I waited. For one agonizing moment, the V shifted. Then she rolled over—still fast asleep.

Time to go.

We eased the door open, and Maeve looked down the hall.

"Move. We're going to be late."

Late?

I zipped up my jacket and tucked my hair back, and took one last look at the V before we slipped out like two ghosts. I had walked out that door eighty-one times before, but somehow, this time, I knew I was not going to return the same person.

Breathe, Simone. But even the cold air could not stifle the heat in my cheeks.

We crept down the stairs and out onto the lawn. I had memorized the layout of the school, and knew the location of every camera and motion sensor—but Maeve did not seem to need my help. She darted from dark corner to dim corridor as if she had done this a million times, moving with such elegance that all my concerns over getting caught soon vanished. Based on her path through the shadows, I guessed the rose garden was our destination, as the stretch of fence there was fronted with bushes and trees—but instead, we took an unexpected turn toward the arts building.

We got to the corner of the building and stopped behind a wall of dense boxwoods, where Maeve retrieved a bulky duffle bag that had been covered with leaves and mulch. Then she turned to me.

"We need to keep moving. Bailes will be turning in soon."

We continued, staying close to the buildings and taking advantage of the sprawling shadows that splotched the lawn. The full moon had now entered a front of incoming clouds that supplied us with some much-needed cover. The duffle clinked slightly, and Maeve hugged the bag tightly to her chest, dampening most of the sound with her hands.

As we neared the building that housed the headmaster's office, we stopped and huddled behind a thick hedge, and Maeve looked up at his window. The light was still on. She glanced at me as I caught my breath.

"Any second now," she whispered.

As if on cue, Headmaster Bailes came to the window—perhaps to survey the grounds one last time before bed, now that the late news was finished. Sophie the cat jumped up on the sill beside him and appeared to do the same. After a moment, both turned away, and nine seconds later, the light went out.

"Let's roll."

Maeve grabbed my arm, leading me to the winterized rose garden in the southeast corner of the grounds. Just beyond the tangles of cut stems stood a locked wrought-iron gate topped with pointed fence posts sharp enough to ruin anyone's day. We inched behind a thicket of trees, stopping in front of the iron bars.

"What took you guys so long?" came a soft voice.

"She took a second to get moving, but we're okay now," Maeve quietly replied. I leaned over her shoulder to catch a glimpse of a dark figure approaching the other side of the fence.

It was Jilli. She was also dressed in dark clothes, and smears of charcoal adorned her petite cheeks. A woolly black hat was trying to hold all her hair, although several strands had escaped.

Jilli? But how did she get on the other side?

Rule 2, Section 12b of the Claymoore Code of Conduct flashed through my mind—*Students may not leave the campus after dark without written permission from an administrator.* But I had no time to think twice. In the next instant, Maeve grabbed one of the bars of the fence and twisted it. To my surprise, it came loose—and I realized it had been cut at the top and bottom before being wedged back into place. Maeve removed its neighbor in the same way and passed the duffle bag to Jilli, nearly toppling her, and we both passed through. Then Maeve turned and carefully placed the bars back in position. We were free.

Free.

The crisp night air filled our lungs as we ran through a series of alleys and side streets. I had been out late in Paris dozens of times—thirty-nine, to be exact. That city was like a flowing river, full of turns, falls, and constant motion. You had to swim to keep up. But while Paris seemed to fall into bed with makeup still on, stubbing out a cigarette, London at night was in order and tucked away just so. It was resting, like a slumbering beast—which made it even more exciting to prowl about.

Not a word was said as we swiftly navigated the softly humming streets. Moving in a zigzag pattern, we soon managed to travel over a kilometer from Claymoore. I was starting to get a little winded, and increasingly curious about our destination. Maybe there *was* no real destination—just a night going rogue on the town. But in that case, why had Maeve brought a bag? *No, there must be a purpose. But what?* Questions flooded my head, but I dared not make a sound.

We stopped in a dim alley, and Maeve carefully hid the duffle bag in the shadows, then approached a weathered brick apartment building. Without hesitating, she leapt up and pulled down the fire escape.

"We're going up. We've got a moving target tonight, so I need a signal."

Jilli and I exchanged a searching look. Then, with a shrug, she moved to follow Maeve up the creaking ladder. I paused for a split second, then clambered up behind them.

The iron rungs of the fire escape were hard and cold—clearly not built for comfort. We navigated up eight stories of balconies and stairs, mindful of apartment lights flicking on and off. The night air was cool and full with the thrill of a mystery. I wondered what was waiting for me at the top.

By the time I reached the cold pebbles that covered the roof, I was breathing heavily. Maeve and Jilli were already perched on the edge of the building, deep in conversation as they gazed out over the city. I came up alongside them.

"Okay, so what's next?" Jilli asked. I was aching to ask questions too, but Maeve hadn't given the word, and I had to prove she could trust me. Plus, I was out in the field now. I needed to be careful.

"We wait," replied Maeve.

She stared out over the city. The fog was starting to lift, and I watched her eyes follow something two streets over. Then the clouds parted, bringing London into full view: Big Ben, the London Eye, Tower Bridge, and even the top of Westminster Abbey. I had seen this skyline countless times before, but tonight, it felt brand-new to me.

For the next thirty-seven seconds, the three of us gazed out over London, the city lights illuminating our faces. It was stately, tranquil, even regal, and for a second, I forgot why I was there in the first place.

"Should be any second now," Maeve said. "We should be . . . *ah! What?*"

Without warning, the streetlamps and buildings began going dark, each borough turning off in random order, one by one. Within eight seconds, the glow of the city had vanished entirely.

"What's going on?" Jilli shrieked.

Maeve grumbled and started to pace. "I don't know. That wasn't supposed to happen. We'll never see it now." She sighed. "Maybe it's a bust for tonight."

My brows knit. I knew the Maestro had been planning more outages—but what could that have to do with Maeve and Jilli?

Suddenly, a distant section of the city turned on, and like a brushfire, lights swept over the horizon. As quickly as it had gone out, London was restored.

Maeve looked down at her mobile. "Come on, come on," she whispered. A message popped up, and she raised her chin to look out over the city. "Any second now," she muttered.

Jilli and I both followed her lead, staring out into the still night. Not three seconds later, we saw the lights on a single street three blocks to the north flicker on and off twice.

"That's it. Let's go," said Maeve.

We quickly climbed back down the fire escape, and Maeve grabbed the duffle bag before setting off. "Almost there, wolves. Hustle!" Maeve called as we jogged down the block.

Wolves? I looked at Jilli, who giggled and let out a faint howl.

Seconds later, we ducked into a shadow-covered, cobble-stone-lined alley so Maeve could check her mobile again. The temperature had dropped about three degrees, though my heart rate more than compensated for the cold. *Who's texting her, anyway?*

Jilli glanced at me and smiled. "Don't worry. Maeve knows what to do."

As if on cue, Maeve received another text message. She read it quickly, then secured her mobile in her front pocket. Then she turned to us.

"Okay. We're going to have forty-five minutes to pull this off. In a few seconds, the street cameras will cycle off, and then we go."

I couldn't stay quiet any longer. My stomach was in knots, and even my scalp was getting sweaty. I felt like I was going to pop. "Go? Go where?" I stammered, breaking my silence for the first time.

But if I'd feared Maeve would send me back for breaking her rules, my worries were unfounded. Instead, her face lit up with a smile as she turned away and pointed to a double-decker bus parked across the street. "There."

What? I thought. *That's strange. Why would we go there? And why would a bus be parked here for the night?*

Maeve turned to me. She was so close, I could have counted her freckles if they hadn't been hidden under the thick charcoal. Her eyes were wild again.

"Do you believe in truth? Do you believe truth will bring justice to the world?"

I blinked, bewildered. For the first time, here was a question I genuinely didn't know how to answer. Of course truth was important, and ethical—but spies dealt in dishonesty. I hadn't told the whole truth about the Chocolatiers' Ball, or why I'd come to Claymoore—and I also knew more about a certain red-headed art teacher than I let on. Maybe some truths could be kept secret until they were needed.

But I also had to play along.

"Of course. Of course, Maeve! The—"

"The truth always comes out," she said.

My heart shuddered, and the night went still. That phrase had been burned in my mind since last summer. *That's exactly what the Red Fox said! How much did he tell them? Why are we doing this? And what's in the duffle?*

Maeve glanced at her mobile, which was counting down the seconds. "You're a good artist, Simone, and we've really needed somebody since Claire disappeared. You might even be better than her."

Wait. *Claire? Was she a part of this, too?*

"Don't worry, we won't get caught. Just follow my directions and stick to the plan," Maeve whispered.

In the next instant, I heard the security camera above us move from side to side.

"That's it. Go."

We ran across the dormant street to the other side of the bus, where Maeve told me to get on her shoulders. Then Jilli scaled us and slid onto the top floor of the bus. We passed up the bag, and I stood on Maeve's shoulders while Jilli pulled me up. Finally, Maeve took a running start. She jumped, and I grabbed her hand to help her join us.

"The perfect canvas, don't you think?" Maeve pointed at the red metal roof as she found her footing on the top of the bus. Jilli opened the bag, and for the first time, I saw that it was full of paints and brushes. No wonder it had been so heavy. My stomach dropped.

What am I doing here? The adrenaline was starting to fight with my conscience as the gravity of where I was, what I was doing, and who I was with settled in. *What if somebody sees us?*

But Maeve gave me no time to think. "Do you know the painting *Philistines* by Jean-Michel Basquiat?"

Of course I did. It was a masterpiece of contemporary art, and

I knew every line and brushstroke. I nodded.

"We're going to paint it. Right here," Maeve said with a smile.

"What? Why?"

"Because that's what we do. Hurry, we only have forty-five minutes."

My mind would not slow down enough to properly evaluate the situation, but I knew I had to placate her. I had to find out what these two knew about Claire. Without another thought, I forged ahead. "Okay. Yeah. Let's do it."

For the next thirty-two minutes, with Jilli as our lookout, Maeve and I worked in perfect harmony, jumping over each other, moving paint over our "canvas," and sharing brushes with surgical precision. A line here, a splash of paint there; color, color, color. I loved every second, and something about Maeve put me completely at ease. My mind turned off, and I was immersed in the moment. No rules, no accountability, no one to answer to—just art.

As I finished my last line, Maeve stood, exhausted but triumphant, and took in the painting. "That's it. It's done."

The three of us came together and gazed over our creation. It was perfect—the blocking, the color palette, the details, all of it. My hand was shaking, and I dropped my brush. There was no going back now.

What have I done?

Jilli whistled. "A car's coming. Duck!"

The three of us lay flat as a car moved down the street. Its headlights illuminated the night as I recalled distant memories of hide-and-seek with Mia and the V. It was exhilarating, and for the first time since being onstage in Vienna, I felt alive.

The car slowed a bit before passing us, but it finally motored by and turned left at the corner. As its taillights faded, the three of us laughed into the cold.

"Okay, Jilli, you're up," Maeve said.

As I watched, Jilli dipped a brush into the can of red paint and added what appeared to be a wolf's head at the corner of the painting. Then she stepped back to examine her handiwork.

With that, all my assumptions were confirmed. Maeve and Jilli were not just copycats looking to post something on social media. They were the real deal—the Red Wolves of London—and now I was in on it.

"It still looks like a wolf," Maeve quipped. Jilli turned to her, mouth drawn into a pout.

"You don't have to keep rubbing it in. You know I'm practicing!"

Maeve shrugged playfully. "It's fine. After all, it's kind of our calling card now."

Wait. "It's not supposed to be a wolf?"

Jilli shook her head. "I'm not a very good artist. That's why we needed to find someone else after Claire left." She looked down at the signature and sighed. "It's *supposed* to be a fox."

A fox?

A surge of clarity broke through my excitement. My stomach churned, and the hairs on my arms stood on end. Of course. How could I ever have doubted? The Red Wolves: Maeve, Jilli, Claire—

And pulling the strings, *la Volpe Rossa.*

Bad Girls

T he morning sun was starting to creep into the dormitory, the light desperately trying to penetrate the dense fog that had gathered as Maeve, Jilli, and I crept back to Claymoore through the dark London streets. On the way home, Maeve had explained that the director of London's public bus transport was considering easing safety regulations and cutting drivers' pay to make up for budgetary shortfalls. Several people in government had been in his ear to make quiet changes. But safety could not be overlooked—and when it came to making this point, *Philistines* was the perfect fit. The director would certainly have some explaining to do.

As for me, I didn't sleep a wink. The evening's events had burned themselves into my mind. I could barely believe it: Maeve, Jilli—and at some point, Claire—were the Red Wolves of London—and la Volpe Rossa was at the heart of it. He must have recruited this cohort last term, and was now deploying them to tag corrupt corporations that were deceiving the public. It didn't feel right. *Vandalizing buildings? He's better than this.* And what did that have to do with the Maestro and his Key?

I studied a few specks of paint lingering on my hands. Part of me wanted to wash them off at once, but another wanted to keep them intact as memorials of a watershed evening, one I would never forget. I felt older that morning, as if a part of my childhood had faded away into my old toy box back home. I wondered if anyone would realize.

The V was my first concern. We'd been friends forever, and she would be the first to notice if I was acting strangely. After slipping in before dawn, I'd managed to return the watch to my wrist with her none the wiser. As she stirred in bed, however, I steeled myself.

The V turned over in bed and peered at me. "Morning, Simone." Catching sight of me, she frowned. "Hey—are you okay? You look kinda jazzed."

Not good enough. I would have to do better. "I'm fine. Had a restless night."

"Yeah, I thought so. I woke up once and you were gone. Where—"

"Oh—I was in the bathroom. I must have eaten something funny," I interjected quickly. *Thank goodness she didn't notice the watch!*

The V seemed to accept this, because she yawned and rolled over for what would no doubt become another fifteen minutes of rest. I sat back in bed, my heart still pounding with the last remnants of adrenaline lingering in my system. I wasn't proud to have told my friend a lie—but it was only a small one.

It didn't take long for news of the Wolves' latest work to swarm through the city. Traffic helicopters soon noticed the bus as it traveled along the Westway, and within minutes, two news copters were circling overhead and pictures were pasted all over the internet. People lined up along the route and hung out of windows to try to catch a glimpse of the bus as its still-unsuspecting driver trundled through town, presumably wondering what all the fuss was about—a fleeting touch with fame that he soaked up until his supervisor finally got through to him over the radio after about thirty minutes.

At brunch, I picked at some scrambled eggs and sausage. Despite everything I knew I had to investigate, I was still engrossed in the previous night's adventures. The crisp night breeze, the dim lights—the freedom! A shiver went up my spine at the mere possibility of another night out. My guess was that last night's events had been a test of my loyalty to the Wolves—a first step. Had I passed?

The V leaned over. "So, what are we going to do today? Do you think we could go shopping or something? Christmas is coming fast." The V had taken a handful of supervised shopping trips with other girls, but she'd been scheming over a more thorough retail adventure with me for weeks, arguing that she simply couldn't leave London without having purchased something bespoke.

I managed a smile. "Don't you remember? We're going to Father's store this afternoon for a soft launch. Now that construction is mostly finished, they've started to bring in more stuff for the actual production. Father said we could pretend to be customers and order anything we like. I'm meeting Jilli to study first, and Father is sending a car for us at two o'clock."

Apparently this news wasn't exciting enough for the V, because as I spoke, she scanned the room, searching for some new drama. Evidently she found some, because in the next moment, she jammed a sharp elbow into my side.

"Jonas is looking at you!" she exclaimed.

Ugh. Not this again!

By noon, the fog had cleared, and the weather was surprisingly bright. It was hard to concentrate on schoolwork with everything milling about in my head—but Jilli and I had secured written permission to leave campus for the afternoon, and there was no way I was going to pass up this opportunity.

Four streets west of Claymoore, an enclave of retail stores and eateries that attracted local families stood along Booth Street. UK

Coffee Roasters was our destination of choice, given its dependable bustle and choice baked goods. Today, the café was packed with chatty families brought out by the sunny weather, and the air carried the scents of roasted coffee, freshly baked biscuits, and dried lavender sitting in pots on each table. I could lose an entire day in here with a good book.

But I wasn't here for pleasure. On the heels of our night on the town, I hoped Jilli and I could relax and get to know each other better. Maybe she would open up.

Right now, however, Jilli had her nose buried in a book. Though I was pretending to write in my journal, I was actually stealing glances at her and strategizing how to drum up a conversation about the Wolves.

Still, old habits die hard, and as I scanned the room over Jilli's shoulder, I noticed two men sitting ten meters from us, doing—well, nothing. They had no mobiles, no newspaper, neither tea nor coffee—they were just sitting. *Odd. Might want to circle back to them.*

"So . . . Maeve seems nice." It was all I could come up with, and it felt lame, but Jilli still looked up from her book and smiled. "Do you guys go out—"

"*Shh!* We never talk about that in public, ever," she said sternly. She fidgeted in her chair and looked around the café. "So—tell me about you and Jonas!" she demanded loudly.

Oh, no. "Umm. He's just some boy in one of my classes. That's all."

Jilli laughed. "Yeah, 'some boy.' Every girl in the school has a crush on him. I'm not surprised he likes you. You're a catch."

A catch? I doubt it. I frowned and glanced back at the conspicuous men. I didn't recognize them from the Ministry, and Eloise would have briefed me if she was sending agents to London. One of them was staring.

An agent wouldn't be staring.

My heart began to pound in my ears. There was only one answer—they had been sent by the Maestro.

We need to get out of here, and fast.

My eyes locked on the occupants of a neighboring table: a well-dressed woman with her three children. The Ministry trained junior spies to engage with adults if compromised in the field. Without an escort, Jilli and I were sitting ducks. Maybe this family could provide some cover.

"Excuse me, but I absolutely love that brooch you're wearing," I said to the woman.

She placed her mug on the table and smiled. "Well, thank you, dear. Isn't that nice of you to say." Her children paid little attention to the exchange. "Tristan! Please sit down," she called to her unruly toddler.

I looked casually over at the two men. Their eyes were still fixed on me.

I made eye contact with the woman and smiled back. "There has to be a story behind it. I love Victorian jewelry. Did I overhear that your name is Love? Mrs. Love, I presume by your stunning ring."

Jilli had taken notice of the conversation and closed her book.

"Oh, why, yes—a family ring from my husband," Mrs. Love replied as her boys started to wander. She looked us over quickly. "You two are dressed smart. Students of Claymoore, I presume?"

"We are—but where are my manners? I'm Simone—Simone LaFray—and this is my friend Jilli."

"LaFray! The family opening the chocolate shop on Sloane Street?"

"Yes, Mrs. Love, that's our store. We're very excited about it."

Jilli turned her head and squinted at me. "What are you doing?" she whispered. I turned to her and shook my head.

"So are we!" Mrs. Love exclaimed. "My boys simply cannot wait for the grand opening."

"Of course," I said. "Neither can we—after all, even the Queen herself will be in attendance."

Mrs. Love's gaze passed over her children. "Is that so?" I could practically see the wheels turning in her head. "Well, it was wonderful to meet you, but we must be off. Some more shopping to get to," she said.

As she collected her boys and moved toward the door, I leaned across the table. "We need to go, now!" I whispered.

Jilli seemed caught off guard, but she nodded. "Okay."

I looked back over Jilli's shoulder. The men were gone. *Strange. Maybe nothing. Still, we better get back to school. I have to be at the store in an hour.*

We pushed our way through the crowded shop and jumped out onto the pavement after the family. The crisp air splashed our cheeks as we pulled down our woolly hats and took out our gloves. Across the street, a white van had parked. It had no plates.

We need to move.

I looked up and down the block. Suddenly, Tristan pushed through us to catch up with his mother. Mrs. Love saw us and gave a quick wave. "Let's go this way," I said.

We made it halfway up the street before the men reappeared, no more than six meters behind us and quickly closing in. I grabbed Jilli's hand.

She jumped. "Simone—what's going on?"

"Oh, nothing. We can't be late, that's all," I replied.

We hurried up the crowded pavement, my heart pounding. I tried to pull up my sleeve, but my gloves were making it impossible. *Keep moving.* I glanced back and saw the two men, now only three meters behind. I had to do something.

"Excuse me, Mrs. Love?" I called after the family.

She stopped and turned. "Well, if it isn't the girls from Claymoore. What is it, dear?" she replied.

We stopped jogging and nestled close behind her and her boys. I caught my breath and let go of Jilli's hand. "You forgot to tell me about the brooch. I simply cannot stop thinking about it."

"Well, let's see. It was my godmother's, and when I was . . ." she began as we continued up the street toward Claymoore.

I glanced back just in time to see the men climbed into the van. The driver stared at me as they slowly pulled away. We were safe for now—but it had been close.

I turned to Jilli, who was now holding hands with two of the young boys. Exhaling in relief, I tuned out Mrs. Love and played through what just happened in my head. There could be no doubt now. *The Maestro knows I'm here—and he wants his Key back.*

"These chocolates are not chocolatey enough!" Sugars bellowed. Ashes blew across the half-eaten sample as she extinguished her cigarette.

"I assure you, this is the same recipe we've been using for decades!" Father replied, checking the temperature in the display cases out front. The bags under his eyes suggested he hadn't slept in days, but his exhilaration was obvious nevertheless.

The air in the store was fragrant, the scents of sweet sugar, peppermint, licorice, and of course, chocolate filling every breath. Months of work were nearing their end, culminating in a breathtaking display primed for a party. Cleaning crews had been working around the clock to get the store scrubbed and polished from top to bottom. Since the Queen herself had confirmed her invitation, additional preparations were being made and others scaled up for the royal arrival: the enormous sugarwork chandelier had been further adorned, and a fresh staff in new uniforms were lined up for inspection. The chocolate fountain was now functional, the silver bowls covered with rich milk chocolate that flowed like silk into an enormous, swirling basin, giving off an intoxicating aroma that mingled with the other sweet scents. Despite her constant complaints, I was sure Sugars was loving every second, and couldn't wait to cut the ribbon with the Queen at her side—oh, and Father, of course.

"I brought a change of clothes," said the V, dusting off the sleeves of her Claymoore blazer. "I can't assume the role of a customer in these! I look like I'm twelve. I want to look like a real customer, not a prep school girl."

I shook my head and smiled. While I appreciated the V's zest for realism, I suspected her anticipation of the store being flooded with social media influencers might have something to do with her desire to project a more mature look.

"I like our uniforms," I said. "They make us look British—don't you think?"

"Maybe—but what if I'm asked to pose for a paper? Don't you think a—"

"Bonjour, Simone!" boomed a voice from behind me.

I turned with delight. I had known this voice my entire life.

"Monsieur John!" I squealed as memories of 7 Rue Clodion flooded my heart. I ran to him and wrapped my arms around his waist. As always, his well-dressed figure exuded a sense of dignity. Even the new staff seemed to have taken notice, and were paying him extra respect.

"It's so good to see you. Look at you! You must have grown ten centimeters," he said. "Madame Tris sends her love." I couldn't help but blush.

"Well, I would love to stay and chat—but I'm here on official business. I have to whip this lot into LaFray shape!" He straightened his bow tie with a wink.

I gave him a wink back, and one more hug. "Perhaps some chess later?" I asked. "We could meet in Trafalgar Square."

He quickly nodded. "I was counting on it, mademoiselle. The board and pieces are in my bag."

With a smile, he turned to his staff. "Alright, then; now let's take a look at you all."

"Did you hear? The Queen is coming!" the V yelled as she ran down the staircase. Following Jilli's example at Halloween, she'd helped herself to Miss Hannigan's costume from Claymoore's latest production of *Annie*—a dowdy skirt and sweater adorned with a red boa and rows of long beaded necklaces—and fashioned a makeshift disguise that she said would add to the authenticity of being a difficult customer. Given the financial status of those attending Claymoore, I found their choice of the play quite odd—but for the V, it was now paying off.

People were already starting to assemble in front of the store. Sugars had handpicked a gaggle of social media influencers and attractive young people, allegedly to "stress-test" our operation before the grand opening—but in reality, the staff had been testing round the clock for over a week. This party was just a publicity stunt: a clever, well-staged opportunity to flood social media accounts with multitudes of elegant selfies taken in our shop. Nevertheless, Father wanted us there to share in his excitement—and to try out the treats.

"Have you tried these yet?" the V asked, devouring a small plate of macarons.

Soon enough, Father was working the crowd, and eager guests lined up to pose for a photo of themselves with the candy sculpture in the background. The event was moving like clockwork, everything precise and impersonal. This was not the LaFray's I knew.

I walked up to the counter, where Monsieur John stood behind the clerk with a watchful eye, and asked for one pecan truffle and one lace cookie. The clerk pulled them from the display and delicately arranged the cookies on a napkin before presenting them to me.

I smiled and looked down at the treats. A glance was enough to let me know these were ours: their smell, their colors, their weight all begged you to throw them into your mouth. I closed my eyes and took a deeper whiff. Pure heaven. Father really was going to pull this off.

"Anyone else having trouble posting anything?!" came the frustrated voice of one of the well-polished attendees.

One by one, everyone stared at their mobiles. Monsieur John frowned at the cash register's suddenly frozen screen.

"The internet is down. No service," I heard a man shout from the kitchen.

I looked down at my watch a moment before it began vibrating.

"What do you mean by 'the entire London cellular network'?" I asked Eloise as I paced the pavement in front of the store, staring at her image on my watch's screen.

"The Maestro somehow breached the cellular grid, and nothing is going through. Even government lines are down," she said. "Authorities say they have it under control, and service should resume within the hour."

I frowned. Although the London public's lack of mobile and internet access would have little effect on the Ministry, the Maestro's attacks were becoming more frequent and widespread. Just yesterday, Amsterdam and Sweden had experienced rolling power outages, and the interruptions were putting people on edge. Something had to be done—and soon.

"Two men were following me earlier today," I admitted.

"What?" Eloise's tone sharpened. "Are you sure? What men?"

"I was studying with a friend at a coffee shop off campus, and—"

"Off campus! Simone, you should know better than to go off campus without an adult escorting you, regardless of your watch's ability to monitor you. You have to be careful!"

I paused and looked at the pavement, my heart sinking into my stomach. Eloise didn't even know the half of it. What would she have said if she knew I'd gone out with the Wolves, and that I hadn't even had my watch when we did that? My run-in with the two men had shaken me. She was right. Still—

"We got permission from—"

She cut me off again. "May I remind you, young lady, you are on a mission, and must be aware of your surroundings at all times. After what happened to Claire—" She paused, rubbing her hand across her forehead.

I bristled. I *was* on a mission, and her words reminded me I'd made every choice for the benefit of that mission—to learn about what Claire had been doing, and get her back. Why didn't Eloise trust me to do what I needed to accomplish that? *I can take care of myself! I had the situation under control. I was out with Jilli and Maeve in the middle of London at night without permission, and it went fine. Eloise doesn't even care about the Wolves.* My thoughts turned. Maybe I shouldn't have mentioned Jilli—I didn't want Eloise to focus on her, or Maeve. They were already in deep, and a Ministry inquiry would derail all my efforts.

"What did they look like? Did you get a picture?"

"No, no pictures, but it was the Maestro's doing. I know it."

"In that case, you can't be too careful," Eloise replied. "What about the Key? Any news on that front?"

Of course—the Key. "Nothing yet, but I might have some leads. I need more time."

Eloise straightened her jacket. "It is imperative that you find that key. Failure is not an option here, Simone."

"Yes, madame. I understand."

"Good," she said.

An uncomfortable silence followed.

"So, the store looks great," I said, desperate to inject some levity into the conversation.

"Hm? Oh, yes—the store. Yes, that's wonderful—but something just came over a secured line. I must go." Eloise reached for her phone, and the transmission ended, leaving me feeling confused and upset.

Thump thump thump. I looked up to see a beaming V pounding on the glass from inside the shop. With a triumphant smile, she caught my gaze and waved her mobile in the air. Service had been restored.

———

There was still a chill in the air later that evening as I returned from Trafalgar Square, having won my chess game with Monsieur John in a surprising 3-2 split. He had been off his game, and I could not let that pass. Still, I was baffled by the two critical errors he had made in our last match. *Who moves the bishop twice to open? And why concentrate on the sides?* He must have thrown it. Regardless, it had been great to see him and bottle up a hint of home.

I was making good time moving down Allen Street when I glanced up to see a billboard for *LaFray's Patisserie* looming over me. It was one of fourteen such advertisements posted throughout London, and each one weighed heavily on me whenever I passed beneath it. Having my name splashed across so many advertisements made me feel exposed and pretentious. I still hated spotlights.

Claymoore's tall rooftops loomed in the distance. I sped up, remembering the Maestro's men and Eloise's words. But as I turned a corner, I came face to face with three ominous road-blocks—though not of the type I had expected.

"Where do you think you're going?" asked Kirstin. She was flanked by Charlotte and Michele, who fluttered a pace behind her like a veil caught by the wind. All three girls looked as polished as ever, with braided hair, long wool coats, and black leather gloves.

I slowed my breathing and tried to relax as Michele and Charlotte boxed me in. I couldn't say I hadn't been anticipating something like this after my performance in gym class—but this was not the time.

"We don't know what you're up to, but a few things need to be sorted out," Kirstin said, looking me up and down. "You and your friends, that mouthy Cantone girl and scary Stahl, need to know your place."

"Our *place?*" I replied with confidence, returning her once-over. Mimicking was an effective tool I'd studied a few years back, and it always helped to lead with a question. It was a simple technique for disarming someone—but the growing look of annoyance on their faces suggested it wasn't working this time. I needed to follow up. "Perhaps it's you three who need to know *your* place. I assure you that I'm quite comfortable here. In fact, I need to get back to my room now."

As if on cue, each took a step toward me, and the air started to thin. *Hm. Too much?*

"Sad, ugly little French girl—forgot your hairbrush today?" Kirstin mocked, reaching out to pull a lock of my hair. I continued to look her dead in the eyes. I wasn't going anywhere.

A voice rang out from behind them. "What do we have here? Three bullies out for a walk?" My heart leapt. It was Maeve, with Jilli at her side.

"This doesn't concern you, Stahl," Kirstin said—but the trio began to back away as this new pair casually strolled up and stopped on the other side of me.

"Well, if it concerns my friend, it concerns me, doesn't it?" Maeve's voice was calm but firm. Her reputation preceded her, and these three obviously wanted none of it—but they also couldn't just turn and run.

"Watch it," Kirstin lobbed, raising a fist. "I heard if you get just one more demerit, you're out of here. Then where would you go, charity case?"

Oh, no. That was low, and Maeve stepped right into her face. This was spiraling.

I wedged myself between them and pushed Maeve back, moving her just out of arm's reach. "Just having a bit of a chat, Maeve, nothing serious," I offered to calm the waters. But there was no way Maeve was going to back down.

They stared at each other for another six seconds—and then Kirstin relented. "Just a chat."

Jilli stepped in to supply another buffer. "Look, we need to go, so *bye-bye*," she waved. "Bye-bye, go home. Shoo."

Kirstin squinted and clenched her fist one last time before relenting. "Watch yourself, Simone," she snarled at me, and the three girls turned and proceeded up the pavement.

Victorious, we watched them retreat. I looked over at Maeve to thank her, but before I could, she threw her arm around me and said something that moved me to the core: "Us bad girls gotta stick together."

'Bad girls'? That phrase had never once been used to describe me—never ever. An electrifying rush of empowerment surged through me. Maeve, the most dangerous girl I knew, saw me in this light, and had accepted me as one of her own—one of her girls. While I'd sought her approval, actually receiving it somehow felt so much bigger, so much better than I had anticipated. *Is it*

wrong to feel this way? Will people look at me differently?

Maeve's hand slid off my shoulder, but the heat of it remained, even on that chilly evening. Somewhere deep inside me, a fire had just ignited.

"Thanks," I said at last.

She nodded. "Sure."

Dinner that evening was particularly gratifying. I sat confidently in my chair, my shoulders back and my chin up, still basking in the glow of being called a *bad girl*.

It was a strange feeling. I'd never wanted to be bad in any way, but Maeve's approval made me feel proud and somehow accomplished. Not *bad*, but ... formidable. Everyone looked at Maeve in a certain way—one that seemed composed of three parts fear, two parts apprehension, and one part envy. Would they see me like that too?

I glanced around to notice if anyone was looking at me. A quick scan produced inconclusive results, but oddly, I found the possibility strangely thrilling. *Take a look, everybody.*

"What were you doing in the park anyway?" the V asked as she looked over at the footballers' table. At her insistence, I'd told her the story when she'd asked where I'd gone after the opening—but she'd apparently managed to miss some key details.

"I wasn't in the park. I was at Trafalgar Square, playing chess."

"Uh-huh." Was it just me, or did the V seem oddly subdued? "Have you talked to Jonas today? I haven't seen him anywhere. You must have a lot to talk about."

Ugh, him again. I wish she would just shut up about that. I had to squelch this right now. "Why would I have anything to say to him? He's just some boy."

Apparently this was not the right answer, as the V whipped

around to stare at me with wide eyes. "Just some boy? He's your *boyfriend*, Simone. Everyone is talking about it." *Oh, brother.* "It turns out Kirstin had a crush on Jonas earlier this year, after he was named captain of the team. He's a real catch, Simone. Just think how jealous all the other girls will be!"

To be honest, I didn't care in the least how jealous anyone would be—but this did explain some of the unwanted attention from Kirstin and her minions. A rivalry with her was a distraction I didn't need. I had to finish this now.

"Is that the footballers' table over there?" I asked, standing up and straightening my glasses.

"It's the one in the corner." The V put both hands over her mouth and squealed as I started to walk toward them. "What are you going to do? Do you need me?"

I turned my head midstride and called over my shoulder, "No, this should only take a second."

I marched purposefully across the dining hall. My newfound confidence seemed to be attracting the attention of nearby students, who looked on, eager for drama. School cafeterias were often a venue for trivial altercations, but kids could always sense when something was about to go down, and this was one of those times.

Jonas' friends were starting to whisper in his ear—I assumed to announce my impending arrival, although he'd spotted me several seconds earlier. He *was* quite handsome—but I had already made up my mind. I was on a mission. Four meters away, and I resolved to—*ugh!*

I suddenly found myself in midair. A swift kick from Kirstin's loafer had sent me tumbling head over heels. My glasses flew from my face and skidded across the floor. I hit the ground hard, completely humiliated, and feeling like the furthest thing from a *bad girl*.

I scrambled on the floor, trying to salvage my dignity as the entire room laughed.

Kirstin leaned down. "Watch your step, freak."

I took one glance at Jonas, then ran out of the room as fast as I could.

—————

I sat in my bed in my dormitory, staring out the window. I had been crying for three minutes and fourteen seconds, and I was still trying to figure out why. I didn't even like Jonas—well, not in *that* way—but some foreign emotion was welling up and throwing me off-kilter. *Did* I like him in *that* way? And would he ever talk to me again, after what had happened?

No, that's not it. Pull yourself together.

My embarrassment stung to the core, crushing my new outlook as a tough, capable bad girl. I didn't care that I had tripped in front of people and that they'd laughed at me—well, maybe I cared a little—but none of that would have happened if I hadn't deemed it necessary to publicly rebuff Jonas. I felt mean. *This bad girl thing is tricky. What's happening? I'm crying again.*

The V cracked open the door. "Are you okay?"

I turned my face away, but I knew it was obvious I'd been crying. Letting out a jagged sigh and roughly wiping my nose with my sleeve, I croaked back, "Yeah, I guess so."

She came in. "Here are your glasses. They landed in Michele's soup, but I tried to wipe them off. Are you hurt? You fell pretty hard."

I turned toward her. "Yeah, yeah—I'm fine." I smiled ruefully. "It was quite a scene, wasn't it?"

A relieved smile washed over the V's face. "Oh my God, that was *cataclysmic* in terms of boy drama. You must have been three meters in the air. Are you sure you're okay?"

The gravity of the scene hit me again. It must have been a spectacle to all who witnessed it: a girl full of confidence and swagger being upended by an aristocrat who'd harbored feelings for Jonas all along. *How did I let myself get into this?*

The V pushed my hair back from my face. "It's okay. It's no big deal. Everyone will probably forget about it by dinnertime anyway." She rocked from foot to foot, grinning as if hiding a secret she could no longer contain. "Take a look out the window. He wants to talk!"

I rushed to the window to find Jonas in the courtyard below, waving his hand and signaling me to come down. As soon as I saw him, the embarrassment returned, and my head dropped. It would be a long walk outside.

I pushed open the heavy door and was met by a cold gust of wind. Jonas was standing there in his woolly hat and topcoat, trying to keep warm—and there I was, a shell of the girl who had marched across the refectory only thirty-six minutes ago.

"Hey." It was the only word I could muster.

Jonas smiled in return. "That was some flip in the refectory. Are you okay?"

I didn't remember it being a *flip*, but at this point, I wasn't looking for supreme accuracy in recounting the event. I just wanted to get this over with. "I'm okay. Just fell, that's all."

He looked down at his shoes, then raised his head. "That lot can be pretty mean—you know, Kirstin and her friends. I think they're so used to getting everything they want, they can't handle any competition socially. Don't let them get you down."

Competition? Why would I be competition?

"Anyway, I just wanted to say I'm sorry for what happened and—"

"Jonas, I don't want to be your girlfriend," I blurted out. "I'm just not ready for anything like that. The whole thought of it makes me ill. Not that you're not a—"

It was my turn to be interrupted. "Simone, I don't want to be your boyfriend. I don't think I want to be anyone's boyfriend, to be honest." He began to blush. "Maybe things got confused. I'm not the best at talking to girls, especially the smart ones—and you know how people talk."

What? I was just getting comfortable with the idea that a fellow student saw me as more than just a test answer key—but above all, I was glad to be rid of the awkwardness.

"I just heard you were a good singer, and I liked your painting and wanted to talk. That's all. Oh, and I like books, too. I read all the time at night. Jilli said you guys read a lot. Maybe we could meet in the library sometime or whatever."

A boy that likes to read, and likes art? Wait, maybe—no! "Yeah, that would be great."

Out of the corner of my eye, I caught a glimpse of the V and five other girls pressed against our bedroom window, watching us. But there would be no further drama here.

A smile filled my face, and I straightened my glasses as an overwhelming need to make him feel better came over me. This was a first—but what to do? *Maybe . . .*

"Jonas? This might seem odd under the circumstances, but—can I hug you?"

"Ah—well—okay," he stammered, sliding his hands out of his coat pockets. He stepped forward and we embraced, as a faint chorus of screams rang from the fourth floor.

I returned to the room and disappointed the entire assembly by announcing that Jonas and I had simply agreed to be friends. Somehow, having an "ex-boyfriend" carried even more clout than actually having one, and I was more than okay with this unintended consequence. After what had happened in the refectory, I needed the confidence boost. And most importantly, with all this behind me, I could concentrate on the tasks at hand—find the Key, and get Claire home.

———————

My bed was especially welcoming that evening—a safe place among all the recent drama. My soft cotton pajamas fit just right, my covers were pulled up, and my laptop rested in front of my raised knees as I spoke to Mother.

"Well! That sounds like quite a big day," Mother said as I adjusted my earphones. Lights-out was only five minutes away, and I was hanging onto her every word, filing them away to use to fortify myself after the chaos of the day.

"Yeah, I guess so. Have you heard anything about Claire?"

Mother adjusted herself in her chair. She looked tired again, and her skin shone with oil. I tilted my head and gazed at her. "I'm afraid not, dear. It's as if she just vanished into thin air."

Mia crashed into frame. "Simone! Can I come to the opening? Mother said we can't come—but the *Queen* is going to be there!"

My eyes widened and tracked to Mother. "You really aren't coming? I thought you'd be here."

"Sorry, Simone. I already spoke to Father, and we agreed it's best for us to stay here." I caught the tinge of disappointment in her voice.

"Oh. I see." But I didn't—not at all. I'd never dreamed Mother would miss the opening of our new store. *The most skilled operative in the Ministry, staying home?*

"Goodnight. We love you," Mother said as Mia waved and made faces into the camera.

Our call ended, and I heard the V turn over in bed. I looked out the window. Frost had begun forming in the corners, the moonlight illuminating each crystal. Except for the distant lights of Big Ben and Tower Bridge winking in the background, London seemed frozen in time.

Why isn't she coming? This means so much to Father. How could he want this?

I counted the lights and the rising spires, wanting to be out there, moving in the night air. I needed another night out with the Wolves. Given more time and opportunity, I could connect the dots. I knew I could.

I was adjusting my blanket with a yawn when our door opened. I bolted upright immediately, peering through the darkness.

A welcome figure stood in the shadow. My heart raced as Maeve adjusted her backpack and gave a devilish smile.

"We're going out, Frenchy. Grab your things."

The Zoo

Over the next four weeks, we slipped out three times. The first time, we painted a Campbell's soup can with the label "Murdered Meat" on the side of a trendy food producer in Soho that advertised "All Vegan – All the Time." Apparently, they had not been holding to their promise. The second outing saw a recreation of Haring's *World* with "Don't Pollute" splashed across it; the Chelsea Physic Garden was contemplating a change in their use of pesticides. I hated to cover a piece of the surrounding aged stone wall, but took comfort in the fact that the water-based paint would be no match for a pressure washer. Last, we absconded to Westminster to paint Dali's *Greed and Lavishness* on the building of an insurance company that had recently denied a series of valid claims involving flooding in South Yorkshire.

Each excursion was the same: Maeve would come for me late at night, having previously stashed a bag of supplies somewhere on the grounds, and we would pick it up and meet Jilli behind the rose garden before slipping out. The three of us made a good team, and I found myself enjoying the late-night runs. The Red Wolves' popularity seemed to be growing exponentially, with news crews and paparazzi patrolling the city at night in hopes of encountering a work in progress. But a near miss on our last outing had sent us scrambling to avoid a pedestrian, and though we hadn't been seen, it had been enough for Maeve to temporarily suspend our outings and allow time for the attention to cool down. For the last two weeks, we'd remained at Claymoore—though I could tell Maeve was getting antsy.

Between my classes and the thrill of sneaking out and painting the town with the Wolves, I was so exhausted, I found myself stuck when it came to the second part of my mission: finding the Om-niKey. I hadn't forgotten it, of course—every day, I went to the art supply room, hoping to find it unlocked; and I was becoming something of a fixture in the hallway. I'd even briefly entertained the idea of requesting access to the room directly from Headmaster Bailes. In the end, however, I decided against it. Even though the Ministry had told him about my status as a spy, Headmaster Bailes was the one responsible for employing the Red Fox. Even if Bailes had been completely hoodwinked by the Fox after all, the man was certainly charming—it was enough to make me wary of asking him for help, especially given his tough stance on anything that broke with school tradition.

I would much rather have worked with Ms. Kusma—but she was also keeping a tight grip on her own key to the art supply room. Twice she had accompanied me into the room when I eagerly offered to retrieve paper, paints, and brushes for the class; but each of these opportunities had afforded me only a few minutes to open some jars. I had, however, managed to count them. There were one hundred and six jars in the supply room, and thus far, I'd gone through ninety-five of them—to no avail. But I was close. The OmniKey had to be in one of them. I could feel it.

Without the distraction of our nightly outings, my anxiety was peaking, and sleep had become a nightly battle. I tossed and turned, my covers pulling at me. Tonight, even my feet had begun to sweat under the thick comforter.

It was almost 1:00 a.m. when I heard the doorknob turn.

I sprang up in bed, anticipating—

Maeve—wait. Jilli?

Indeed, it was Jilli's dark, petite figure that moved toward me as I reached for my glasses on the nightstand. "Shhh. We're going out tonight. Maeve will meet us later. We need to get the supplies," she whispered.

Supplies? What's going on? Maeve always had the supplies.

"No time to explain. Let's go!"

I strapped my watch to the V's wrist as usual, then followed Jilli out of the dormitory. We crossed the grounds in silence. *This isn't the way to the fence. Where are we going? Where is Maeve?*

We stopped at the back of the arts building and crouched behind some bushes. Jilli began to feel around the frame of one of the windows.

"Ah, there it is," she whispered as the window tilted forward. "Follow me."

She slid through the window and placed her feet on a radiator, then jumped to the hallway floor.

"Come on, Simone." She waved to encourage me.

"Okay, okay," I replied, backing in.

"There are no cameras down here, but we have to stay quiet," Jilli said, continuing down the hall. I nodded and followed. As we turned the corner, it hit me—*the art supply room!*

A jolt of excitement pulsed through me. Hopefully, I could have a few minutes to sort through the last jars.

When we got to the door, however, it was locked.

"I got this," Jilli said. She pulled two paper clips out of her pocket, straightened them, and placed one in the lower part of the lock.

"Maeve showed me how to do this. A little tension on the bottom . . ." she said, turning the clip counter-clockwise. "Then the other one to push the pins on top." She inserted the other straightened clip. "And turn!"

The door opened.

Picking the lock. Why didn't I think of that?! I could have gotten through these so much faster! But I knew why. Even now, I felt we were somehow violating Ms. Kusma's domain.

Jilli pulled out a flashlight and moved toward the shelves in the back, right next to the jars. *I just need twenty-five seconds!*

As fast as I could, I picked up jars and lifted the lids, committing their positions to memory. I knew exactly which ones I had yet to check, and with every jar, my emotions frothed within me. *Ninety-six. Ninety-seven. Ninety-eight.* It had to be here. A hint of doubt nagged me—it was, after all, statistically improbable that I hadn't yet come across the Key—but I pushed it to the back of my mind. I couldn't give up until the mission was over, until I'd checked them all. *One hundred and two. One hundred and three—*

As I worked, Jilli turned and eyed a pile of large boxes covered by an empty sack. "That's them," she whispered.

One hundred and four. One hundred and five—

I stopped, my hand trembling as it hovered over the lid of the last jar. *This is it. It has to be.* I planted my feet. Weeks of waiting and searching had come down to this. I looked over at Jilli, but she was distracted, wading through the clutter toward the boxes. *Perfect.*

I took a deep breath and snatched the lid off the jar. Then, leaning over, I peered straight down into its hollow belly. As I looked inside, a rush of emotion crackled through my limbs.

The jar was empty.

The breath I'd been holding came out in a rush.

"I—I don't understand. It should be here." Words spilled out of my mouth as I abandoned all subterfuge. *Something's wrong. How could I have miscalculated so badly?* "It should be here!"

Jilli turned the flashlight on me. "*What* should be here?"

I stood in the beam of the light, frozen. Disbelief crept coldly through my veins. "I—I—" I struggled for words. "I . . . lost something here, the last time I came to get supplies—for class. I have to find it." I grabbed the final pot and turned it upside down, shaking it as if the Key would suddenly appear inside and fall out of it. "I have to!"

Jilli frowned, eyebrows arching sympathetically—but she shook her head. "Simone, we don't have time for that now. Maeve's probably already waiting." She grabbed the sack. "Here. Hold this."

I barely registered her words. "What?"

Jilli huffed, now clearly exasperated. "Put that down. You need to hold this open for me!"

I stopped. My whole body ached with disappointment—but she was right. It wasn't just the Ministry; Maeve and Jilli were counting on me too. I didn't know why the Key wasn't here, but I couldn't dwell on that now.

Realizing I was going to have to come back another time, I reluctantly put down the jar and moved to help her.

Jilli opened one of the boxes and removed three cans of paint and a handful of brushes. Mr. Redd must have hidden a stash of supplies for the Wolves last semester. "Okay, let's go," Jilli whispered.

We went back through the hall and shimmied out the window, securing it behind us. Jilli gave me a smile that I did my best to return, but the expression felt hollow, even as it appeared on my face. As we took off, my mind was still back in the art supply room, going through every jar.

I didn't miss one. I couldn't have.

"Where have you been?" asked Maeve as we arrived at the rose garden.

Jilli readjusted the sack on her shoulder. "We got here as fast as we could. Did you get your thing done?"

Maeve's eyes darted to the side. "Yes. No communications

tonight. We're going dark." She relieved Jilli of the sack and said, "No talking. Just stay with me. Let's go."

We ran through the alleys of Paddington, then turned north to cut through Marylebone. My legs were becoming heavy and the cold air stung my lungs, but I was glad of the chance to distract myself. My mind had already made fifty-three passes of the art supply room, and was going for a fifty-fourth.

Finally, we stopped on a knoll in Regent's Park. As we looked out over the dark green, I heard the faint sound of an elephant trumpeting in the distance.

"It's just not fair to keep them penned up in there," Maeve said, shaking her head. "Let's go."

We trudged up the Outer Circle and stopped at a hedge near the entrance to the London Zoo to catch our breath.

The strangeness of our outing was finally enough to pull me out of the art supply room and into the moment. *Wait. Why are we at the zoo? We're not going to set any animals free—are we?*

"See that wall over there, next to the entrance?" Maeve said, pointing. She was talking faster than usual. "We're going to paint a picture of Pipaluk the Polar Bear holding a sign that says, 'Sad Animals Live Here.'"

Jilli and I stared at Maeve.

Pipaluk the Polar Bear? Why are we here for this?

Maeve wilted uncharacteristically under our gaze. Her eyes darted back and forth. Finally, she burst out, "Okay, so I came up with this one myself. I was getting antsy just sitting around. Couldn't wait any longer after, you know, almost getting caught last time. This is an easy one—like a practice run, to get us back into it. Just a quick painting of a polar bear holding a sign, that's all. The newspapers will love it."

When did Maeve start caring about the newspapers? Jilli and I shot each other an uncertain glance, but we nodded anyway.

Maeve moved toward the wall with the duffel bag of supplies swinging from her shoulder. She opened a can of white paint and started on the outline. I pulled a can of black paint out of the bag, and—

"Well, what do we have here?" said a voice from across the street.

Two flashlights turned on us. We froze.

Oh, no. Oh, no. What are we going to do? Heart beating out of my chest, I turned to face the men. The can of paint slipped from my hands.

Beside me, Jilli was fidgeting terribly. She put her hands up, and Maeve gave her a sharp glance. "Don't do that! I have an idea."

"Now what would you three be doing out here on this freezing night with cans of paint? A little art project, is it?" said the taller man. They took a step closer, and the beams of the flashlights moved away from my eyes just enough for me to catch a glimpse of their hats and uniforms. Bobbies.

My mind automatically ran through the protocol for communicating with police officers—but something nagged me. His accent sounded forced. Maybe he was tired?

The men took another step. The beams of their flashlights moved across us, both settling on me.

"You wouldn't be those Red Wolves who're causing all the fuss around here, would yah?" The man's inflection had changed. I squinted to see his name badge. It read "Miller." The other's read "Herlihy." With that accent—no way.

Something was not right. Even their uniforms looked off— the jackets were frayed around the cuffs and collar, and the pants were a different shade of blue. *And why haven't they radioed a report in?*

That was all I needed. *These aren't bobbies. But then, who are they?* I studied their faces. *Are they—*

Recognition flared. *Oh, no—the men from the café! The Maestro—he knows I'm here!*

I turned and whispered, "We need to run. Now!"

Maeve gave me a wink and jerked her thumb backward at the zoo gate. Its rails looked just wide enough for us slip through.

The men took another step, and Maeve yelled, "Go!"

"Hey now, stop!" yelled the other man.

Jilli and I easily slipped through the gate—but as Maeve followed, the heavily laden duffel briefly stuck between two of the bars. Jilli and I rushed to help, and together we pulled it through, even as the men ran toward us.

"What are we going to do?" Jilli yelled. "You said we wouldn't get caught!"

The men had just reached the gate, and began attempting to climb over it. *How did they find me?!*

"Don't worry! I've visited this place like five times before. Follow me!" Maeve replied.

We took off down the paved walkway as the men crested the gate. The zoo smelled like wet hair and dog food. As we ran, I caught the reflections of dozens of animal eyes watching us. Our presence must have been quite unusual.

Without looking back, we took a sharp turn through a tunnel and into the Africa exhibit. On the way, I caught a glimpse of an oversized map of the zoo and committed it to memory. Footsteps pounded behind us.

"They went this way!" one of the men shouted.

Maeve looked around. "They're too fast. We need to hide," she whispered.

I peered down the path and saw something. "In there," I said, pointing at the lemur pen. "Everything else here might eat us. Come on."

We jumped over the railing and hid under some ornamental

trees. Two lemurs watched us as we hunkered down, covered by leaves. The meerkats across from us popped their heads out, interested.

The beams of the men's flashlights darted across both sides of the path. Their lights washed over the tree, but its thick, mossy green limbs draped to the ground like a curtain, keeping us well hidden. *Keep going, keep going,* I pleaded silently.

A lemur took cover under my tree and leapt up in surprise at seeing me. "It's okay," I whispered.

"They could be anywhere in here. Nasty little runts," the taller man grunted in a Polish accent. All illusions were gone. They were definitely with the Maestro.

"Let's wait at the front gate. They'll have to come out eventually."

The lights moved away.

"Simone?" I heard Jilli whisper. I looked out through the dense foliage and saw her, a lemur crouched on her head.

Maeve crawled out of a small hut, followed by six lemurs. "It stinks in there!" she whispered.

Together, we huddled beneath my tree.

"Who are those guys?" Jilli asked. Her eyes were wide with anxiety. "They're not police. What are they?"

"I don't know, but we need to get out of here," Maeve replied.

"There's a camel pen at the end of this trail. It borders the outside wall. I saw it on the big map down there," I said, pointing back the way we'd come. "It should be safe—and maybe we can get over the wall."

"Sounds good," Maeve said.

As we jogged down the lane, the presence of the Maestro loomed large. *How did he find me, and what's next?* One thing was certain: Eloise had been right after all. *It's too dangerous to be out here anymore.*

We arrived at the camel pen to find four camels asleep standing up. I surveyed the paddock. The outer wall had to be two and a half meters high, its stone slick and worn, with no apparent footholds. There were no trees to climb. *Ugh.*

"There," whispered Jilli. A camel stood fast asleep next to the wall.

We jumped the rail and navigated across a ditch that had been dug to keep the animals in.

"Now what?" asked Maeve as we crept up to the sleeping animal.

Jilli smiled. "If we can get up on his back, we can jump to the top of the wall."

Maeve looked incredulous.

"It's worth a try. He's almost right up against the wall. It can't be more than a meter. Give me a boost," said Jilli.

We lifted her easily. The camel remained still. She stood on the hump and leapt atop the wall. "No worries. It's easy," she grinned, apparently pleased with her success. Then she disappeared, leaping down to the other side.

Maeve nodded. "You next, Frenchy. Then pull me up." She boosted me up onto the camel's warm, soft back. As I balanced, however, the camel started to sway.

"Quick. Take my hand," I said to Maeve.

"There they are!" came a shout.

Flashlights turned on us from the pathway.

"Let's go, let's go!" I urged.

I pulled Maeve up as the men started over the railing. It took all the energy I had, but we needed to get over the wall.

"Jump!" yelled Jilli from the other side. The camel was waking up, stomping in confusion at the weight on its back and the presence of the men who ran toward us, flashlights bobbing.

Maeve turned to me. "Time to go, Frenchy. One—two—three!"

We jumped just as the camel sped off. We barely made it—but barely was enough. We stood at the top of the wall just in time to see the men sprinting away from the angry camel, then turned and jumped down.

We'd done it. We had gotten away.

———

For the next few days, none of us said a word about our night at the zoo—even to each other. I attended meals and lessons half in a daze, overwhelmed by the converging pressures present in my life and wishing I could tell someone—anyone—the whole truth.

But I couldn't. Eloise and Mother couldn't know I was prowling London tagging buildings at night, and Maeve and Jilli could never find out that they had gotten within a meter of being captured by the Maestro's thugs. I had to protect them all—from the Maestro, and from each other.

And I had to complete the mission. The stress over my recent failure left me constantly exhausted, and the days seemed to blur together. By the time I realized an entire week and a half had passed, the opening of our store was only one day away—and I still hadn't found the Key, nor even thought of where else I might look.

I've checked everywhere. It doesn't make sense. There were no other places to look. Maybe I missed something? But I knew I hadn't. I could picture every detail of every position of every jar in that room. I'd lifted every single lid, and none of the jars had contained the Key. *But it doesn't make sense! Why would Claire Pilfrey, a junior agent with the Ministry, make so many jars, if not for some purpose? For fun? For—*

Someone was calling my name.

"Miss LaFray. Miss LaFray!"

"Oh—y-yes, Mrs. Boschen. I'm sorry, I was—" I stammered.

"I asked you if you thought the French Revolution was more of a political or societal movement. I thought you may have some insight into this, but perhaps I was wrong? Please pay attention." She paused. "Miss Morrow? Do you have any thoughts on this matter?"

I slumped in my chair. I had never been told to pay attention in my life. Paying attention was what I did best.

But while Madison offered a compelling argument for the societal influence on the French Revolution, my mind wandered again. *Why were we at the zoo in the first place? Just to paint a polar bear? It was too risky. What was Maeve thinking?*

"Thank you, Madison; very impressive. That's it for class today. Please remember to read chapter twelve tonight for tomorrow's discussion. Especially you, Miss LaFray," Mrs. Boschen said. I couldn't wait to get out of there.

As I rushed down the hall after class, Jilli ran up alongside me. "What was that? Are you tired or something?"

"Yeah—just tired. I was up late last night reading," I replied. I *had* been up late— but mostly thinking about when I could sneak out to try picking the lock on the art supply room door. There had to be something in there I'd missed. With time evaporating, I needed to investigate before tomorrow night—but after our last outing, I also didn't want to risk getting caught.

"Maybe you need some fresh air," Jilli said as we turned a corner. "That always wakes me up."

"Hm? Oh, maybe," I said, miserably aware of how distracted I sounded. "Jilli, I'm sorry, but I've got to go. I'm meeting the V in the library." Though it was practically the last thing on my mind, I'd promised to help the V study for our world literature final. The exam was two weeks away, but she was teetering on a C and wanted to make the honor roll. As for me, I hadn't checked any of my grades for the last few weeks. They had no relevance to me now.

"I'll see you later," I said as I started to walk faster. With luck,

I could finish the V's study session in an hour or less and get back to planning. I hoped so.

But luck, it seemed, was avoiding me today—I was just thirty-five steps into my trek before I was interrupted by a vibration from my watch.

Ugh, not now!

———

"What do you mean, 'He wants to trade'?" I whispered.

I huddled breathlessly in a small alcove carved into the library's stony outer walls, having run across the grounds to find a place to answer Eloise's call as fast as I could. The angle of the stonework blocked the view from the nearest security camera, and a leafless tangle of bushes would keep me safe from prying eyes. The only downside was the cold, insistent and unrelenting against my flushed cheeks.

"The Maestro wants to trade Felix for Claire," Eloise elucidated. "We received the communication an hour ago, and both MI6 and the CIA have confirmed it was authentic. As you know, it goes against protocol to negotiate with a terrorist, but we cannot pass up this opportunity. The Maestro wants his son, and I want my daughter. We'll sort out the details later, but don't worry—there's no way they'll be getting away with this."

I processed all the possibilities. "What about the Key? Do I still need to—"

Her eyes, which had been looking at someone to the left of her screen, refocused on me. "Yes. The Key is now your number one priority. It is essential that you find it. Time is running short." She paused. "He wants to swap at LaFray's grand opening."

The opening? That's tomorrow!

My heart sank—but it made perfect sense. Given the pomp

of the evening, the event would be packed, and hard to surveil. "Does Father know?"

"No, not yet. We're debating whether to let him and Madame Fontaine know. It might be too big of a distraction for them. We'll let you know the details later—but for now, this is confidential information. Do you understand that, Simone? Confidential." She straightened up. "And yes, the Queen and her detail will be long gone before any trade. We can't put her at risk." She paused. "Find the Key. We'll be in touch."

With that, the face of my watch went black.

Teeth chattering, I made my way to the front of the library and pushed the heavy oak door open, then I shook off the cold in the vestibule. I would have to process all the implications of what Eloise had told me—but I couldn't do it now. Not yet. There was too much on my mind.

"Over here," the V whispered, waving a book at me.

I placed my backpack on a chair and sat down. She smiled.

"Okay, I'm ready," she said. "I've been studying, so let's have it."

I began to dig in my backpack, but my mind wandered again, back to the zoo and the men shining their flashlights on me.

"Simone? Hellooo," the V said. "Where's the quiz?"

Oh, no! Four years ago, the V and I had started a ritual at Trinity: Before every exam, I would make up a multiple-choice test for the V for which every answer was C. She said it increased her confidence to get full marks each time. This time, however, it had completely slipped my mind. *How did I forget? I never forget anything!*

"Oh, V—I'm sorry. It just slipped my mind," I said.

"Slipped your mind? What?" the V answered in disbelief. She peered at me. "Geez. What's going on?"

I didn't know why, but something in her tone rankled. "Nothing!" I snapped—a little more curtly than I'd intended.

I winced, and the V blinked in surprise. "I didn't mean any-thing by it. You just seem so—so distant. We only have a few more weeks here, and my grades are a big deal to me."

"I'm sorry, V. I could make something up now?" I offered.

"Girls? Is everything okay over here?" asked Mrs. Bickford.

"Yes, ma'am," we whispered in unison.

The V started shoveling her books into her backpack. "I'm go-ing to find Madison and ask her to help me with this. See you later, Simone," she said, standing up.

As she walked away, I buried my face in my hands and exhaled deeply.

Am I doing the right thing? I wondered as the V's footsteps grew fainter. *I could just sneak into the supply room tonight, find the Key, and get out of here. I don't need to sneak out anymore, or keep secrets from my friend.*

I dropped my hands and straightened my glasses. I glanced over at the reference section and remembered the first time we'd snuck out. It had been great—the freedom, the friendship, the ex-citement. Was it bad to feel this way? I liked Maeve and Jilli; I just wished we weren't sneaking out anymore. It was too dangerous, and I didn't want anything to happen to them. Suddenly, every-thing was closing in on me.

What do I do?

I was grateful when the day was over and I could nestle in bed. Since receiving Eloise's message, I'd spent the entire latter half of the day mired in the uncharacteristic brain fog that had descended on me ever since I'd failed to find the Key, full of mixed feelings about the opening and the mission. I'd go back to the storage room and look through the pots again in the morning. For now, I couldn't wait to clear my head and get some well-deserved rest.

The V was already fast asleep, and Kirstin had finished her final rounds nearly an hour ago. The fourth floor of Beresford Hall was silent, slumbering. Frost was forming on our window as a gentle breeze pushed against it. My mind relaxed as thoughts of the store back home began lulling me to sleep.

Then a familiar voice brought me back.

"Frenchy, we're going out," Maeve whispered in my ear.

Dante's Inferno

Maeve told me to meet her and Jilli at the fence before she slipped away into the shadows. For a few moments, I contemplated staying—but I couldn't let them go alone. I couldn't disappoint them.

I tore the covers off myself and leapt out of bed. As I picked my jeans off the floor and rummaged for a turtleneck, the familiar rush returned. With great care and a practiced hand, I took off my watch and attached it to the V's wrist, careful not to wake her. This time, the face didn't even blink. *Excellent. Now, where is my—ah!*

My backpack, overstuffed with books and papers, lay on the floor across the room. I strode over and dumped it out. *I'll clean that up later.* I put my arms through the straps and pulled it tight to my back, buckled the now empty sack, and crept to the door.

My mind was a blur, and I paused to steady myself. *Breathe, Simone.*

"Where are you going?"

I spun like a whip. The V had sat up in bed and was reaching for her glasses. Euphoria became panic as blood rushed to my head.

"Ah—nowhere! I mean—to the bathroom, that's all," I fumbled out. *No, no, no!*

"Why do you have your backpack?" She turned on her lamp. I was doomed.

"And why are you dressed? What's going on?" the V asked, voice steadily rising in volume. Her questions would be unrelenting. I had to say something fast.

"It's really nothing. Some of us go down to the yard at night and, umm, watch the bats. It's pretty nerdy." I regretted the lie as soon as the words left my lips.

"Bats! Can I come?" shrieked the V.

Oh, no! I'd forgotten the V loved bats. My mind tripped back to our fourth-year zoology project. Our presentation had earned us a ninety-eight percent, but the real joy was in exploring Paris at night with our mothers. Felton's myotis was the—*ugh. Focus!*

"I'll get dressed!" the V added, vaulting out from under the covers.

"Ah—I don't think that's a good idea. It's kind of a small group," I replied with mounting frustration—to no response. Instead, the V turned her attention to the racks of clothes hanging in her closet.

"A bat club! I had no idea. What should I wear?"

"It's not a club, V; it's just something dumb we do sometimes!" I hissed. But she was undeterred. She got dressed in ten seconds, donning a neon windbreaker that could be seen from a mile away.

This was bad. There was no way Maeve would let the V go with us—and if I showed up dragging the V, she might leave me out, too. *Ugh, V!*

"Hey—what's this?"

My attention snapped back to the V, who was staring at her wrist—and my spywatch, right where I'd left it.

Oh, no!

I was plummeting down the rabbit hole, and having no success grasping its slick sides. "I didn't want Mother to track me and see I was out of the dorm." The words spilled out—the truth, but—

"So why didn't you just leave it on your bed or something?"

Touché.

I was running out of ideas, and becoming more flustered by the second. "I don't know. I guess I didn't want to misplace it or something." A terrible answer.

The V's smile faded into a confused expression. "What? That makes no sense. You never forget or lose anything, ever. What's going on?"

"It's really nothing, V. Can't I just tell you in the morning?" I snapped. Two minutes and forty-six seconds had elapsed since Maeve had vanished into the night, and time was ticking. My conscience raged in an inner debate. *Just stay in your room. (It's safe.) Or walk outside and look for some bats. (What if there aren't any?) This is going badly. (I'm sweaty.) Play it safe (What about Maeve?) and go to bed. (I'll toss and turn all night.) You're not a little girl anymore. (You're . . . a bad girl?) Freedom! (Yes, freedom.) You're on a mission. (Yes, a mission, a mission . . .)*

The desire to leave was pulling me outside with herculean force. *Tick, tick, tick—*

Just go!

"We'll talk about this—bat, or whatever—club thing tomorrow," I said, pulling the door open and darting out. *Maybe if I hurry, she won't be able to follow.*

No such luck. I got four steps down the hall before the V was on my tail. *What am I going to do?*

I slowed, and the V caught up. "Where are we going?" she whispered too loudly as we tiptoed through the dim hall and down the stairwell.

"V, you can't come tonight!" I snapped—but there was no way she was turning back. My stomach churned, my frustration flaring. I wanted to be free in the night more than anything—but the V was standing in my way. I couldn't let her come with us. I still didn't know what was next for the Wolves, or what they might be capable of, but I could handle myself. The V, on the other hand, could get into real trouble if we ran into anyone again. *What to do?*

As we emerged onto the lawn, the cold enveloped us, and the V let out a sneeze loud enough to wake the dead—as if the brightness of her coat weren't enough. My mind raced as the inner debate rolled on. *Do I go back? (No! Yes. Maybe?) Call it a night? That's the smart thing to do. (But what about Maeve? She'll hate me.) Go back and go to bed. (But what about the mission?) Forget about all this and go back. (I don't want to!)*

Wait—my watch! It can't leave the campus. It was still on the V's wrist, but I had to be careful.

"V, please go back to the room. I'll tell you everything tomorrow, but you *have* to go back."

She peered at me and smiled as we broke into a jog. "No way! This is the most fun I've had all week. Bat Club is awesome!"

Frustration turned to anger. My hands were now drenched with sweat, and every centimeter of my stomach was in knots as we got closer to the rose garden. *It wasn't supposed to be this way!*

"What's she doing here?" Maeve whispered, as the two girls appeared from behind the hedge, both of them carrying a pair of heavy bags. Jilli let out a gasp.

The V stood there looking like she was waiting to enter an amusement park, full of anticipation and excitement. Maeve looked her over, then turned her eyes on me. "Simone, can I talk to you a second?" I knew she wasn't really asking.

"Where are all the bats? Did anyone bring a flashlight or binoculars?" the V asked, obliviously scanning the sky for darting *Molossi.*

Maeve pulled me aside and leaned in close. "She has to leave, *now!*"

"I tried to tell her—"

"No. You don't understand; she needs to leave right now! This is a big night, Simone. A big night." Her eyes were wild. "We can do this without you, but we need to leave now. You got me?"

My head spun as I turned to look at the friend I had known forever. The pressure was overwhelming—but I had to go. Maybe I would find out more about Claire, or maybe I would just fit in for one more night, but I had to.

"Tell her to leave," Maeve ordered.

My heart sank. Could I say that to my friend? *You can still go back to the room, Simone,* a small voice said. *It's not too late.* But no. Maeve loomed over me, and I understood. There was no other way.

A foreign ugliness welled up inside me. *Is this how a bully feels?*

"Nobody wants you here, V, so just go back!"

As soon as the words left my lips, I was overwhelmed with shame. I had never spoken to the V like that before. She stared at me like I was a complete stranger.

"What did you say?" she eked out. "Simone, I just want to—"

My heart was breaking. "Did I stutter? You need to leave, V; nobody wants you here. Now beat it!"

The V's hands flew to her mouth, and her shoulders slumped forward. Tears started to form as she slowly turned away.

The few flames of anger that remained vanished as my heart lost all warmth. I'd just crushed my best friend. For one wild instant, I fought the urge to console her and disclose everything: being a spy, Claire, the Wolves, everything. But I couldn't. It was too late.

As I watched her walk back to our dorm, dejected and sobbing, the depth of our friendship was made clear to me. The separation from her was palpable, the longing to reconnect made everything in me ache. I knew she would never look at me the same again. Tears streamed down my face, and not even the frigid wind could keep them from dripping off my cheeks.

What have I done?

———

We hurried down a shadow-peppered Bedford Gardens. The rush of excitement I had hoped to find was absent, replaced by an unshakeable hollowness. The air felt stagnant, the city lights looked dull, and as I focused on the back of Maeve's sweatshirt, I felt nothing at all.

"Keep up, Simone!" Maeve hissed. Her eyes were on her watch. "Only three streets to go."

Dimly, it occurred to me that the V may have taken off my spywatch and thrown it onto the yard, or even smashed it to pieces. I couldn't say I would have blamed her. It was clear that I was going to have a lot to explain.

"One more street, guys," Maeve called out.

I finally roused myself enough to take in my changing surroundings. Maeve had led us into a residential neighborhood—and a particularly nice one at that. The low iron fences and shiny green lampposts sparked recognition in me. *Wait a second—we're on Aubrey Walk.*

We stopped under a well-trimmed cherry tree, which gave us the most cover, and I tried to catch my breath and assess what was in all these bags. By my estimation, Maeve had brought at least twice the amount of paint we'd used on the bus.

"Are you okay?" Jilli whispered in my ear, placing her hand on my shoulder.

I was not okay—not even close—but I had to see this through. I mustered up a forced, "I'm fine."

Maeve rifled through the bags, revealing an arsenal of paint and art supplies.

"Tonight will be our masterpiece—our finest tagging yet. We have less than an hour before a patrol car passes through. The closest one is two streets away, so we need to start now." *How could she know that?*

Maeve cracked open a can of dark red paint. "Not only has the Fontaine Company been flooding the world with candy made in sweatshops, but the owner is corrupt to the bone. You know the stories, don't you? You know how many lives she's destroyed; you know the . . ."

Maeve kept going, but my mind had turned off. A year ago, I might have been the first person to raise a protest against the Fontaine Company. Sugars had been terrible to Father—mean, vindictive, and vile. She'd tried to run us out of business for years, buy us out. But now . . .

Numb confusion overcame the excitement of the moment as my alliances collided. *I can't believe it. And today of all days! How could I have let this happen? Why am I here?*

". . . So that's why we're going to paint *Dante's Inferno* on the street right in front of Fontaine's house. Chenavard's masterpiece recreated for all to see," Maeve concluded in a sinister tone.

Dante's Inferno. It made perfect sense. The image of the painting was burned into my psyche, and I recalled every brushstroke. Before, without being coaxed, I would have composed it in perfect detail. Now, however, my palms were sweating, and my nostrils were heavy with the unmistakable smell of petrichor. A storm was moving in, or at least a heavy fog.

I reached for a brush, dipped it in paint, and held it up. But my fingers wouldn't move.

As I stood numb, the extended silence must have been getting to Maeve. "I know this might be hard for you, with your father and all," she coaxed. "But you have to see the bigger picture. We need to know you're with us. Truth above everything. Remember? We need to know, Simone! *Are you with us?*"

I took a deep breath and stared at the blank road. For what felt like the first time in weeks, clarity flooded my mind. *No. This isn't why I'm here. Agents don't vandalize property. Why am I doing the work of the Fox? I'm better than this.* An image of Mother appeared in my head, which was suddenly full of memories of home—my parents, Gigi, Mia, our shop on Rue Clodion, and of course, the V. I thought back to my best friend smiling, comforting me, bringing out the best in me. This smart, beautiful, and unconditional beacon of joy in my life was hurting because of me. In the face of that, being a bad girl had lost all meaning. I needed to make this right.

The paintbrush fell from my hand, splattering against the pavement.

"I have to go."

I turned and ran as fast as I could into the stark night.

"Simone!" Maeve hissed desperately, unwilling to raise her voice on the quiet street. "Simone!"

But I didn't turn back. I had to go find my friend.

I was halfway to Claymoore when the fatigue of the evening took hold. Loafers were not the best shoes for running. My feet were sore, and my calves were cramping. I couldn't go on.

I slumped down on one of the frigid benches lining the street. An illuminated LaFray billboard loomed over me, and I couldn't help but wince.

I put my head in my hands. The V and I had never fought before. It struck me then that I had never apologized to her before either. *Would she even want to talk to me? Would it just make things worse?*

My doubts bloomed into full panic. *How am I going to explain what I was doing with Maeve? Should I tell her I'm a spy, get everything out? Would she even believe me?*

For the next hour and twenty-seven minutes, I thought over what I could say to the V—connecting every detail, every action, and yes, every lie. Still, I produced nothing. But my legs were once again ready for travel, and this bench was providing no further inspiration. It was time to go.

Managing a steady jog, I found myself outside of the Claymoore gates in just under twenty minutes, winded and emotionally bankrupt. I found the break in the hedge and passed through the fence, replacing the iron bars behind me. I crept across the grounds and turned the corner to ascend the steps to our dormitory—

—only to come face to face with a very unwelcome silhouette, waiting for me.

"Miss LaFray, I will remind you of our policy concerning students leaving the campus," Headmaster Bailes said, coming into the light. "It is nearly three a.m., young lady, and you have much to explain. To my office, immediately."

Oh, no. Bailes knew why I was at Claymoore, but I couldn't imagine him bending the rules for anyone.

Things couldn't possibly get any worse.

I followed the headmaster across the frosted lawn like a scolded puppy. *This isn't me; this isn't me. I've never been in trouble in my life!* My training overtook my uncertainty, and interrogation tactics flashed through my head. My calves had started to cramp again, and my sweaty shirt clung icily to me.

As I walked up the stairs, a thought sent a jolt through me: *What if the V is up there? Did she rat us out?* I'd never imagined the V as vindictive—but I'd never imagined I could've said what I'd said to her, either. If she had let the headmaster know what I'd done, I couldn't help but feel I certainly deserved it.

As we got to the top of the stairs, however, I was relieved to see the headmaster's office was dark. He snapped the light on as he entered, then hung his jacket on the coat rack and placed his tweed cap on top of it before taking a seat behind his enormous desk.

Rigidly, I followed suit, sliding into the tiny chair opposite him. As I did, Sophie the cat woke with a start, jumped off the padded velvet cushion where she'd been sleeping, and circled the room before taking a seat on the headmaster's lap.

"As you know, Miss LaFray, here at Claymoore, we have a code of conduct. Our rules are not open for interpretation, nor are they suggestions. Demonstration of character through conduct is the hallmark of this institution, and I simply cannot tolerate this behavior. Granted, I do not know whether your actions tonight were merely part of your work for the Ministry—"

They were! I wanted to say. It was the truth. But the Ministry didn't know I'd been sneaking out either. In fact, I'd deliberately tried to hide my outings with the Wolves from them. They couldn't vouch for me.

I was trapped—caught like a wolf in a snare.

"—but as I was not informed, I am inclined to think not." He paused, then said, "I take your silence as an affirmation. Understand that as headmaster of this school, I must consider the well-being of all my students, and I cannot have them thinking they can flout the rules without consequence. Do you know what the punishment is for sneaking off campus at night, Miss LaFray?"

I did. I had memorized the entire student manual. "Expulsion, sir."

"Expulsion, indeed." The word sank through my mind and lodged itself in my stomach like an iron weight. "A length to which it pains me to have to go—especially given your otherwise spotless record. Miss LaFray, in all my sixteen years as headmaster here, I've seen some bad eggs. I've dealt with some substandard individuals. But you do not strike me as a troublemaker. And given your, let's say, *unique* enrollment, I have my doubts that you were the only one to go rogue tonight."

Uh-oh.

"Believe me, this is not the first time a group of students has skipped out for a night on the town. We didn't have time to do a full sweep after your prefect alerted me she'd found Miss Cantone crying alone in your room—"

My heart clenched. *Oh, V . . .*

"—but I can only assume others were involved. Therefore, in this singular instance, I am willing to negotiate a lighter punishment for you—on two conditions."

For a moment, a spark of hope leapt up in me—but it was short-lived.

"First, I require from you the names of any and all students who snuck out with you tonight, and the reasons you did so. Furthermore, you will compose a letter of no less than ten pages expressing your full contrition for this event, addressed to me." The headmaster's eyes flashed. "I will not be made a fool. If I do not have those names by dinnertime tomorrow, make no mistake: you will be expelled."

The spark dissolved into a tingling numbness. I collapsed limply against the back of my chair, my mind feeling as if it were melting into a puddle of mush. From the headmaster's lap, Sophie the cat stared at me with a look of disdain.

What a mess.

Eggs Benedict

The sun barely broke through our dormitory windows as morning came. A cold gray light cast a pallor over London, and the air was heavy with the threat of rain. Storm clouds were starting to gather in the distance, dark and thick.

Early morning was typically my favorite part of the day, but this morning, I couldn't shake off the despair and shame I felt. For the last few hours, I had wrestled with my actions and tried to formulate the perfect explanation—but nothing held together. The words fell apart like a house of cards. I sat on the edge of my bed, vulnerable, fidgeting, and anxious, feeling fragile and unrefined. I had no experience with something like this, and I hated it.

Across the room, the V rolled over in her sleep. My watch was still on her wrist, and I caught the reflection of pulsing red light bouncing off her white pillow. *Red!* Adrenaline flooded me—and then I realized I was in no position to address this problem. I would have to deal with it later.

The V's eyes opened, and my stomach dropped. She yawned and rubbed her eyes, and for a moment, it seemed as if nothing had happened—but in the next instant, I saw the weight of the prior night return. This was not the V I knew. Her face held no reassurance, no endless curiosity, and no joy.

"G-good morning, V," I offered.

In response, she turned her nose up and crossed her arms over her chest. Her typically ever-present smile was replaced with an unfamiliar scowl.

"Don't talk to me."

"Okay. Sure. That's fine. That's . . . fine," I stammered.

A moment of silence passed.

"So, did you have fun?"

"V—" I began; but the words I'd wanted to say evaporated on my tongue. I tried again. "No. It was horrible." Maybe if she knew how much trouble I was in, I could get through to her. "Headmaster Bailes caught me coming back in, and in all likelihood, I'm going to be expelled."

The V gasped, and her brows scrunched up in confusion. *So she didn't know about Kirstin coming by.* But if I'd hoped for sympathy, I saw none in her eyes. "Well, that sounds about right!" she barked. "And what about your new best friends? Are they getting expelled too?"

Outside, rain had begun to fall, lashing the glass windowpanes. A lump rose in my throat.

"Why did you say those things last night? Why were you so mean? Were you trying to show off or something?" The V wiped a hand across her nose. "It isn't fair. I was your friend *first*—your only friend!"

Her words pierced me like arrows, but I couldn't blame her. It was true: the V was my first and only real friend. She had every right to be upset.

"I know. It's—it's complicated, V."

"Complicated!? I don't see what's so complicated. You start to hang out with some other kids, and suddenly you can't stand to be around me. That's not complicated! How could you say that?" She started to cry.

A wave of guilt crashed over me, paralyzing me with its weight. My tongue felt like a brick in my mouth. "I know! I was stupid." I'd never referred to anything I had done as *stupid*. "I didn't mean to hurt you, I promise. Can you forgive me?"

But she just shook her head.

"Yeah, it *was* stupid, and really mean, and—no, I don't forgive you! You were like my sister, Simone!" She turned away from me again, and my heart broke.

'Were'?

Now we were both crying. Every cell in my body ached. Wiping the tears from my eyes, I looked at the spywatch on her wrist, hoping it wasn't transmitting audio.

"Everything alright in here, losers?" Kirstin's mocking voice caught me by surprise. She always seemed to show up at the wrong time.

"Ugh. We're fine. Can't you leave us alone?" the V said, wiping her cheeks.

Kirstin fixed her eyes on the V like a lioness spotting a tired gazelle. "It looks to me like you babies are crying for your mothers. Homesick, are we?" she asked in her most pretentious tone.

"We're not homesick, you frump!" the V snapped. "This is none of your business. Now bounce."

Kirstin pursed her lips. "Fine. Sit here and cry your eyes out. I don't have time for this nonsense." She slammed the door behind her with a bang.

But the brief interruption, however unpleasant, had helped clear my head. I knew what I needed to do. My friendship with the V was more important than anything in the world—even the Ministry. I had to come clean, whatever the consequences.

"V, I have to tell you something, but it has to remain between us. Do you swear?"

The V craned her neck to look back at me and sniffed. "What?" She blinked. "Sure, I guess. Is this about Jonas?"

I wished it had been about Jonas—but there was no going back now. I collected myself and sat up straight. *No more secrets.*

"You might not believe me, V, but I'm an *espionne*." My words came out in a rush, my heart pounding. There—the box was open.

She scoffed. "Yeah, right—and I'm a robot sent here to take over the world."

"It's true, V. I'm a spy with the Ministry of Foreign Affairs. You know—where my mother works?"

"I don't believe you." Her face was blank and hard.

"It's true. I've been training there for years. I'm an analyst. That's why I needed to come to Claymoore—to find out what happened to Claire Pilfrey, my boss's daughter. She's gone missing," I said hurriedly.

"Claire? The artsy girl?" The V shook her head, growing frustration clear in her voice. "Why are you making this up?"

"I'm not. This is what I do, V. I figure stuff out for the Ministry. I notice everything, I see everything, and I can't forget anything. Jilli and Maeve were good friends of Claire, and I've been trying to figure out what happened to her by learning more about them. I had to get close to them. But—" For an instant, I teetered, then plunged ahead. "Maeve, Jilli, and Claire were the Red Wolves of London. After Claire vanished, they wanted me to take her place. It would've been too dangerous for you to go with us last night. I had to do something. I hate myself for it, but I couldn't put you in danger. I couldn't." Tears flowed down my face. "I love you like a sister, V, and I couldn't let anything happen to you."

If anything, the V looked even more skeptical and betrayed. "That can't be true. What danger?" She shook her head. "If there was danger, you should've taken me! I could've helped you. I've always stuck up for you! I—"

"I couldn't. I'm sorry." I rushed on. "I'm being monitored all the time. I have a watch that lets the Ministry know where I am. I couldn't go out with it—not with what we were doing. But if it doesn't detect a heartbeat, a distress signal goes out. Agents would be here in less than five minutes." I took a breath and gestured to the spywatch, still on the V's wrist. "I had to leave it behind with someone. You were the only person I could think of. Please, V."

The V held up her wrist, as if noticing the watch for the first time. She turned it from side to side, taking in the still-flashing red light.

"What? This?" She frowned. "That's crazy. What about when you take showers?"

"I punch in a code that disables it, and reactivate it when I put it back on. It senses my heartbeat and reads my blood pressure. If the data is inconsistent, my supervisor will remote in."

"'Remote in'? You mean like a mobile call?"

"Yeah, a video call; and then it scans my retina."

The V sat up in bed, her expression changing from inquisitive to skeptical before settling into a morose frown. "No." She shook her head firmly. "No. I don't believe you. You're not a spy, you're just a weird girl that likes books and knows everything. And there's no way Maeve and Jilli are the Red Wolves."

In that moment, I knew there was only one way to convince her. *Breathe, Simone.*

"Take the watch off. Take it off and put it face down. Let's see what happens."

The V studied me, her eyes searching for lies. Then, with a shrug, she took off the watch and laid it on the bed.

For the next three minutes, we sat in silence. The flashing red light shifted to white, signaling the emergency protocol was underway. Four minutes and three seconds later, I pointed out the window, and the V glanced over and saw what I had already noticed out of the corner of my eye: three men in gray trench coats were running across the grounds. One of them was speaking into his wristwatch.

The V's brow furrowed.

"What's going on?" she murmured. She stumbled back from the window and stared at me in disbelief. I could see her eyes widening as she started processing the truth.

"No way. You're really a spy?"

I nodded, and her mouth fell open.

"I knew it. I *knew* you had a secret!" she said. "I never doubted you for a second! I could tell because—"

Heavy footsteps cut her off, beating down the creaking wooden floor of the hall outside. In the next instant, our door flew open as the three men barged in, frowning, and fixed their eyes on me.

The next thirty minutes were a swirl of confusion as I was swept into a private study room for questioning. After we finished the identity protocol and the agents determined I hadn't been physically harmed, the mood in the room lightened—but not for long.

Soon one of the agents placed my computer in front of me and turned it on. The screen came to life—to reveal a steaming Eloise, glaring at me.

"What is going on there? You had me worried sick! We cannot have you going missing—tonight is the night, and we need to be sharp. You know the protocol, Simone. What happened?"

As I collected my thoughts, one of the agents chimed in. "The watch checks out, madame. No errors."

Ugh. There went the simplest explanation. *Think of something!*

"Well?" Eloise asked.

Think faster!

"I—I just took off my watch so I could take a shower. I guess I wasn't thinking—I had a restless night. Sorry."

Eloise gaped. "Took a *shower?* You take showers every day. Is your head right?"

The agents slunk into the hallway, where I caught a glimpse of Headmaster Bailes lingering before they closed the door. I felt a leap of gratitude for their discretion.

"Yes, madame. It's just . . . it's just that the V and I had a big fight. It was awful, and I don't want to get into the details. I'm just sick about it, and I didn't sleep much, and—"

"Dear, friends have disagreements from time to time—it happens. I am not too old to remember fallings-out with my school friends. At the time, you think the world is ending, but in reality, it's just another day. You'll both get over it soon enough," she said. "Ordinarily, I might place you on leave—but that is not an option. Do I have to remind you what is at stake tonight?" She didn't. "This is *not* the time to lose your head. We need you to be focused. No mistakes!"

I nodded. "I'll pull it together. I've been a little scatterbrained lately," I admitted.

"See that you do." With that, the screen went dark.

I sighed and slid my computer into my backpack, then hopped off my chair and put my ear to the door. As I'd spoken with Eloise, the agents had been talking with Headmaster Bailes in the hall. Now I heard their muffled voices through the thick wood. Apparently a couple of kids had noticed the agents running across campus, but no one had paid them much attention. One of the realities of having royals and wealthy kids at your school was that security guards were commonplace. No one would have guessed the men were there for me.

I leapt back from the door as footsteps approached. It opened, and Headmaster Bailes stuck his nose in, flanked by the agents.

"You may return to your room, Miss LaFray—and remember, I want those names by dinnertime."

One of the agents stepped forward and buckled a new watch to my wrist. "This one stays on."

On the way back to my room, I texted Mother to let her know I was okay. No doubt Eloise would have informed her of the alarm as well, and probably that I was alright, too; but I wanted her to hear it from me. I missed her dearly, and didn't want her to worry.

"What happened?" the V asked as I walked in. She was still hidden beneath her covers. "Did they hurt you?"

I peered down the hall and closed the door. "No, of course not. I'm fine."

She seemed reassured—at least enough to wriggle out from under the covers. "I'm still mad at you, you know."

"I know, and you should be. I hate myself for saying those things as much as you do. I just didn't know what else to do."

With a sigh, the V swung her feet over the edge of the bed and faced me.

"Look, I don't care that you didn't tell me you're a spy or whatever. I just never thought you would talk to me like that. I'm your best friend, Simone. Those girls don't know you like I do. I was your friend *first*."

An exhausted tear slid down my cheek. "I know. Like I said, I'm sorry, and I'm always going to be sorry. It was mean, regardless of the reason for it, but I hope you understand."

"Yeah, I do. I guess." The V began to swing her legs restlessly back and forth. "So, why didn't you tell me you were a spy? I tell you *everything*. Don't you trust me?"

"It's not that. It's just part of the job—you know, going under-cover. And . . . I guess I liked having a secret, too." The V was so much more boisterous than I was—it was one of the only things I'd felt put us on equal footing.

"A secret?" The V shook her head. "That's one heck of a secret. I don't have a secret that would even come close to that." She swung her legs back onto the bed and let out a long, tired sigh.

"I guess I just want to be alone for a while. Tell everyone I'm tired or something when you go to brunch. I need some sleep."

"Yeah, okay. I'll tell them," I replied.

I started toward the door, then paused. "V?"

"Mhm?"

"The new store . . . it's opening today. Will I still . . . you know. Are you still coming?"

She settled back into her covers and closed her eyes, seeming exhausted by the whole ordeal. "I don't know, Simone. At this point? I really don't know."

I stared at her as she sank into sleep. I'd thought she was coming around, if her fidgeting was any indication. Still, watching her, I knew it wouldn't be so easy to put this behind us. Words could sting, and my horrible behavior would not soon be forgotten. I'd hurt her, and she needed time to process the bomb I'd placed in her lap.

"Eggs Benedict?" asked the hostess as I placed my plate on the dining hall counter.

Brunch at Claymoore rivaled that of a five-star hotel: eggs, pancakes, waffles, meats, and a wide range of fresh fruits, all at our fingertips. A small chalkboard sign declared eggs Benedict the special of the day, but I did not feel worthy of such a decadent dish. The regret I felt for the V hung over me like a dark cloud, sad and heavy.

"Just toast and fruit, please," I replied. I wasn't the faintest bit hungry, but I wanted to respect the V's wishes for some time alone.

I received my food and instinctively turned toward the third table on the left—but my pace slowed to a near halt when I saw Maeve and Jilli. From a glance at the news, I'd gathered they'd finished their painting without me last night, and the work of the

Wolves was again the source of much chatter. Local TV stations quickly picked up the story of *Dante's Inferno*, and the Wolves' newest painting had even made that morning's cover of the *Times*. Sugars had been contacted for an interview, but had declined to comment—no doubt since she was so busy with the launch of the new store later today. I privately guessed that it agonized her to keep quiet; she would have adored the attention, and probably couldn't care less about somebody painting the street in front of her home. In fact, on any other day, she might even have appreciated the opportunity to spin the vandalism into her own brand of publicity.

"Good morning, Frenchy. You look rested," Maeve said as I set down my tray.

I didn't—not in the slightest—but maybe if I haphazardly buttered my toast to avoid making eye contact, she wouldn't realize it. I just didn't think I could stomach any more disappointment today. Even if Maeve wasn't my first friend—even if she'd tried to get me to betray my father's business partner—I'd thought she was becoming *a* friend, and I didn't have many of those. My stomach tightened at the thought of her turning her back on me, even though I knew I'd done the right thing.

Maybe Harper was right. Maybe everything is more complicated than I imagined.

I sighed and finally risked a glance up—just in time to see Maeve lean in.

"You left us in a bad spot last night," she whispered through gritted teeth. "I had to paint faster than ever, and we almost got caught. The night watchman saw us and chased us for fifteen minutes. Do you know what—"

"The headmaster wants me to turn you two in," I broke in.

Maeve sat back in her chair, stunned. Jilli's eyes widened.

"He caught me when I was coming back in. He knows I

wasn't alone. He wants me to give him the names of everyone who snuck out by dinnertime . . . or I'll be expelled."

"What? Expelled?!" Jilli exclaimed. "I can't get expelled!" She turned to Maeve and whispered, "I can't get expelled, Maeve! My scholarship, my parents—"

"You're not going to get expelled, Jilli. I won't let that happen." Maeve's tone was firm, and she turned to me. "We won't let that happen, will we, Simone?"

I didn't know what to say. I didn't want to get them in trouble—but the thought of getting myself expelled from one of the most prestigious schools in the world wasn't exactly appealing either. How would I explain that at Trinity? Would Trinity even take me back?

For the next two minutes and twelve seconds, silence reigned. Finally, Maeve broke the tension. "How did he catch *you,* and not us?"

I shook my head. "I'm not sure. I stayed out for a while, so I don't know if I came back before or after you. I don't even know how he knew we'd left. But I do know Kirstin checked my room. Maybe she told the headmaster I was gone."

"Why didn't he expel you on the spot? Isn't there some rule about that?" asked Maeve.

I shrugged. "I guess he's giving me some leeway because I'm a foreign student. Maybe he likes me," I replied, trying to inject a hint of humor.

Jilli was holding her stomach and breathing fast. She hadn't touched a bite of her food since I'd sat down. Across from me, Maeve sat and ate her breakfast quietly, as if she had already accepted her fate. There was nothing else to say.

Suddenly, my new watch buzzed. *What now?*

"I've got to go." I stood, and their silent gazes followed me. "Don't worry—I'll let you know what's going on as soon as I can.

I just have a lot to take care of—the store's opening tonight, and I have to—" I couldn't tell them about the Key. "—I just have a lot to do. I'm sorry."

I strode away with my untouched plate, willing myself not to look back. Even so, I felt their eyes on me all the way down the refectory.

———

After returning my plate, I ducked into a study room down the hall, activated my watch, and waited. The screen buzzed to life.

"Simone!" Mother exclaimed. "What in the world is going on there? I've been on the phone with Eloise three times today. I've never been so worried—and now I hear you're going to be expelled? Expelled!" She paused to collect herself. "What's going on? Eloise said you had a fight with the V. This isn't like you."

My shoulders slumped. "It's too long to explain. You're going to have to trust me, Mother. I'll explain everything when I get home. For now, can you just tell me about home, the store, Gigi? Anything."

A sympathetic smile moved across her face, and she acquiesced. In the next eight minutes and two seconds, she caught me up on the goings-on around the store, Mia's holiday production of *A Christmas Carol,* and taking Gigi to get her nails trimmed. I soaked up every word, visualizing it all with absolute clarity. I could have listened to her for hours. Finally, the world made sense again, if only for a little while.

"It's going to be fine, dear," Mother added as she finished. "We'll work this out. I've survived bigger catastrophes than this." I was grateful for the reassurance. "For now, try to focus on the Key for a few hours. Do you have any leads there?"

My stomach fluttered, and I looked at the floor. "No, but I've got to find a way to get into the storage room again. It's the only place left that makes sense. Claire fired over a hundred biscuit jars while she was here. That *has* to mean something—but I've checked them, and there's nothing in them. Maybe I missed something."

"Well, you only have a few hours. You better get busy," Mother said. Her tone softened. "Anyway, it's a big night tonight! Father is expecting you at six o'clock sharp, and Eloise will be calling you for the final briefing at three-thirty. Simone, whatever happens, know that I love you—and remember: *Protéger les Gens.*"

The call ended, and I closed my eyes and took a deep breath. Mother was right. I had so much left to do—and I couldn't stop now. *First things first, Simone: find the Key. No matter what happens, you are getting into that storage room.*

I fished two paperclips from my backpack and put them in my pocket. With conviction in my step, I marched to the storage room—only to spot a gray-haired janitor taking out the trash in Ms. Kusma's room. There was no way I could pick the lock with him around.

I froze. For an instant, I considered aborting the mission and coming back later—but then my mother's words from the time we'd spent on the roof at 7 Rue Clodion flashed through my mind. *Don't be afraid of change, Simone. Change happens—but the strong are ready.*

I approached him and leaned against the doorframe.

"Excuse me, sir, but do you mind if I sit in here for a bit? It's quiet, and no one interrupts me."

The man jumped. "Well, hello there, miss! I didn't see you." He smiled at me. "Ms. Kusma likes her room locked for the evening. I'll be back in a few minutes, but the place is yours until then."

"Thank you."

I slipped past him. The room was cold and empty, the smell of chalk and acrylic paint mixing with a hint of turpentine and fresh paper. I took my usual seat and—so as not to waste time—started contemplating what I might write in my letter to the headmaster as I waited for the janitor to move on. The student in me was sensitive to the fact that expulsion was on the table—a punishment like that would certainly leave a mark on my permanent record. Another part of me, however, wanted to craft a blistering letter detailing Claymoore's numerous shortcomings, and why I would accept his expulsion as a badge of honor. But that might take too long.

I gazed up, past the shelves of paint cans and stacks of blank canvases. *There must be over a hundred thousand dots of paint on that ceiling.* I studied every color, searching for new patterns between the paint drops as I contemplated the decision I had to make. Should I rat out the other Wolves?

I debated the merits of the arguments for and against, balancing the impact of expulsion on my permanent record. It was a serious matter, especially since I'd never been in trouble before.

Ultimately, however, the choice was easy.

No matter what else they had done, Maeve and Jilli had given me something that could not be taken away. They'd taught me rules could be broken, and to never let anybody push me around. They'd unveiled a stronger part of me, one with confidence and grit—and for that, I was grateful. And though it might be wishful thinking, I hoped that they would be at my side again someday.

Now, I was more certain than ever: Harper was right.

"Miss? I'm moving upstairs, so please pull the door closed behind you if you leave. I'll be back later to lock up," the janitor called from the doorway.

"Yes, sir. I'll be just a few more minutes," I replied.

I waited to hear his footsteps fade. *Now, let's take a closer look at those jars.*

I ran down the hall to the storage room as fast as I could. The door was locked, but I pulled out my paper clips and replicated what Jilli had done before. *Click.*

Yes!

I pulled the door open, flipped on the lights, and walked with conviction to the back of the room and the heaps of jars. Picking one up, I examined it from every angle.

On initial inspection, it looked no different than it had the many times I'd come down here over the past few weeks. I slowly turned it in my hands, looking for clues—markings, etchings, patterns that might have indicated a puzzle singling out one jar or another, or directing me to a special hiding place. But there was nothing.

Think, Simone. My hands were growing cold. *Think—wait. My hands!* I had never had the opportunity to hold one of Claire's jars for this long before—but now, after a couple of minutes, I noticed what I'd missed. The jar was pulling the heat from my hands.

I inspected the glaze on this jar, and then the others. All of them were the same: thick and dark, with a cool gray tone. *Claire must have added aluminum to the glaze to interfere with the Key's transmitter. That's why nobody could locate it!* She could have dropped the OmniKey into any one of these jars. With a similarly glazed lid on top, the Key would be safe and sound, with no signals leaving the jar.

But I'd already checked all the jars—and they were all empty. My gaze swept around the room. *Did I miss one?* It couldn't be. I had checked every possible place in this room where a jar could be hidden, counted every single one of the misshapen vessels, and I was sure of their exact number. *Still, it doesn't make sense. If she made so many, and she was so good at art, why are they all so distorted? Wouldn't she want a sturdy container? Were they under-fired?* Claire would have needed to fire the aluminum glaze at a lower heat, so as not to melt it; but that shouldn't have affected the initial firing of the clay. *Unless—*

And in a flash, the answer came. The reason Claire had made so many jars. The reason they were misshapen. The reason I hadn't found the Key in any of them. *Of course! She didn't make the jars to put the Key* in *them like a cookie. She could have made one jar to accomplish that. She was trying to fire the Key into the* ceramic itself! The heat would have had to be high enough to bake the ceramic, but not high enough to damage the Key. *All the misshapen jars—she was experimenting! But—which one worked?*

I looked over the piles of jars in front of me. There was no time to examine them now, and no way I could take them all with me.

With a sudden rush of clarity, I knew what I needed to do. It was something I never would have contemplated before, something that would have gotten me in huge trouble—but I didn't have time to worry about that now.

And besides, I was going to get expelled anyway.

I went back to the door and peeked outside. *I hope nobody hears. This is going to take a while.*

I closed the door and flipped the lock. Staring at the rows of jars, I started to think of the V and what I had done since coming to Claymoore: sneaking out, getting expelled, and disappointing so many people I cared about. A fire began to rise, and I rolled up my sleeves and adjusted my glasses. The bad girl was back.

Over the next three minutes and twenty-two seconds, I smashed jars and lids on the floor like a bull in a china shop. Two at a time, I threw them as hard as I could, working my way from the front of the room to the back. Shards of ceramic flew everywhere. With each explosion, I thought about all the worries, all the mishaps I'd endured.

Soon, over a hundred jars lay broken on the floor, the debris scattered throughout the room. There was only one left. I stopped and took a deep breath, inspecting it closely. In the right light, the glaze had just a hint of red. *Could this be it?*

All my theories hinged on this. With both hands, I raised the jar over my head and smashed it to the floor with all my strength. *Tink!*

I brushed away pulverized dust and shards of ceramic to uncover a polished steel card, exactly as I'd envisioned it. *There you are!*

I flipped it over and studied it. It gleamed, reflecting the fluorescent lights above. *This is what everyone is so worked up about?* It looked so nondescript—but then again, looks could be deceiving.

As if on cue, my new watch started to vibrate. I clutched the Key hard in my right hand. *Have they already picked up its signal? Do they know I found it?* Even for the Ministry, that would've been difficult—the outer walls of the buildings here were solid stone. *I guess I'll find out.*

I activated my watch's video feed, and a stern-faced Eloise appeared on the screen. "Simone, dear. Are you ready for tonight?"

She definitely didn't know about the Key. I nodded, trying to push down a sense of giddiness, and barely able to contain the grin that threatened to come to my face. "Yes, of course," I replied as calmly as I could. I could hardly wait to share my success. "Have there been any changes or modifications to the plan?"

"Just two. We concluded that the third-floor balcony is not going to be a suitable observation point for you. You need to be in the center of the room and able to see the entire area. After analyzing the room several times, we've decided that the best place for you is in the chandelier."

What? I supposed that did make sense. I would be out of sight among the sugarwork and candy, with a bird's-eye view of the shop. Excited by the prospect of blending into the scenery, I finally allowed myself to grin. "Okay—but how do I get up there?"

"After your performance, you will change into a discreet outfit and head to the attic. There is a trapdoor that opens to the inside of the chandelier. You will open it and shimmy down. It should easily hold your weight, and we affixed a small seat within the chandelier this afternoon."

"Okay. Sing, change, go to the attic, and rappel down. Got it," I said distractedly, rolling the Key in my hand. I couldn't wait one more second. "Eloise, you aren't going to—"

"Simone, it is imperative that you concentrate on the task at hand. Focus, young lady. We don't want any gaffes here," she interrupted.

Her words stopped me cold, and I frowned. *Gaffes?* It wasn't like my mentor to be so snappish—but then again, Eloise hadn't been acting like herself since Claire had vanished. *Oh, right—Claire!* In my excitement at finding the Key, I'd nearly forgotten the purpose of the night, outside of the opening of our store: the swap. Eloise must be frantic at the chance of getting Claire back at last. *Maybe I'll keep the Key to myself for now.* Eloise had enough to worry over. Anyway, between the Fox, the Maestro, and the Ministry, it wouldn't hurt to have an ace up my sleeve—or resting in my pocket.

"Understood. What's the second change?" I replied, trying to let go of my excitement.

"Oh, yes. The Maestro demanded his son be seen inside the store. I'll escort him so that anyone searching for him can get a good look. This will lure him out. Be ready, Simone," she said.

Eloise's face disappeared as the call ended, and my excitement returned. We had a plan—but before I left, I had a few more tasks to accomplish.

I put the Key in my pocket and returned to the art room. There, I grabbed a pen and a sheet of paper from Ms. Kusma's desk and wrote:

Dear Headmaster Bailes,

I accept your consequence of expulsion, and will have my personal effects removed from the premises in short order. Although I must be moving on, I appreciate the opportunities that were afforded me here at Claymoore.

Fondly,

Simone D. LaFray

P.S. Kirstin Kerns is a horrible person and should be stripped of her prefect title immediately. Documentation is forthcoming.

"Miss? Are you still here? I need to be locking up now," I heard from outside the door.

Phew! Great timing. "Okay," I replied. *Yes—I am* definitely *done here.*

I returned to my dorm as fast as I could, and slowly opened the door. The V was still asleep, snoring under the covers. Quietly, I threw my school clothes into a bag and tossed it onto my bed, then gathered my personal items and placed them carefully into my backpack. Now there was just one thing left to do.

As I slid the envelope under the headmaster's door, I knew there was no going back. There was nothing left for me here—I had found the OmniKey, and Claire was on her way home. Bailes would never know Maeve and Jilli had snuck out. And besides, I had a grand opening to get to.

I can't believe it—I'm going to be in a chandelier!

God Save the Queen

As I rounded the corner onto Sloane Street, a wave of growing excitement hit me. I had presumably just been expelled from the most prestigious preparatory school in the world, my best friend was still mad at me, and now that it was outside Claymoore, the key I was carrying was undoubtedly broadcasting a tracking signal to the Maestro. I could only hope his desire to get his son back would be stronger than his desire to get the Key—at least for now.

What a day!

Dusk moved over London, bringing with it a hint of fog. The fierce morning rain had let up, and a gentler evening drizzle had unsurprisingly been forecast—though the weather was the least of my worries. I had to admit London had grown on me, even if I'd managed to mess everything up.

I moved closer, bracing myself for the force of the crowds. Father had warned me every news outlet in the world would have reporters outside the store, waiting to interview Sugars and catch a glimpse of the Queen eating our chocolates. The opening was the talk of the town, and Sugars had made sure it would be the party of the year.

On my sixth step, I spotted the dark, unmarked van where Eloise and a small army of Ministry operatives were holding the Whisper. I had spent a lot of time in these rolling fortresses—but today, I would be in the field.

Peering down the street, I made out the top of Father's head through my fogged glasses. He was dressed to the nines in a crisp white maître's uniform with polished brass buttons—but despite his impressive presentation, he couldn't help but bounce on his toes, waving his hand over his head. "Simone! Simone!" he yelled.

I started to walk faster. *Wait a second.* Father's usually floppy locks had never even been close to perfect, but now it seemed his hair had been cut and carefully styled. As I adjusted my glasses for a better look, a section of gelled hair came loose and fell back across his face. *That's more like it.*

As I approached, he put both hands on his hips and smiled hugely. I stood in front of him for a second before he reached out and gave me a sorely needed bear hug. He could be embarrassing—but not today.

"Now let me take a proper look at you." He pulled back to take in my outfit. Since I'd left my former uniform and campus clothes behind at Claymoore, my only option had been a pair of heavily wrinkled khaki pants and a faded sweatshirt that had spent the last month balled up under my bed. "You look great!"

Only my father could think so. I looked like a frumpy stowaway on a lost boat.

"I'm so glad you're here," he said. A wry smile came over his face. "Tough day at school, huh?"

Ah. So he knew of my expulsion—but for whatever reason, he seemed to be taking an enormous amount of pride in it. In an odd way, I supposed I could understand. *How many parents can say their child was expelled from the Claymoore School?*

"Don't worry, Simone. It's going to be fine. It just so happens a few schools showed me the door in my day. You don't need them, and they were lucky to have you. Now, on to bigger and better things!" he said. He drew me into another hug and lowered his voice to a conspiratorial mumble. "Eloise said all the arrangements have been made. So, you are going to be in the chandelier, hm? That's brilliant—but be careful. The trade is supposed to happen during my presentation, and the Queen will have returned home by then. I hope this works."

He always made everything okay. My heart felt full, opened. I had been contemplating what to say to him today for some time. The new store was a source of great anxiety for me, and it was time for me to come clean.

"Father, I have to say something."

He got down on one knee to give me his complete attention. "Well, I hope it's not a surprise. I don't think my heart can take any tonight."

"No, nothing like that." I took a gulp of air, then babbled, "I really didn't want you to open this store. I wanted our lives to stay the same—but mostly, I wanted us all to be together. I don't like change, and being apart from you and Mother is the worst. Mia and Gigi too," I said.

He grabbed my hand. "Simone, you know that—"

I cut him off. "I know. But that doesn't matter now. I was wrong. This is your dream. You've always been behind me, and I want you to know that I'm behind you, one hundred percent."

He smiled back at me and gave me another hug.

"Louie! Louie!" came a shout from the store. Monsieur John was clutching a clipboard, two clerks chirping in his ears.

Father stood and pulled his jacket taut. "Sugars has a dress and a pair of shoes for you in the staff room. She's also brought in someone to do your hair and makeup. She wants us to dazzle." He pushed my hair from my face and said, "You look more and more like your mother every day."

Really? By my account, which was seconded by many, Mother was among the most beautiful women in Europe, if not the world—in no small part thanks to her unshakeable confidence. A confluence of intelligence, achievement, and strength, she had no equal, and never searched for a compliment. She didn't need to. I could only hope to be like her.

Warmth spread through me, cutting through the night's chill, and a genuine smile emerged. I missed Mother more than ever, but tonight, I was going to make her proud. I was going to bring Claire home—and capture the Maestro, too.

As I went through the security detail, a steward reminded me not to shake hands with the Queen and her entourage, nor to speak before being spoken to. Afterward, a royal surrogate made me practice my curtsy. I needed no such refresher, but it did help in shaking the cold. The attention was extravagant, but I tried to appreciate the glamour.

Sugars had acquired a pale leather McQueen ensemble for me to wear. I was in awe of the hand-painted flowers and flawless fit. The look was beautiful, but though it was an honor to wear one of his masterpieces, I still couldn't wait to get out of it. I wanted to get to my perch and get to work.

Thankfully, there was a small pocket in the skirt where I could store the Key. I wasn't about to let it out of my sight.

"Simone, dear!" yelled Sugars, spotting me from the front of the store. She looked like royalty herself, in a gold sequined gown and chignon hairdo. Photographers had circled around her, and she shooed them back as I came to greet her. "And this is the star herself, all the way from Paris—Simone LaFray!"

The flashbulbs turned to me, and I was blinded by the barrage. I lifted my hands to cover my eyes, but I was too late. I would see spots for the next two minutes and eight seconds.

"*Bonjour à tous,*" I mustered, waving.

"Isn't she magnificent! Now, let me show you all the chocolate fountain. Right this way," Sugars added, expertly deflecting the attention from me and beckoning the cameras into the heart of the store.

"Simone," I heard a familiar voice say. Monsieur John was motioning me over to the microphone. Even though we were forty-three minutes from opening, the store was packed with people making last-minute adjustments and adding more chocolate to the fountain, which would be filled to its maximum capacity of 4,107 liters of premium chocolate. Its size completed the illusion that the store was actually a fully functional chocolate factory—and in just over an hour, I would be suspended above it, hidden within the chandelier.

Monsieur John greeted me with a warm smile. "You look amazing, Simone. Would you like to adjust the microphone?"

After a quick hug, I did just that. I'd start with "Le Marseillaise"—a song I'd only sung before in school. This occasion was quite different. "God Save the Queen" would follow. I was confident in the traditional arrangement—though to be honest, I just wanted to get this over with.

I glanced at my watch. More than half an hour remained. *Well, a private warm-up couldn't hurt.*

I navigated through the crowd to the back of the bustling store, eventually meeting two of the Queen's security detail flanking the service door. I gave them a gentle nod as they opened it.

The alley behind the store offered near-ideal acoustics—well, as far as cold alleys went. *Deep breaths.* My full warm-up took eighteen minutes and eleven seconds, which flew by fast as I focused on the mission ahead.

Oops. I hit a wrong note, which scattered two doves that had been perched on a trash can. *Breathe, Simone.* The smell of chocolate wafted into the alley as a clerk came out to throw some trash in the skips. "Good luck," the man said.

With my senses now flooded with the family's chocolate, my mind was transported to 7 Rue Clodion. The patisserie I grew up in was clear in my mind—the way the floorboards creaked when I walked in, the golden glow of the late-day sun cascading through the front windows, and the jingling *clang* of the door's bell. Depending on its alignment and the force of the door, it could ring anywhere between a C and a D sharp.

My diaphragm expanded, and I began to sing a lullaby from my youth. My posture relaxed, and I felt the notes in every fiber of my being. The lyrics rolled out smoothly, and my body found a welcome ease. "Showtime."

I knocked, and the security guards opened the door. Affixing my earpiece, I walked back into the store with supreme confidence. The aroma of chocolate had reminded me that whatever the outcome of the swap, this was Father's night. I had to make it great.

The room was packed, but I could see Monsieur John standing on a stool, looking for me. He spotted me and waved frantically, mouthing, "The Queen is here! The Queen!"

I wedged my body through a sea of reporters, well-wishers, and clerks toward the front of the store. The Queen and her entourage were just meters away, and I heard Sugars welcoming her. I couldn't see more than a quarter meter ahead of me as I nudged through the crowd.

Finally, I broke through—and stumbled to my knees. A brief hush fell over the crowd.

Oh, no. Why did I have to fall?

"Well, that was quite an entrance," said the Queen.

I stood as fast as I could, dusted off my knees, and gave a proper curtsy. "Y-your Majesty!" I fumbled out.

She smiled at me and took a confident step closer. "So you are the talented young lady that has the world by the tail?"

"Yes, your Majesty. It's a pleasure to have you in our store," I replied.

"Well, it's a beautiful store, dear—and we are so glad to have you here in London."

The Queen turned to the reporters, and their cameras' flashbulbs exploded to capture an image of the two of us together. The photos would later be printed in the papers— the Queen looking poised as always, and me standing beside her like a confused tourist.

The party made its way to the front door, where a bright yellow ribbon had been strung for the ceremonial cutting. The crowd once again consumed me, pushing me away from the Queen. I found another stool and tried to see over the masses, and managed to spot the top of Father's hat and Sugars' rather prominent hairdo, but not the Queen.

The flashbulbs went off again, and a roar went up from the crowd. I could tell from the rotation of Father's hat that he was looking for me, but this was his moment—and besides, I needed to get to the microphone.

Keep it together, Simone. Sing the songs, and then get into position.

The flashbulbs continued for another minute before Sugars directed everyone to turn and form an audience for my performance. I stood at the microphone next to the chocolate basin, counting down the seconds. As a small space opened in front of me, my mind returned to Paris. *You can do this. It's just like singing to the rats in the subway. Just breathe.*

With all eyes on me, I took a deep breath, pictured Mother, and gazed out at the crowd. The notes leaped from my mouth. My tone was clear, and my breathing even and true. For the next minute and eight seconds, I captivated the crowd, catching the voices of Father and Monsieur John singing "*Marchons, Marchons*" amid the guests. As I ended my song, a shower of applause rained down around me.

Eeeek! went my earpiece, briefly startling me.

"Everything is in place, dear," Eloise whispered. I tapped the face of my spywatch twice to acknowledge the message and re-adopted my stance for the next song.

As expected, "God Save the Queen" was nothing short of a showstopper. To match the celebratory mood of the evening, most of those in attendance started to sing after the fourth line, and the atmosphere soon began to feel more like that of a pub than a patisserie. This time, when I hit the last note, raucous applause erupted as several Union Jacks and French Tricolors unfolded from the rafters, releasing a deluge of confetti onto those standing below. In the commotion, Father stepped forward, beaming proudly, and I opened my arms to receive him. He gave me a proper hug and kissed both my cheeks, and at that moment, the world felt right again.

I had done it.

But the night wasn't over. I stepped away from the microphone as Father knelt to give me another hug.

"I've got to get changed. I'll see you later," I whispered. He nodded back, the smile never leaving his face.

The attention turned from me as an army of servers appeared from the back room, carrying silver trays towering with sweets— fresh macarons, truffles, chocolates, and calissons. The crowd pounced on the delicacies. It was the perfect distraction, and I bee-lined to the staff room.

Someone had moved my dress bag from a heap in the hallway and hung it on a row of hooks meant for aprons. As I stepped closer, I noticed an envelope pinned to the front. It read:

> Simone,
> I felt confident you would not disappoint.
>
> > Best,
> >
> > Sugars
>
> P.S.: The dress is yours, and the shoes too.

I changed quickly, zipped up the bag, and smoothed out the

front. My dress was beautiful, but I was far more comfortable in my surveillance clothes. The pants had four zippered pockets, so the Key would be secure as I shimmied down the chandelier.

Moving upstairs was a challenge with so many people moving about, but I slipped through gaps and between knees. In less than four minutes, I scaled the steps to the attic. My flashlight found the trapdoor, and I gently opened it to gaze down at the crowd.

I tugged lightly on the ceiling anchor, testing the sturdiness of the candy chandelier. Even as late as yesterday, the builders had been having issues balancing the weight of the enormous fixture as Sugars added more and more embellishments. The exact weight of the final product was impossible to determine at this stage, but by my calculations, I would be just fine.

I grabbed the chain and dropped my legs down, crossing my feet over the links. It held. Slowly, I inched down and took my spot within the sugary sculpture. The seat was small and uncomfortable, and I had to sit cross-legged. I was now cocooned within a menagerie of vibrantly colored sweets thick as a hedge—completely hidden. The sweet smell was intoxicating, and none of the three hundred and eight visitors below knew that a twelve-year-old was suspended nine meters above them. *Here we go.*

"I'm in place," I whispered into my watch.

I was just in time to see the Queen leaving. Sugars and Father thanked her for coming, and two full minutes of pleasantries were exchanged as flashbulbs once again erupted. Then, with a proud flourish, Father opened the grand double doors.

The Queen turned to address the crowd one last time. She gave a wave, smiled, and made her exit, to thunderous applause. Sugars flashed Father an ecstatic smile as he closed the doors behind her entourage.

Phew. That was one big distraction done with. *Time to go to work.*

If the swap went as planned, Eloise and the Whisper would enter the room in twenty minutes. Once the Maestro had eyes on his son, he would be given half an hour to release Claire. If Claire didn't arrive within thirty minutes, the mission would be aborted, and we would go home empty-handed. It was a game of chicken—but even the simplest games could go wrong.

For the next twelve minutes, I surveilled the room with absolute focus. My perch was becoming even more uncomfortable as I wiggled to find the right spot—but the view was excellent. Guests mingled, and the staff moved efficiently in and out of the kitchen. Sugars and Father worked the room, taking every photo opportunity that arose. The lights pulsed with a warm, almost buttery glow. Suspended above it all, I relished every second. I was like a ghost in the room: observing everything without needing to interact. It was perfect.

Well—aside from the V's absence. No matter where I looked, I didn't spot her in the crowd. I couldn't believe she'd missed the opening, and couldn't help but feel responsible—even if it had been her choice.

"Simone, we are about to exit the van. The Queen and her entourage are now eight minutes away, and seem to have had a lovely evening," Eloise allowed. Then her tone grew grim. "Remember, the Maestro will not be working alone, so we need to make sure everyone in the room is accounted for. We have not ruled out any last-minute stunts."

"Yes, I know," I replied. "Eloise?"

"What is it? Is something wrong?"

"No, nothing. I just wanted to say thank you," I said.

"Thank you? For what?"

"For having faith in me. I'm not going to let you down."

She waited a moment before responding. "I know, dear. I know. Get ready. We're coming in." And my watch went dark.

Right on schedule, Father started a chocolate demonstration in the grandiose pastry kitchen. I'd watched him extol the virtues of chocolate all my life, and knew how good he was at it. For the next thirty minutes, all eyes were sure to be fixed on him. No one would notice another person entering the room. It was the perfect time for the swap.

Father took his place behind an enormous marble island. "*Dames, messieurs, garçons,* and *filles* of all ages! Your attention please, and welcome once again to the magnificent LaFray's!" He raised an oversized whisk and a metal spoon over his head, and the crowd applauded. *Very nice.*

This distraction also made it much easier for me to examine the crowd. I launched into the same sequence I'd followed in Vienna: left to right, three over, one up, one down, two back, repeat, over and over until the whole room checked out. No sign of Claire.

As I watched, Eloise entered, arm in arm with the Whisper. They were both dressed appropriately—Eloise in a green dress and sparkling drop earrings equipped with microphones like the ones I'd worn at the opera house; the Whisper in a charcoal suit—and they easily passed as partygoers in the crowd. Indeed, they fit in so well, it took me three seconds to see the discreet black handcuffs binding the Whisper to Eloise.

Thirty minutes.

I started counting them down. *Twenty-nine. Twenty-eight.* The mood was becoming raucous as the champagne flowed. The volume of the room had risen twenty decibels since the Queen and her detail had left. *Nineteen. Eighteen.* It was easy to follow Eloise as she moved through the crowd. She was working the middle of the room and avoiding the sides. If the Maestro had a lookout or camera in the room, he'd know his son was here.

Seven. Six. I checked my watch. *Less than five minutes left. Where are you, Claire?*

Just then, the lights dimmed. This was it. *Focus, Simone!*

My spywatch came to life. "Simone! An agent has reported an unknown girl in the crowd. Can you confirm?" Eloise's voice was frantic and hopeful.

I hastily scanned every meter of the store. "No, I don't—wait." I could barely see a new silhouette standing behind a licorice display in the far corner. I needed to move over to get a better look.

"Is it her, Simone? Is it Claire?"

"I don't know. I'm trying to see." I leaned over as far as I could to catch a glimpse—and as I did, a *crack!* came from above.

Oh, no!

The chandelier cable was starting to give way. With each passing second, the wires were fraying. But I still couldn't see.

Just a little more—

The figure moved back a few centimeters behind the column, but it had to be Claire. It had to be!

Tink! Tink! Tink! The coupling of the chain and the anchor was coming apart at an accelerating pace. This was bad, very bad.

Just one . . . more . . .

Too late.

The chain broke away—and below me was a sea of chocolate.

My heart dropped as gravity transformed the sugary chandelier into a 72.4-kilogram meteor. *Brace yourself, Simone, you're coming in hot!*

I hit the chocolate basin dead center. The chandelier exploded on impact, and liters of liquid chocolate splashed over the crowd like a tidal wave. Colorful sugared embellishments shattered like ceramic, rocketing in all directions as everything, including the enormous windows, was covered in chocolate and candy.

I was bruised all over, and my ears rang. As I peeked over the rim of the now empty fountain, the results of the decadent explosion became clear. Most of the crowd was frozen in place, soaked and silent; but a few were beginning to wipe their eyes and faces. I felt for the Key in my pocket, and was relieved to feel its smooth metal sides. *I have to get out of here!*

I ducked beneath the lip of the basin again and made my way to the back to jump out, away from the dazed crowd. Dripping milk chocolate from head to toe and nursing my bruises, I dashed behind a display of hard candy, where I wiped off my face and glasses and scanned the chocolate-soaked assembly. Some were starting to laugh, and others stood still stunned.

Slowly, any lingering embarrassment faded, and the laughter grew. Sugars seized on the opportunity. She lit a cigarette and stood triumphant, bathed in chocolate, with candy fragments all through her hair.

"Now, that's an opening!" she yelled.

I wiped the face of my watch, knowing Eloise would be on the line in a matter of seconds. Not only was the store now covered in chocolate, there was no Claire. The mission was a failure.

Sure enough, in the next five seconds, Eloise buzzed in.

"What happened?" she demanded. "Did you see him?"

Him? I was so stunned myself, I couldn't understand what she meant. "You mean Claire? No, I didn't see her," I replied. At that very moment, I caught another glimpse of the figure I'd thought was her. The height and shape were right, even the hair color—but this lady was in her early twenties. *Oh, no!* It wasn't her after all—just a guest. My heart plummeted like the chandelier.

"This was a complete failure. Oh, I'm a mess. My hair! I'll have to clean up. Meet in the truck in five minutes," Eloise instructed. Even through the static of the radio, her disappointment was palpable.

Equally dejected, I mustered up a solemn reply. "Yes, I know. I'll clean myself up and be out shortly." The hollowness in my chest was almost as painful as the new bruises welling up under my shins. I'd been so sure we were going to find Claire. I couldn't imagine how Eloise must be feeling. Even handing over the Key couldn't possibly be enough to make up for this loss.

Father spotted me and weaved toward me through the crowd of stunned onlookers. His perfect hair was matted with sugar, and a streak of chocolate decorated his forehead. "Simone!" he yelled. "Are you alright, dear? Are you hurt? Wow! That was quite a ride."

"I'm okay—maybe a bruise or two, but I'm fine," I said. "I'm so sorry—I ruined everything! The store, the mission—it's all my fault."

"Oh, no, dear, no! It's not your fault. Sugars kept adding to the chandelier. None of this is your fault—and besides, they'll be talking about this opening for years." He smiled with an ease I hadn't seen since the Chocolatiers' Ball. The pressure was off. "Besides, after we wrap this up, I'll be on the plane with you, and we'll be in Paris by dawn. We're going home, Simone." He placed both of his hands on my shoulders and gave me a wink.

"*Home*," I murmured—but the sting of losing my friends, getting expelled, and failing to return Claire still lingered.

Father reached behind his back and handed me a bag full of chocolate-soaked paper towels. "Do you mind throwing this in one of the skips out back, dear? If we don't get started right away, we'll be cleaning up chocolate for days," he added with a laugh.

Wordlessly, I took the bag. He was right—if it was allowed to set, all this chocolate would become much harder to clean up. *Well, might as well do something productive.*

Still drenched myself, I opened the back door and was met with a gust of frigid wind. The temperature had dropped four degrees, and the air was moist and thick. I pulled the door closed so as not to let in the cold, and walked forward with purpose—only to hear a matching set of footsteps echoing mine.

Someone was out here.

"Finally. I've been waiting for you since the show started."

A figure peeled away from the darkness and came into the light. I didn't recognize him at first, but the thick German accent was unmistakable. *The Maestro!*

I dropped the trash bag and reached for my watch.

The Maestro held up a small black device. "Ah, ah. I'll be taking my key now—and don't bother with that watch," he said. "It won't do you any good—I've jammed it. Besides, we need to get going."

Going? "I'm not going anywhere with you!" I barked back at him.

He seemed unexpectedly surprised. "You know who I am?" he asked.

I ignored him. This was my chance! "Where is Claire Pilfrey?"

The Maestro gave me an odd look.

"How should I know? Who is this Claire?" he replied. Then recognition dawned in his eyes. "Ah—you must mean Eloise Pilfrey's daughter."

'How should I know'? What is he playing at? "Of course I do! Don't pretend you don't know! You kidnapped her two months ago and—"

The Maestro interrupted, his voice curt and agitated as he stepped forward. "Little girl, I don't know what you're talking about, but I can assure you I have no idea where this Claire is. Perhaps you should ask Eloise." He pulled out a digital storage device. "I'm here to trade *this* with your beloved Ministry. But as luck would have it, you, Miss LaFray, have found my Key—my greatest invention. A remarkable device, don't you think? Challenging to build, one of a kind. However, I trusted it to the wrong person."

His words confused me, but I knew one thing: *He's not taking me anywhere.*

"Of course, he was ultimately right, which is of grave concern—but he didn't have to steal it and hide it away at that school. A slippery fellow, that Fox."

My heart nearly stopped. *The Fox and the Maestro were working together?* Of course. I'd half suspected it, ever since I'd learned he was at Claymoore. But—

Right about what? And why would the Fox steal the Key, if he and the Maestro were working together?

But I didn't have time to ponder. The Maestro moved closer, eyes narrowing. "You are the one who lured in my son back in Vienna. Very clever—but now the tables have turned. Not only have you returned my Key, but here you are—a bargaining chip to bring Felix home."

He started toward me. I steeled myself to run—and then a welcome voice broke through the night air.

"Everything okay, Frenchy?" Maeve asked, walking out of the shadows. Jilli and the V followed behind.

My heart swelled. My friends had come for me!

Maeve glanced at the Maestro. "Who's your friend?"

"We've been looking for you, Simone. Are you okay? Word on the street is something exploded," Jilli added. She stepped forward, joining me at my side.

The V stepped toward me, and reached down to squeeze my hand.

"Geez, Simone. I know your dad's a chocolatier, but maybe a little less chocolate next time?" she said, taking in my ruined clothes. I was so glad to see her, I didn't even care that she was making fun of me.

"I thought you weren't coming," I said.

"What—and miss the Queen? Are you crazy?" the V asked. "I was basically waiting outside the entire time. Turns out Maeve and Jilli were, too." She glanced at them. "When we saw each other and heard what happened, we figured, well, safety in numbers. After all, Wolves travel in packs." She winked.

"You girls need to move along. This is none of your business," the Maestro ordered; but I saw the hesitation in his eyes. "Go back inside and bring your friend some towels. Can't you see she's a mess?"

Maeve moved behind me and placed her hand on my shoulder. "I don't think so. You see, us Wolves gotta stick together."

The night went still, and I felt I grew a meter in height as I fed off the energy of my friends. All the anger, all the disappointment, all the fire welled up inside and galvanized. At that moment, I was invincible. I was my mother's daughter, and I was back.

Maeve leaned forward, and a shiver of recollection passed over me as she whispered, "Show him what you got."

"Enough of this! You're coming with me, Simone!"

The Maestro lurched forward, and I grabbed his right arm, deflecting his hands as he lunged at me. With an upward thrust, I tucked my shoulder into his chest and pulled.

I drove him down to the cold cobblestone—*umph!*—and all the air left his lungs.

"Get him!" yelled Maeve, and my three companions pounced. Fists and feet flew every which way. The Maestro didn't stand a chance.

"They're out here!" came a voice.

Four agents burst through the door, with an elated Eloise behind them.

"We got him! We got him!" she shouted into her mobile. *Who is she talking to?* Claire was nowhere to be seen—but Eloise laughed in delight, as if it was all over. *What?*

"Maybe I could get used to this spy stuff," said a proud V. She was sitting on the Maestro's back and attempting a selfie. "Sit still, would ya?" she said to him.

"Okay, girls, we'll take it from here," said an agent. Together, they pulled the Maestro off the ground.

"No! You have no idea what they are capable of—what they have done. They're coming back, and they must be stopped!" the Maestro yelled as two agents led him down the alley into a waiting van.

What? Who's coming back?

Maeve pulled me aside, away from the gathering crowd.

"The V told me you cleared out your dormitory back at Claymoore," she said. "I take it that means you're expelled?"

I nodded. "I never really got an official pronouncement, but sort of did it myself, in a letter. So maybe it's more like I quit?"

Maeve looked at me with that combination of pride and respect I had come to value so much. "Thanks for not ratting us out. Jilli and I need to stay at Claymoore—at least for another year or two."

What? Why?

Maeve's demeanor shifted. "You know what I'm talking about, right? You know. You're one of us."

I slowed these words as they entered my ears and remembered all the entanglements being one of *them* created. Did I want to be one of them? *What if Eloise finds out and I have to leave the Ministry? Am I sure about this?* But as I looked into Maeve's eyes, I knew: I had to see it through.

Yes.

Maeve put her arm around Jilli, and they smiled in unison at me. They were my friends. "Yeah," I replied, "I think so."

Maeve stared deep into my eyes. "I don't think you do—but maybe by the end of the night, you will. Someone wants to meet you tonight, Simone. In the South Tower of the bridge, the one by Potters Fields Park. You'll find him there. He's waiting for you."

I stood there, oblivious to what was unfolding around me as a flurry of agents escorted the Maestro away. The world held its breath, and a spark of excitement shot through me.

"*La Volpe Rossa,*" I whispered, and Maeve nodded back.

A New Light

A throbbing blister was forming on my left heel as I rushed down Tooley Street. The night had turned a few degrees colder, and a steady breeze settled in. London was battening down the hatches in preparation for a deep freeze, and I was covered in hardening chocolate, hoping that the answers I sought would be waiting for me at Tower Bridge, only two streets away.

My thoughts spun out of control, and my body was sleepy and spent. Belatedly, I realized I'd rushed off so quickly, I'd forgotten to give Eloise the Key. In a brief moment of panic, I reached down to feel for it in my pocket. My fingers found its hard edge, and I exhaled a cloudy sigh of relief into the freezing air. *Still there.*

As I reached the base of the South Tower and stopped to catch my breath, I looked up to take in the forbidding stone walls. It occurred to me that this was a dreadful place for the Fox to want to meet me. If he really was up there, he'd be trapped with no way out, and Eloise just minutes away. He had to know that—but perhaps he was the one setting a trap.

Taking one last breath to clear my head, I stepped inside.

The entryway was as cold as the outside, and dimly lit. I looked up the curving stairwell. The ascent would be grueling, but I couldn't turn back now.

My calves were screaming by the time I reached the top of the tower. There was only one door between us now.

This is it.

I put my hand on the wooden door. It was even heavier than I'd expected, but I managed to push it open. *Oomph!*

The small room within was dim and cold. One of the six windows was thrown wide to welcome the frigid night air. To the right of me, I made out a few chairs and a desk.

"Rough night?" The words emanated from the far corner, syrupy and refined, without pretense or empathy.

The Fox stepped out of the darkness, dressed in a herringbone suit fit for a king. His tie was perfectly knotted, and his shoes shone in the moonlight—a picture-perfect presentation in stark contrast to my chocolate-soaked and now partially frozen outfit. His hair was coiffed, not a single strand out of place—but the color was even more vibrant than it was in my memories. Red, blazing red.

He gazed at me with a peculiar expression that almost suggested a sense of pride. Something about his face was familiar to me: the gentle slope of his nose, the corners of his eyes. I memorized every millimeter of him.

He moved to peer out the open window. Time was short. We both knew it.

"If the reports are accurate, the Maestro is now in custody, and Sugars Fontaine has a lot of cleaning to do," the Fox began with a laugh. He seemed somehow amused, as if all of this had been a delightful game. "The Maestro—not a bad chap. Perhaps a little misunderstood."

I sucked in cold air and tried to catch my breath. I'd gone over what I was going to say to him a hundred times on the trip over—but now, with him right there, no more than four meters in front of me, I found myself tongue-tied.

I managed to get my voice to work. "Where is Claire Pilfrey? And why were you and Maestro working together?"

"Why, Miss LaFray! What an accusation. As you know, we may not have much time. I thought you would want to discuss something more *meaningful*. Something far more interesting," he replied, stepping away from the window. I noticed him glance at my watch as he took a step closer. "I presume you have the Key?"

A jolt went through me, and I fought not to let it show. "Why did you steal it from him?" I said carefully, trying to keep my tone level.

But his eyes lit up anyway, as if he saw right through me. "You *do* have it. Magnificent, isn't it? The key to any computer or server in the world. The Maestro had been working on it for years, and finally finished it about a year ago. He was gloating about it for weeks. Beyond the compulsion to see it for myself, I needed to confirm something I had been fearing for some time. Something horrible that—"

He was trying to distract me. I cut him off. "*Where is Claire Pilfrey!?*"

He recoiled, but recovered quickly. "She's fine now. A good girl, that Claire."

'*Good girl*'? The words were familiar. *The message in the storage room—it wasn't for me. It was for Claire!*

"I had to rescue her from a particularly untenable situation," the Fox continued. "As I'd feared, she was next. It took me months to find her, but nobody on this Earth can hide from me—nor hide anyone from me. In any case, she's safe, and very sound. In fact, she's just sixty meters that way, in the North Tower, waiting for her mother to retrieve her."

"What?" I didn't understand. He had to be lying. "Why did you take her? What were you doing with her?!"

He let out a theatrical gasp. "Why, dear, I've already told you— she was *taken*. Taken by the worst lot of people. Of course I had to rescue her. You'll be finding out about them soon enough. Too soon, I'm afraid." He paused, shaking his head with a faint smile. "Did you really think *I* took Claire? Is that what Eloise told you?" His gaze dropped, and I barely heard his words: "Well, that does make sense now. What a pity."

I could hardly believe his audacity. "Of course you took her! You were her teacher, and you—"

"On the contrary. Claire Pilfrey was on a, let's say, *highly classified* assignment with the most unsavory lot on the planet. Eloise was fully aware of where she was, who she was with, and what she was doing the whole time." He hesitated, and a whiff of his cologne filled my chocolate-washed nostrils. The combination was hideous.

"I, however, couldn't bear to have her in their clutches. We'd thought they were gone, but . . ." He paused, then seemed to think better of something, and abruptly changed the subject. "Your painting on that bus was magnificent. Really elevated Miss Stahl's work, don't you think? Oh, she has a unique talent, to be sure—but you, you are the real prize." He shot me a look laced with sudden concern. "How are you, dear? Where is your mind these days? How is your mother?"

The mention of Mother stoked rage in me. I took another step toward him.

"My mother has nothing to do with this. She's home and—"

"And I'm sure Eloise preferred it that way! Don't you understand yet? This was all just a big distraction, Simone! You were the bait! Bait in a most dangerous game."

"What are you talking about? I'm not *bait*." I paused to collect myself. I couldn't let him rile me—there was no telling what he was capable of.

But the Fox just laughed. "I'm afraid you were. She played you like a Stradivarius, Simone. She's ruthless. Had she known your mentor's real motive in sending you to Claymoore, Julia would have never allowed you to go—hence the misdirection. She was betting on your mother's compassion."

Julia—Mother. I latched onto it. "What do you know about my mother?"

He stood stoic as the night breeze ruffled his hair. "The Maestro has some very *unflattering* information about the esteemed Eloise Pilfrey—information that would not only end a decorated career, but bring shame to *la Republique*. That Key you are holding supplied this information—and if she gets her hands on it, she can cover all her tracks, erase everything. She knew where Claire was all along—so she created this ruse to place you at Claymoore, find the Key, and draw the Maestro out at the same time. I'm sure her performance was Oscar-worthy—*longing for her missing daughter*. Of course she knew the Maestro would come for you. You aided in the apprehension of his son in Vienna, and the Maestro was not going to let that go. You were dangled in London like a worm on a hook."

My blood started to boil at his words. Without thinking, I unzipped my pocket and pulled out the OmniKey. *Was my life worth this? This thing?* I stared at it in my hand, emotionless.

A grin slowly spread over the Fox's face.

"Yes. The truth is, dear, Eloise used you; and you certainly did not disappoint. You got rid of her problem—and I'm guessing that after her interrogation of the Maestro, a charge for the kidnapping of one Miss Claire Pilfrey will surface, along with at least twelve other crimes. No one has compassion for a kidnapper. They're reviled. It's all very clever on her part. Not only did she capture him, now she's going to frame him and send him away for the rest of his life. And to place the cherry on top, you found the Key, and with that in her possession, all her dirty secrets will be washed away. A pretty tidy ending for Eloise—don't you think?"

I processed every word, running through the possibilities. *It can't be.* "You're a thief and a liar. I don't believe a word you say. Eloise is my friend, and Mother—"

"Eloise and your mother are nothing alike. Know that," he interjected firmly, his tone abruptly serious.

"You don't know my mother! She helped try to catch you at the—"

"Oh, dear, no. Your mother had no intention of catching me at the Musée d'Orsay. In time, this will all make sense to you, but trust me, nothing about that day was as it seemed. It all had to be done that way. We had no alternative."

"What are you talking about?" I shook my head. "Just more lies. You can't know my mother!"

"Wrong again, I'm afraid! Your mother and I have a rather, let's just say—*special* relationship. At the time, we were trying to communicate under less than ideal circumstances, and the painting was the only way. Your mother wanted to send me a message, and I had to get it." For the first time, his bravado faded. "This whole time, it was hiding right under your own nose—or rather, on the back of a canvas. *Blue No. 2* has an under-canvas, just like the painting I left back at Claymoore—and everything you need to know, everything you want to know, is written on it. In a letter, from your mother to me."

No. He's lying. Mother would never communicate with the Fox—and even if she did, she wouldn't hide it from me!

"As you know, I once again have old *Blue* in my possession. Yes, stored away in a most secure spot—and only I have the combination. But I realize now that you need to see it—see it in her own handwriting. When you see the message, you will know what to do. The painting and letter behind it will steer you to your new path, Simone."

My anger flared again. "You're lying again. You could paint anything and send it to me. You could paint anything to—"

Crash!

The heavy doors almost flew off their hinges under the force of an array of agents, flanking—

"*You!*" screamed an enraged Eloise.

I turned so fast, my chocolate-covered glasses flew off and slid across the floor.

"Step away from him, Simone. You have no idea how dangerous this—this filth is," Eloise said as the agents fanned out across the room. "He would think nothing of taking you. Back away and let us do our jobs."

Instinctively, I obeyed, retreating from the Fox. A glimmer of metal flashed from my clenched hand. Eloise glanced down—and suddenly, her expression turned to joy.

"The Key! You have the Key! Simone, you've done it!"

My heart felt like it was beating out of my chest. A gust of cold night air whipped through the room, and I began to feel queasy. My knees trembled, and my vision blurred, then faded. *What is happening?*

Time seemed to unfurl in slow motion. Sight, sound, hearing, all dimmed—but in that moment, free of all physical sensation, I sensed something overwhelming. Something that needed no analysis or interpretation, something so unmistakably clear that my other senses weren't necessary to observing its truth. Then it was gone, and the gravity of moment returned.

But the Fox had noticed. Before I could react, reeling, he sprang forward and grabbed my shoulders. "What did you see? What did you see, Simone?!"

The agents froze, apparently unsure whether I was being taken hostage. But I knew he wouldn't do that. In fact, it was now clear to me—perfectly clear—that every word from his mouth had been the truth.

I could not muster a word. The Key slid out of my hand and dropped to the floor with a *clink.*

But the Red Fox paid it no mind. Instead, he knelt and whispered, "Simone. *Remember what I said about the painting.*"

In the next instant, the agents lunged. One of their elbows

clipped my back, and my shoe, still covered in hardened chocolate, slipped out from under me. My trance was broken as I found myself falling. I tried to catch myself, but there was nothing to grab.

The last thing I saw before my head hit the ground was the Red Fox vaulting out the window, fifty-five meters down into the frigid Thames.

———————

By the time the *Licorice Whip Quatre* landed in Paris at precisely 8:42 the next morning, all the newspapers and online outlets had picked up the story, flashing headlines like "Ministry Captures Cyberterrorist," "Kidnapped Girl Returned!" and "World's Greatest Thief Plummets to His Death."

Claire was found in the North Tower without a scratch on her, but was taken to the hospital for observation anyway. Eloise was beyond excited at having her daughter returned and the OmniKey in hand. It all worked out for her—exactly as the Fox predicted. I was happy Claire was back safe and sound, but I could not help but feel a growing distance from Eloise. She sent me a text as the airplane took off. "Great job, Simone!" it said. "You did it!" But her words rang hollow.

As our plane taxied toward the private terminal, I saw Mother on the tarmac, standing in front of a Ministry car. I grabbed my bag and ran to the front. Mark opened the door and my ears popped, but all I cared about was mother, just a few meters away. As soon as the stairwell was secured, I ran down it and into her waiting arms.

"I missed you, bug," she said. She hadn't called me that in years. Tears started to well as I absorbed the scent of her clothes and faint smell of coffee on her skin. I was home.

"I'm so proud of you," she added. She grabbed my bag off the ground and put her arm over my shoulder. "Let's go home."

As the car pulled away down Rue Clodion, my head ached, and my heart reached out for the Fox. Everything he had told me was coming true—but he was gone, presumed dead. Though his body hadn't been found, a Gieves and Hawkes herringbone suit had washed up on the west bank of the Isle of Dogs an hour before we landed. Even after everything that had happened, the news shook me more than I cared to admit. As impossible as it seemed that he could have survived that fall, it seemed equally impossible that he could be dead.

And what about Blue No. 2*?* If he was dead, the painting would be lost forever. A thief of his caliber would have sealed it away somewhere safe.

The next day, Mother and I went to the Ministry for the debriefing, which lasted more than four hours. Although Eloise was still in London, she texted me four more times conveying her appreciation, and we videochatted once. I had only one request of her in the wake of my achievement, and though it initially met some resistance, she ultimately granted it to me.

Mother, Monsieur Leon, and I went over the mission in exhaustive detail, and the fallout was exactly what the Red Fox had foretold: the Maestro was being charged with kidnapping and a series of other high crimes. In all likelihood, he would never set foot outside a prison for the rest of his life.

Claire had offered a harrowing story about being abducted and forced to perform a series of physical and mental tests by an unnamed group of captors. The authorities assumed they were the associates of the Maestro, which further sealed his fate. She was set to be released from the hospital later that day, although Eloise planned to keep her in London. Strangely, her file never mentioned her rescue by the Fox.

Agents questioned me about my time with the redheaded thief—but given what I'd heard, I wasn't about to tell them everything. Instead, I offered foggy details of a stressful conversation that had ended with me knocked out on the floor. I was consistent in my fabricated account, and Ministry agents had no reason to doubt me. His words, and the identities of the Red Wolves, were safe with me for now. Somehow, I had the feeling Harper would approve.

In fact, soon after I'd finished the briefing with Eloise, Junior Agent #4 had sent me a congratulatory text: "Nicely done. I wish I could've seen it! Sorry I couldn't be there this time—but I look forward to working with you in the future – H." Her words were the best I could have hoped for from the Ministry—and her timing was, of course, perfect.

As for the OmniKey, it would remain with the Ministry for now, though its ultimate fate was as yet undetermined. The existence of such an influential item made many in power understandably nervous, and I didn't doubt they all wanted a say in what would happen to it.

I spent the next few days resting and contemplating the last several weeks. The whirlwind of emotion had left me exhausted. Technically, we'd accomplished our mission: Claire was found unharmed, I'd located the OmniKey, and the Maestro was in jail. But I felt no joy. For me, this case was far from over.

There was one bright spot in my dreary solitude. Jilli and the V videochatted with me every day, and though she didn't join them, even Maeve occasionally made contact, always ending each of her rare text messages the same way: "Miss you, Frenchy." Whenever I received one, I couldn't help but smile. They were my friends—all of them—and I was sure we would meet again.

A few days later, I woke to a dull winter morning's light washing through my blinds. Gigi rolled over with a wide yawn, curling up against me. She had been sleeping in my bed ever since my return from Claymoore.

"Knock, knock." Mother cracked the door open. She carried two fresh cups of chamomile tea on a tray, and an old Advent calendar Aunt Emma had given to me on my third Christmas. It was my favorite.

"Feeling better?" she asked, setting the tray on my nightstand. I nodded. "I'm sure you have lots of questions. I don't know if I have all the answers, but there is something else we need to talk about first."

Mother hung the calendar on the back of my door. Then she came to the bed, brushed the hair out of my face, and sat beside me. Her ease filled every corner of the room.

"Life is moving very fast these days, isn't it? One moment we're sweeping up the store and walking the dog, and the next we're defusing bombs, catching thieves, or saving the world." She let out a small laugh. "This is our life, Simone. Our priorities are clear— although family is always first, always." She took a sip of tea and returned her cup on my nightstand.

"I know I haven't been myself, and I'm sure you have concerns about that too." My heart fluttered, and I braced myself for one of those grown-up moments. *Please let things be alright—I can't take any more bad news.*

"Simone, I'm pregnant. You're going to have a baby brother."

Pregnant? Of course! That explained everything: Mother's fatigue, her absence from the field. It made perfect sense. *Why didn't I think of that?*

"There were some complications, but everything's fine now. He's due right around your birthday, so I'll be spending a lot of time at home." Mother looked at me questioningly, and for a moment, I was reminded of Father's hopeful look as he searched for my approval before the opening of the new LaFray's. "Well? What do you think?"

For the first time in months, a deep tension had lifted from my shoulders as memories of recent unpleasantness evaporated. *A baby brother.*

"That's the best Christmas gift ever," I replied.

For the next thirty minutes, Mother held my hand as she went on about the morning sickness and trials of pregnancy. I didn't mind—in fact, I relished every second. At last, joy had returned to 7 Rue Clodion.

Over breakfast, Mia recited her Christmas wish list and reminded us all that her holiday performance was only three days away. But she couldn't hold her excitement about being a big sister. "Can you believe we're going to have a little brother? I think we should name him Leonardo."

"Hmm. Doesn't quite sound right, does it?" Mother replied. "We have plenty of time to pick a name. Something strong."

"I was thinking Louie Junior," interjected Father. We all turned and looked at him, holding back smiles. "What?" he replied cheekily.

He turned to face me, his tone changing from comical to serious. "So, Simone—the store is decorated, but we need to have things in order for the big week. You know how the holidays are. Tris must have over a hundred orders already—though it's nothing compared to the demand in London."

I grinned. In fact, our store in London had sold out every day since the opening, and the news of the chocolate bomb had become something of folklore. Ever the opportunist, Sugars was thrilled at the publicity, and had already started to run advertisements with the tagline *LaFray's—Experience the Wonder!* It worked: her timetable moved up, and she'd already planned for new stores to open in Rome, Madrid, and Amsterdam. The coming year would be like no other for the LaFray family.

I rose from the table. "Well, I better get started. It sounds like we have a lot of work ahead of us."

"I'll be down in a little bit. I need to finish breakfast and clean up first," Father said. He took another bite of his eggs and sipped his coffee.

Reinvigorated by the news of my baby brother, I made the walk down the back stairs with my backpack, looking forward to a few hours of mindless sweeping and cleaning. When I got to the kitchen, I snapped on the lights. My familiar apron hung right where it always had—second peg from the left. I tossed the loop over my head and grasped the ties to pull them tight. Both were badly frayed, with just enough fabric left to wrap around me and tie a slouching bow in the front.

My mobile buzzed. It was Jilli and Maeve, requesting a video call. I swiped the screen to answer.

"There you are, Frenchy," Maeve said. Their heads barely fit in the frame.

"We miss you! How are things in Paris?" Jilli asked.

"Good! Things here are good. Just working in the store," I replied.

"I brought Maeve home with me for the holidays! She *loves* the country," Jilli said, her tone laden with good-natured sarcasm. Maeve rolled her eyes. Then their faces turned serious, and Maeve leaned forward.

"They haven't found him yet. You know—*him*. There are police and agents all over the river looking for him. A few even came to Claymoore to talk to Bailes."

"Yes, that's what I heard. No sign of his body anywhere. You didn't talk to any agents, did you?" I asked.

"No! Of course not. We're too smart to get caught. We have to stick together on this," she replied.

The girls looked at each other as sadness crept over their faces.

"I just can't believe it. I can't believe he's gone," Maeve added.

"You didn't see anything?" asked Jilli.

"No. One second he was standing there, and the next, he was gone."

Almost a minute passed in silence.

"Well, we can't just sit around and feel sorry for ourselves. There's still work to do. He would've wanted it that way." Maeve nodded. "Take care, Frenchy—and Happy Christmas."

"Happy Christmas. I'll text you later," I added.

As the screen went dark, my thoughts drifted back to the mission. I longed for the thread that tied it all together—Eloise, Claire, and especially the Fox. I still wasn't sure how to feel about him. If he was truly gone, I had only his last words to me to go on—which meant I would have to find *Blue No. 2*. But where had he stashed it? And what would I discover if I found it?

I recalled the Fox's words about Mother, and his claims that they had communicated. I wanted her confirmation so badly—but I couldn't ask her now. Mother was pregnant and happy, and with me home, the family was safely together again. Her world was perfect, and I couldn't do anything to upset that.

Pushing these thoughts from my head, I took a deep breath and gazed around the store. This was the LaFray's I loved—everything cozy and familiar, with no impulse items and no chocolate fountain. Christmas made it even better, with the addition of a large gingerbread house on the counter, a tree in the corner, and red ribbons adorning the ovens. I breathed it all in.

Tap, tap. A knocking sounded at the front of the store. The V was peering in through the frosted glass, her hands cupping her eyes. Her time at Claymoore had ended two days ago, on the heels of a successful finals week. She'd even made the honor roll.

"Wow, the store looks great!" she said as I closed the door behind her. She shed her wool coat and tossed her hat on the counter. "You won't believe what happened after you left!"

For the next fifteen minutes, the V filled me in on the comings and goings at Claymoore. I was happy to catch up—but mostly, I was just glad to hear her voice.

"... but the best was when Kirstin got fired and Jonas replaced her as prefect. She pitched such a fit, the headmaster had to have her escorted to a quiet room to chill out. It was awesome!" the V said. "Hey—is it true that you got expelled? There was a rumor that you actually just quit—but, you know. Whatever."

I smiled. "Yes. Well, I have not been asked to return."

"Yeah. So, I guess it's back to Trinity after the holidays?"

But I couldn't wait any longer. There was something I had to say. "V?" I broke in. "You know I didn't mean any of that stuff I said that one night. I was frustrated and just wanted to keep you safe. I would never—"

"Simone, I know. You don't have to say anything, I know what you were doing. Everything is fine. We're going to get on each other nerves sometimes," she replied. "Besides, I'm like a spy now, too. Are we going on another mission soon?"

"Mission? Well, I don't think ..."

"I gotcha—but I'll be ready. You can count on me," she replied. "Hey—I got you a Christmas gift. You can open it now if you want."

My heart warmed. "I have something for you, too."

"Really? Can I open it?"

"Well, you can if you want. Or maybe you'll never open it." I walked over to my backpack, which was sitting under the apron rack, and pulled out a sealed dossier. It read: "French Civil Documents, Articles 343—Sealed Adoption Records." Though she'd initially resisted, Eloise couldn't deny my request after I'd proven instrumental in the return of both Claire and the OmniKey.

I walked back to the V with the envelope in my hands.

"Here it is, V. Your adoption file. It's yours if you want it."

Her eyes opened wide, and her lip started to quiver.

"I—I—I—" she stammered.

"It's okay, V. You don't need to read this today. I just knew that . . ." I trailed off as tears started to roll down her flushed cheeks.

"No, it's fine. I know you're trying," she cut in. I waited for her to say something, and she gave a little laugh. "Well, I guess it's all in here, huh?" She took the package out of my hands and stared at it, gauging the envelope's weight. Tears fell as a lifetime of emotions collided. Then her breathing slowed, and she smiled.

"No, you keep it." She looked up at me with adoring eyes. "After I got home, my family—they knew I'd been thinking about my birth parents a lot, and Mom said we needed to clear the air. Dad went on about waiting for me and how I'm a miracle and stuff like that," she stammered. A smile crept across her face. "They said when I'm ready, they'd tell me everything—they'd even take me to visit Korea. Maybe someday I'll ask, but not now. Not today."

She handed the envelope back and smiled.

"Oh—now for your present!" she insisted, pulling out a small wrapped box. "Open it, open it!"

I ripped off the wrapping paper to reveal a white jewelry box, which I quickly opened.

"Oh! It's a—"

"It's a Red Wolf pin. Isn't it cool? Maeve made them in art class. One for her, one for Jilli, one for you—and one for me." The V paused. "Yes, one for me. I'm an honorary member now. I put it on my backpack."

I gazed at it as all the memories of Claymoore returned. "I love it, V," I said, pinning it to my apron. We met each other's eyes and smiled, and all was right again.

"Happy Christmas, Simone—but I've got to go. Mum is having some neighbors over for cocktails. I'll text you later!" she said, giving me a hug.

I shut the door behind her and flipped the lock. All worries evaporated while I watched my best friend skip down the street.

I turned from the window. The sight of the holiday trimmings adorning our tranquil store brought a smile to my face, and I let out a deep breath. The burden of the Fox and Eloise would have to wait—for now, the joy of a baby brother and the bliss of being home for Christmas surpassed all.

A *click!* echoed from the back of the store.

"Mia, is that you?" I shouted; but no reply came. *I must be hearing things.*

I strolled back through the store to grab a broom, looking down at my wolf pin with pride. Memories of prowling around London at night returned, and I let out a low, quiet howl. My heart was full.

As I entered the kitchen, my eyes were drawn to the desk, which was overflowing with clutter. While I was gone, the staff had piled incoming letters upon it, and I would have to—

Wait. It can't be.

I stopped cold, and my body went numb. I rubbed my eyes to make sure I wasn't dreaming.

Hanging perfectly level above the desk was *Blue No. 2.*

Acknowledgments

The joy of writing these words is more gratifying than I can express. Writing a book is a challenge, and the time spent can be long and grueling. A hardy few were in the trenches with me from the beginning, and several more have shaped my life in ways too numerous to count. I will try my best to thank them accordingly.

Thank you to my dad, Tom, for giving me a lifetime of support, unending curiosity, and the stubbornness to never walk away. Thank you to my boys, Patrick and Michael. I'm proud of you both, in so many different ways. And thank you to my dear friend Andy—the Wahlberg to my DiCaprio.

Thank you to my editor, Erin Harpst. You are extraordinary. Thank you, friend. A big thanks to my team at Brandylane Publishers: Allison Tovey, Michael Hardison, Grace Ball, Kelly O'Neill, and Robert Pruett. I am grateful for you all.

Over the last several years, I have come to cherish a community of talented writers and artists who defy the limits of rational support. First, I'd like to thank my less attractive twin, Ash Knight, who is truly the biggest dork in the world. I appreciate you, Boogie. Also many thanks to the most fearless hustlers in the game: Halo Scot, A.C. Merkel, Ross Young, Tanweer Dar, Anya Pavelle, Lali A. Love, Julie Kusma, Derek R. King, Joanne Paulson, J.G. MacLeod, Claudia Oltean, Ginger Quinn Rogers, Tristan B. Taylor, Serena Hassan, Helena M. Craggs, D.W. Harvey, Victoria Marswell, and Mario Dell'Olio. Pizza for everyone!

Last, but not least, to Ali Stables—cheers!

About the Author

S.P. O'Farrell is the award-winning author of the *Simone La-Fray Mysteries*. When he isn't writing, he is championing special education, the performing arts, and numerous environmental initiatives. He lives in western Maryland with his wife and two sons.